THE SOUL OF THE ROBOT

THE
SOUL OF THE
ROBOT

by
Barrington J. Bayley

ALLISON & BUSBY
London

First published in Great Britain
by Allison & Busby Limited
6a Noel Street, London W1V 3RB

ISBN 0 85031 145 4

Printed in Great Britain by The Anchor Press Ltd
and bound by Wm Brendon & Son Ltd
both of Tiptree, Essex

For Mike Moorcock – "the eternal champion"!

I

Out of pre-existence Jasperodus awoke to find himself in darkness.

Seldom can a sentient being have known such presence of mind in the first few seconds of its life. Patiently Jasperodus remained standing in the pitch-blackness and reviewed his situation, drawing upon the information that had been placed in his partially-stocked memory before his birth.

He became aware that he stood unaided inside a closed metal cabinet. The first intelligent action of his existence was to grope forward with his right hand until he found the knob on the inside of the cabinet's door. He turned, and pushed. Then he stepped out to inspect the scene that met his eyes.

A man and a woman, well worn in years and dressed in smudged work smocks, stared at him shyly. They stood close to one another, like a couple who had grown old in each other's company. The room smelled faintly of pine, of which wood workbenches and other furniture were fashioned: chairs, cupboards, a table and an assembly rack. Cluttered on these, as well as on floor, benches and hooks, was a disorderly array of components and of the curious instruments betokening the trade of an electronics craftsman.

Although the room was untidy and somewhat shabby, it had a warm, homely atmosphere. Its disorder was that of someone who had his own sense of method, and Jasperodus already knew how efficacious that method was.

His glance went back to the elderly couple. They, in turn, looked at him with expressions that tried desperately to mask their anxiety. They were gentle and blameless people, and in Jasperodus' eyes rather pathetic since their eager expectations were doomed to disappointment.

"We are your parents," the wife said in a hesitant, hopeful voice. "We made you. You are our son."

She had no need to explain further, for Jasperodus knew the

story: childless, and saddened by their childlessness, the couple had chosen this way of giving their lives issue. They looked to Jasperodus now to bring them as much joy and comfort as an organically born flesh-and-blood child might have done.

But like many an ungrateful son, Jasperodus had already made his decision. He imagined better things for himself than to spend his life with them. Jasperodus, the hulking, bronze-black all-purpose robot they had created, laughed harshly and moved purposively across the room to the door. Opening it, he walked out of their lives.

Looking after his retreating back, the man put his hand comfortingly on his wife's shoulder. "We knew this could happen," he reminded her gently. It was true that they could have made their offspring with a built-in desire to cherish them; but that, they had both decided, would not be the right way. Whatever he did, it had to be of his own free will.

Yet, after their long, patient labours, their parents' anguish was real. Jasperodus had some theoretical knowledge of the world, but no experience of it. His future was as unpredictable as his past was blank.

"What will become of him?" the woman said tearfully. "What will become of him?"

2

The rambling cottage stood alone in extensive countryside. Jasperodus took a direction at random and simply kept on walking. He walked first across a tiny patch of land that supplied his parents' meagre needs. Two robot agricultural machines were at work, one harvesting high-yield crops of grain and vegetables and the other tending a few animals. More of his father's handiwork, Jasperodus did not doubt, but they were primitive machines only, built for specific work. They compared to himself as a primitive insect compared to a man.

Five minutes brought him through the smallholding to rolling woods and wild meadows. Confident that if he kept going he would eventually meet with something more in keeping with his new-born sense of adventure, for the time being he contented himself with simply enjoying his first few hours in the world, admiring his body and all the faculties his parents had given him.

Jasperodus' form was that of a handsome humanoid in bronze-black metal. His exterior, comprising flat planes mollified by brief rounded surfaces, aspired to a frankly metallic effect. To alleviate the weightiness of this appearance he was decorated all over with artistic scroll-like engravings. Altogether, his body exuded strength and capability.

His face he could not see and so had to postpone his inspection of it. His senses, however, he could explore freely. He switched his eyesight up and down the spectrum of radiation, well beyond the octave of light visible to human beings. His audible range was equally broad. His sense of smell, on the contrary, though adequate, was not as sharp as in many men and certainly did not approach the acuteness of some animals. As for his sense of touch, it was perfectly delicate where it concerned dynamics, but he was to learn later that it lacked the delicious touch-sensations that were available to organic beings; it meant nothing to him to be stroked.

Touch-sensation was a field his father had not mastered, indeed it was the trickiest problem in the whole of robotics.

His repertoire of sensory inputs was rounded off by a superb sense of balance and movement. Jasperodus would have made a skilful dancer, despite his weight of about a third of a ton.

All in all he was probably one of the finest robots ever to be built. His father, a master robot-maker, was well-qualified for the task; he had learned his trade first of all in a robot factory in Tarka, later spending nearly a decade creating unusual robots on the estates of the eccentric Count Viss. Finally he had enrolled with the supreme robot designer of them all, Aristos Lyos, for a further three years of special study, before retiring to this remote, pleasant spot to create the masterpiece that would fulfil his life. Jasperodus could well imagine the old man's devotion, as well as the inexhaustible patience of his wife, who had prepared the greater mass of repetitious micro-circuitry.

Insofar as the machinery of his body went, all that Jasperodus had examined so far was of the finest workmanship, but not unique. More mysterious was the formation of his *character* . . . Here his father had shown his originality. It would have been an easy matter to endow him with any type of personality his parents had wished, but that would have defeated the object of the exercise, which was to give rise to a new, original person of unknown, unique potentialities. Therefore, at the moment of his activation, Jasperodus' father had arranged for his character to crystallise by chance out of an enormous number of random influences, thus simulating the chance combination of genes and the vagarious experiences of childhood.

As a result Jasperodus came into the world as a fully formed adult, complete with a backlog of knowledge and with decided attitudes. Admittedly his knowledge was of a sparse and patchy kind, the sort that could be gained from reading books or watching vidtapes. But he knew how to converse and was skilled at handling many types of machinery.

He knew, too, that the planet Earth was wide, varied and beautiful. Since the collapse of the Rule of Tergov (usually referred to now as the Old Empire) some eight hundred years previously there had been no integrated political order. In the intervening Dark Period of chaos even knowledge of the planet's geography had become vague. The world was a scattered, motley patchwork of states large and small, of kingdoms, principalities, dukedoms and manors. And although a New Empire was arising in the south of Worldmass – the great continent comprising most of Earth's dry surface – that saw itself as a successor to the old and destined to resurrect its glories, the machinations of the Great Emperor Charrane made slow progress. The rest of the world heeded him but little.

On and on strode Jasperodus. Night fell. He switched to infrared vision, planning to walk on uninterrupted into the day.

After some hours he saw a light shining in the distance. He switched back to normal vision, at which the light resolved itself into a fierce beam stabbing the darkness and moving slowly but steadily across the landscape, disappearing now and then behind hillocks or stretches of forest. Eager to investigate, he broke into a loping run, crashing through the undergrowth and leaping over the uneven ground.

On topping a rise, he stopped. He found himself looking down on a track comprising parallel steel rails. The moving headlight rounded a curve and approached the culvert. Behind it followed a chain of smaller lights, glimmering from the windows of elongated, dulled-silver coaches with streamlined fluted exteriors.

He instantly recognised the apparition as a train. But its speed, he imagined, was unnaturally slow for such a machine—barely twenty miles per hour. Suddenly he heard a staccato chattering noise coming from the train, first in a long burst, then intermittently. The engine? No ...

Machine-gun fire.

Jasperodus slithered down the embankment. The windowless leading coach swept majestically abreast of him, wheels hissing on the rails; locating a handhold he swung himself easily on to the running-board that ran the length of the outer casing.

He edged along the brief ledge, pressing himself against the curved metal skin of the vehicle and looking for a way in. Up near the roof he found a square sliding panel that made an opening large enough to admit him. Gracefully he levered himself to a level with it and dropped feet first into the brightness within.

He landed in a narrow tunnel with a rounded roof. At once

the machine-gun started up again, making a violent, deafening cacophony in the confined space, and he staggered as bullets rattled off his body. Then there was a pause.

The big machine-gun was stationed at the forward end of the long corridor. Behind it squatted a man in blue garb. It appeared to Jasperodus that he was guarding the door to the control cab. He glanced to the other end of the corridor, but it was deserted. The gun controlled the passageway completely; the man's enemies, whoever they were, were obliged to stay strictly out of sight.

Again the machine-gunner opened up. Jasperodus became indignant at the ricochetting assault on his toughened steel hide. He pressed swiftly forward against the tide of bullets, lurching from side to side in the swaying tunnel but closing the distance between him and his tormentor. At the last moment the gunner scrambled up from his weapon and clawed at the door behind him. He had left it too late. Jasperodus took the machine-gun by its smoking barrel and swung it in the air, its tripod legs kicking. The guard uttered a single grunt as the magazine case thudded dully on to his head.

Jasperodus stood reflectively, looking down at the blood oozing from the crushed skull. He had committed his first act in the wider world beyond his parents' home. And it had been an act of malice. The machine-gunner had posed no substantial threat to him; he had simply been angered by the presumptuous attack. Letting fall the gun he opened the door to the control cab. It was empty. The train was fully automatic, though equipped with manual override controls. The alarm light was flashing and the instrument board revealed extensive damage to the transmission system. The train was in distress and evidently making the best time it could.

Steps sounded behind him. Jasperodus turned to see a grinning figure standing framed in the doorway and cradling a machine-gun of more portable proportions. A second new arrival peered over his shoulder, eyeing Jasperodus and gawping.

Both men had shaggy hair that hung to their shoulders. They were dressed in loose garments of a violently coloured silky material, gathered in at waist and ankles and creased and scruffy from overlong use. The sight of Jasperodus made the grin freeze on the leader's face.

"A robot! A goddamned robot! So that's it! I wondered how you clobbered the machine-gun – figured you must have come through the roof."

He brushed past Jasperodus and into the cab, slapping a switch after a cursory study of the control board. Ponderously the train ground to a halt.

Just then Jasperodus noticed that a gun in the hands of the second man was being pointed at his midriff. Impatiently he tore the weapon from the impudent fellow's grasp, twisted it into a useless tangle, and threw it into a corner. The other backed away, looking frightened.

"Cool it!" the leader snapped. Jasperodus made no further move but stared at him. After a glance of displeasure the man turned away from him again, bent to the control panel and closed more switches. With a rumbling noise the train began to trundle backwards.

Then he straightened and faced Jasperodus. "Say, what are you doing here?" he said in a not unfriendly tone. "Why did you kill the guard?"

"He was shooting at me."

"Who owns you? One of the passengers? Or are you freight?"

"No one owns me. I am a free, independent being."

The man chuckled, his face breaking out into a grin that creased every inch of it.

"That's rich!"

His expression became speculative as his eyes roved over Jasperodus. "A wild robot, eh? You've done us a favour, metal man. I thought we'd never shift that bastard with the machine-gun."

"How did the train come to be damaged?" Jasperodus asked. "Are you its custodians?"

"*Now* we are!" Both men laughed heartily. "We made a mess of things, as usual. She kept going after we detonated the charge. It should have stopped her dead. We damned near didn't get aboard."

While he spoke he was scanning the rearwards track through a viewscreen. "My name is Craish," he offered. "As well you should know it, since you may be seeing a good deal of me."

The significance of this remark was lost on Jasperodus. "Robbers," he said slowly. "You are out to plunder the train."

13

Again they laughed. "Your logic units are slow on the uptake," Craish said, "but you cotton on in the end."

Excitement coursed through Jasperodus. Here was the tang of adventure!

After a short journey Craish once more brought the train to a halt. He flung open a side door.

They were parked on a length of track that rounded a clearing in the all-encompassing forest. Here waited more of Craish's gang. With much noise and yelling they set about unloading the train, unlocking the container cars and carelessly throwing out all manner of goods. On the ground others sorted through the booty, flinging whatever took their fancy into small carrier vehicles. The procedure was ridiculous, thought Jasperodus. The freight train was a large one. Its total cargo must have been very valuable, yet the bandits would be able to take away no more than a small fraction of it. The band was badly organised, or else it knew enough to keep its nuisance value within limits.

Craish returned to Jasperodus, who still stood watching from the running-board of the control cab. "Go and help my men unload," he ordered.

The order was given in such a confident tone that Craish obviously had no doubt that it would be obeyed unquestioningly. Jasperodus was affronted. Did the man think of him as a slave? Craish was walking unconcernedly away. Jasperodus called out to him.

"Where is this train bound?"

The other stopped and looked back. "The Empire, eventually. It's a trading train, sent out by Empire merchants. It stops at towns on the way and barters goods." He looked askance at the robot, wondering why he needed to ask this question.

"What will you do with it? Leave it here?"

"Nah. Send it on its way. So they'll never know where we jumped it."

With that Craish walked away. Jasperodus pondered. The prospect of a trip to the Empire excited him but, he reminded himself, the train was crippled. Still, he could if he wished stay with the train on its long and monotonous journey, although he would meet with the opposition of the bandits, who plainly would not want witnesses to their deeds wandering abroad. Also, there

14

might be trouble when the train reached its next stop. All in all, it might be better to stay with these ruffians. As his first real contact with human beings they were already proving entertaining.

Accordingly he contributed his superhuman strength to the unloading and sorting of the cargo. Eventually the forage trucks were filled to capacity and the bandits, who numbered about twenty, seemed satisfied. Some of the discarded cargo was actually put back on board; the rest was gathered in a heap and set alight, an inflammable liquid being poured over it to make a good blaze. As the huge bonfire glared fiercely at the sky the marauders brought forth another kind of plunder from the train's single passenger coach : prisoners, all female as far as Jasperodus could see, linked together by a rope tied around their necks, jerking and protesting. The train pulled out, limping painfully under automatic control towards its distant destination.

They all set off through the forest. The forage trucks had big balloon tyres that enabled them to roll easily over the rough ground, but most of the men walked, as did the prisoners. The forest sprawled over rocky, hilly terrain through which they travelled for more than an hour. Finally they debouched into the bandits' camp : a dell formed like an amphitheatre, having a large cave at its closed end.

The night was warm. Before long a fire was started in the centre of the dell, casting a glimmering light over the proceedings. Goods spilled to the ground as the forage trucks were tipped on their sides; the men began to go through the plunder like children with new toys, draping themselves with sumptuous raiment, shaking out bolts of expensive cloth, playing with the new gadgets and so forth. Jasperodus gathered that later most of it would be sold in nearby towns. But not, he guessed, the bottles of liquor : specially prized articles that were passed from mouth to mouth and emptied rapidly.

Casting his eye over the strewn booty, Jasperodus spied an object of immediate interest to him : a hand mirror, included among the valuables because of the gems that adorned its frame. Quickly he seized it and settled by the fire; now at last he would be able to see his face.

He had feared that his father might have given him the grotesque mouthless and noseless face seen on many robots, or even

15

worse, that he would have committed a much greater travesty by sculpting a human face. The countenance that stared out of the mirror reassured him. It was a sternly functional visage – and, of course, it was immobile – but it was more than just a mask. Following the general conception of his body, it consisted mainly of machined flat surfaces and projections that gave it a solid but intriguingly machicolated appearance. A square-bridged nose ended in simple flanges perfectly adapted to its function as an olfactory device. A straight, immobile mouth, from which Jasperodus' booming, well-timbred voice was thrown by a hidden speaker, was so well placed amid the angled planes of the jaw that it fitted naturally and without artifice; as did the flat, square ears, which contained an arrangement of small flanges serving the same purpose as those of the human ear : the abstraction of direction and stereo from the sound they received.

Eyes glowed softly by their own red light. Finally, the whole face was lightly engraved with the same intricate scrolls that decorated the rest of the body.

Jasperodus was well pleased. His was a non-human, robot face, but somehow it seemed to express his inner essence : it looked the way he felt.

Craish arrived and found him gazing into the mirror. Laughing, he tipped up a bottle and poured liquor over Jasperodus' torso. "Admiring yourself, metal-man? A pity you can't drink."

Jasperodus laid down the mirror, but did not speak.

Unabashed, Craish sat beside him and swigged from the bottle. "We can certainly use you," he continued. "You're strong, and bullets don't bother you a bit. You look like you're worth a lot, too – your owner must be plenty sore to lose you. You'll stay with us from now on, understand?"

He spoke in the same matter-of-fact tone in which he had ordered the robot to work at the train. Jasperodus ignored him. Nearby, one of Craish's men had laid down his sub-machine-gun and he picked it up to examine it. It was simply-constructed, but its design was good : merely a barrel, a repeater mechanism, a short stock and a handgrip. On one of his father's lathes Jasperodus could have turned one out in less than an hour. The magazine was spherical, slotting over the handgrip, and contained hundreds of rounds.

"An effective device," he commented, slinging the gun over his shoulder by its strap. "I will keep this."

"Hey, gimme my gun, you damned robot," objected its owner explosively. "Who do you think you are?"

Jasperodus stared at him. "You wish to do something about it?"

Craish intervened in a sharp tone. "Wait a minute! If I want you to carry a gun I'll tell you, metal-man. So put the gun down. Just sit there and wait for your orders."

"You are very good at giving orders," Jasperodus said slowly, turning his massive head.

"And you're good at taking them. You're a robot, aren't you?" Craish frowned uneasily. "A machine." He was perplexed; robots, in fact any cybernetic system, had a natural propensity for obeying orders that were firmly given, but this one showed an unnerving individuality. Advanced machines, of course, would tend to be more self-reliant and therefore more subject to individual quirks, but not, he would have thought, to this degree.

"Say," whined the deprived bandit, "this hulk doesn't take any notice of us at all. It just sits there defying us. It must have a command language, Craish."

Craish snapped his fingers. "That's it. Of course." He turned to Jasperodus. "What's your command language? How does your master speak to you?"

Jasperodus had only a vague idea what he was talking about. "I have no master," he replied. "I am not a machine. I am an original being, like you. I am a self."

Craish laughed until tears started from his eyes. "That's a good one. Whoever manufactured you must have been a kookie to write that in your brain. Where are you from, by the way? How long have you been loose?"

"I was activated this morning."

"Yeah?" Craish's merriment trailed off. "Well, like I said, give the man back his gun."

"Do you think you can take it from me?" Jasperodus asked him acidly.

Craish paused. "Not if you object," he said slowly. He deliberated. "Were you thinking of staying with us?"

"I shall keep my own counsel."

17

"Okay." Craish motioned to the plaintiff in the case. They both got up and left. Jasperodus remained sitting there, staring into the fire.

Soon the revels entered a new phase. The bandits turned their attentions to the women, who up to now had been standing in a huddled group to one side. Their menfolk had all been slaughtered on the train, and they looked forlorn and apprehensive, remembering the recent horror and anticipating the mistreatment to come. Now they were dragged into the firelight and their ropes removed. They were forced to dance, to drink. Then their kidnappers, one by one, began to caress them, to throw them to the ground and strip them. The light of the flames flickered on gleaming naked bodies, and very quickly the scene turned into an orgy of rape.

Jasperodus watched all this blankly, listening to sobs and screams from the women, to growls of lust from the men. Carnal pleasure was foreign to him, and for the first time he felt sullen and disappointed: the experience of erotic sexual enjoyment was something his parents had not been able to give him.

True, the enjoyment the bandits found in forcing women against their will, in hearing their screams and cries of protestation, he could to some slight extent understand. After all, there was always satisfaction in forcing, in dominance. But the frantic sensual pleasure of desire gone mad, that he could not understand.

Again, it was not that he lacked aesthetic appreciation. He knew full well what beauty was, but unfortunately that did not help him in the sphere of eroticism. The aesthetic qualities of the naked female bodies now exposed to his view did not exceed, in his opinion, the aesthetic qualities of the naked male bodies. Clearly the sexual passions they aroused in the breasts of these ruffians was a peculiarly animal phenomenon that was closed to him.

It came to him, while he watched what the men were doing to the women, that he possessed no phallus or genitals of any kind. Yet his parents had definitely envisaged him as a son, not as a daughter or as neuter, and his outlook was a strictly masculine one. He glanced down at himself. So that the absence of male genitals should not invest him with an incongruously feminine appearance his father had placed at the groin a longish box-like bulge that gave a decidedly male effect, rather like a cod-piece. Unlike a cod-piece, however, it hid not phallus and testicles but a package of circuits concerned with balanced movement, corresponding to the spinal ganglia in humans.

Throughout the night the sleepless Jasperodus watched the frenzy in the firelight and brooded. Any stimulation he managed to gain from the spectacle of continued rape (and later, of resigned abandonment on the part of the women) was vicarious and abstract; the purely mental observation of a pleasure which, he was sure, he could never share.

3

At dawn, while the camp was still in a drunken sleep, Jasperodus roused himself. He made his way back along the route he had come until striking the railway track. Then, taking the direction followed by the crippled train, he set off, walking between the rails with his sub-machine-gun clanking lightly against his side.

The sun rose to its zenith and found him still walking. By the time it sank into mid-afternoon the wild countryside was giving way to cultivated plots. The people here were evidently not rich and lived sparsely. Although some of the fields were worked by rather tatty cybernetic machines, in others human labour guided powered ploughs and harvesters, or even scratched the earth with implements hauled by animals.

The further he went the more the forest thinned, until eventually the landscape consisted entirely of farmland. Draught animals had disappeared by now. The farms were larger and only machines were at work. The cottages of the outlying farms were here transformed into more expansive houses, and altogether the scene was a pleasant one of peaceful rural life.

Without pause Jasperodus walked on into the night and through to the next day. At mid-morning he was entering a town.

Judging by its appearance it was of some antiquity, and probably dated back to the Old Empire, for on the outskirts he saw a clump of ruins that he guessed to be at least a thousand years old. In its present form, however, the town had probably taken shape about five hundred years ago. Its streets were narrow, twisting and turning confusingly. The buildings, many of them built of wood, crowded close together and had a cramped appearance.

Jasperodus strode easily through the busy lanes, enjoying the bustle of commerce. The open-fronted shops were doing a brisk trade and the people cast scarcely a glance at the tall man of metal who passed in their midst.

But he was not ignored by everyone. As he approached the town centre a sharp, peremptory voice rang out.

"You there – robot! Stop!"

He turned. Approaching him were four men, uniformly apparelled in sleek green tunics, corded breeks, and green shako hats surmounted by swaying feathered plumes. Their faces were hard, with cold eyes that were used to seeing others obey them.

"No robots carry weapons in Gordona. Hand over that gun."

Jasperodus pondered briefly and made the same decision that had guided him on the train – that although he had the power to resist, he would learn more of the world by complying. He surrendered his weapon.

The men moved to surround him, preventing him from keeping all of them in view at the same time. Like the bandits, they displayed no fear of him despite his obviously powerful person, which loomed a good half head taller than themselves, but appeared to take his acquiescence for granted. He noticed, too, that the passing citizens gave the group a wide berth.

"Who owns you?" the leader demanded. "Where are you going?"

"No one owns me. I go where I please."

"A construct on the loose, eh?" said the man, looking him up and down, "A fine-looking construct, too. Follow us."

"Why?" asked Jasperodus.

The man shot him a look of surprised anger. "So you question the orders of a king's officer? Come, robot, come!"

Not comprehending, Jasperodus walked with the quartet along the thoroughfare. Shortly they came to a stone building that stood out from the smaller, poorer buildings on either side of it. Jasperodus' guides led him inside where, behind a large counter of polished wood, waited more men similarly attired to themselves.

"Found a footloose construct in the street," Jasperodus' arrestor announced. "Take him to a cell and put him on the list for this afternoon."

Not until now did Jasperodus seriously sense danger. "I am no prisoner!" he boomed. The sergeant behind the desk blew a whistle. At his summons two big robots blundered into the room: hulking great masses of metal even larger than Jasperodus. Though

21

their movements were hardly graceful they closed in on him with practised speed and attached themselves one to each arm with an unbreakable grip.

Jasperodus' struggles were useless. The metal guards dragged him down a stone corridor into the depths of the building. "Why are you doing this?" he growled. "What crime have I committed?" But the guards remained silent. He guessed them to be dim-witted machines, suitable only for such low-intelligence tasks as they were now performing.

A door clanged open and he was thrust into a small cell. Eyeing the stone walls, he wondered at his chances of breaking the stone with his fist. Unhappily, he saw that it was steel-backed. Nor was that all: the guards snapped massive manacles on his wrists, restraining him by thick chains that hung from the ceiling, so that his arms were forced above his head and he was left dangling in the middle of the cell.

An hour passed before the door opened again. Into the cell walked a small, dapper man with a sheaf of papers under his arm. The newcomer sat down on a tabouret in the corner, keeping a safe distance between himself and the prisoner.

Placing his papers on his knee, he took out a writing instrument. "Now then," he began amiably, "this should take only a few minutes."

"Why have I been brought here?" Jasperodus asked thickly. "What plans have you for me?"

The man seemed surprised at his ignorance. "We here in Gordona do nothing without observing the proper form," he said indignantly. "Robot property cannot be impounded without legal proceedings."

"Your words are nonsense to me," Jasperodus told him with exasperation.

"Very well. I will explain. As a footloose robot you are to be taken into the King's service in the state of machine-slavery, or as the legal term has it: construct-bondage. Your case comes before the magistrate this afternoon, and I am the lawyer in charge of its presentation. As a self-directed construct you will be required to be present and may be called upon to answer questions to satisfy the magistrate of your derelict condition. You could even fight the impound order."

"And how do I do that?" asked Jasperodus with growing interest.

"By naming your former owner. If he resides within the borders of the kingdom you could apply to be returned to him. Er, who is – or was – your owner?" The lawyer's pen poised above the paper.

"I have none. Yet neither do I consent to being made a slave."

"On what grounds?"

Jasperodus rattled his chains. "Are men, also, made slaves?"

"Certainly not. On that point the law holds throughout most of the civilised world." The lawyer warmed up as he began to enjoy dispensing his learning. He ticked off points on his fingers. "Sentient beings may not be made slaves. Self-directed constructs are invariably so. Any who, through the carelessness or inattention of their owners, have somehow escaped their master's supervision and wander abroad masterless may be reclaimed by any party much as may a derelict ship. Such is the law. The word 'slavery' is a popularism, of course, not a proper technical term, since a robot has no genuine will and therefore no disposition towards rebelliousness, if properly adjusted."

Jasperodus' voice became hollow and moody. "Ever since my activation everyone I meet looks upon me as a thing, not as a person. Your legal proceedings are based upon a mistaken premiss, namely that I am an object. On the contrary, I am a sentient being."

The lawyer looked at him blankly. "I beg your pardon?"

"I am an authentic person, independent and aware."

The other essayed a fey laugh. "Very droll! To be sure, one sometimes encounters robots so clever that one could swear they had real consciousness! However, as is well known . . ."

Jasperodus interrupted him stubbornly. "I wish to fight my case in person. Is it permitted for a construct to speak on his own behalf?"

The lawyer nodded bemusedly. "Certainly. A construct may lay before the court any facts having a bearing on his case – or, I should say on *its* case. I will make a note of it." He scribbled briefly. "But if I were you I wouldn't try to tell the magistrate what you just said to me. It wouldn't . . ."

"When the time comes, I will speak as I choose."

23

With a sigh the lawyer gave up. "Oh, well, as you say. Time is pressing. Have you a number, name or identifying mark?"

"My name is Jasperodus."

"And you say there is no owner?"

"Correct."

"Unusual. Can you give me details of your manufacture?"

Jasperodus laughed mockingly. "Can you of yours?"

With a mystified air the lawyer left. Jasperodus waited impatiently until at length the robot guards returned and removed the manacles. This time he made no attempt at resistance. He was conducted up staircases, along corridors and into the courtroom, which as near as he could judge was lodged in one of the poorer adjacent buildings.

Jasperodus surveyed the courtroom with interest. At one end a man of mature years sat on a raised dais: the magistrate. In his foreground, to right and left of him, were arrayed in sectioned compartments of panelled wood the functionaries of the court: clerks and recorders, as well as places for lawyers and other representing parties. At the other end were tiered benches, now empty, for a public audience.

Still accompanied by his guards Jasperodus was ushered to the dock, a box-like cubicle with walls reaching to his waist. Meanwhile the dapper lawyer described fairly accurately the circumstances of his arrest.

The magistrate nodded curtly. "Anything else?"

The lawyer waved his hands in a vague gesture of embarrassment. "The construct has expressed an intention to speak on its own behalf, Your Honour." Glancing at Jasperodus, he raised his eyebrows as a signal for him to go ahead.

Jasperodus' argument was simplicity itself. "I am informed that in law no sentient being can be made a slave," he declared. "I claim to be such a sentient being and therefore not a subject for construct bondage."

A frown of annoyance crossed the magistrate's face. "Really, Paff," he admonished the lawyer, "do you have to plague me with pantomimes? What nonsense!"

Paff shrugged a disclaimer.

Doggedly Jasperodus continued: "I know I have self-awareness in the same way that you know *you* have it. I do not speak for other robots. But give me any test that will prove my self-awareness or lack of it, and you will see for yourself."

"Test? I know of no test. What nonsense is this?" Irritable and nonplussed, the magistrate looked for advice towards the functionaries who sat below him.

The technical adviser, a suave young man in a tunic brocaded in crimson, rose to his feet. "By your leave, Your Honour, there is no such test. Any faculty possessed by sentient beings can be simulated by an appropriate machine, and therefore the fact of consciousness itself is beyond examination."

The magistrate nodded in satisfaction and turned to Jasperodus. "Quite so. Have you anything germane to say?"

Jasperodus refused to let it go. "Then how does the law define what is sentient and what is not?"

"That is simple," replied the magistrate with the air of one explaining something to a child. "A sentient being is a human being or a kuron. But not a construct."

"Only natural, biologically evolved creatures can have consciousness," interpolated the adviser, receiving a frown of reproof from the magistrate for his impudence. "Any robotician will tell you that machine consciousness is a technical impossibility *ipso facto*."

Jasperodus recalled that kurons had originally been extraterrestrials, who migrated to Earth centuries ago and had since lost contact with their home star. Now they lived in small communities scattered throughout various parts of the world. He seized on the magistrate's mention of them to pursue the question further.

"Suppose there was brought before you a being from another star who was neither human nor kuron," he suggested. "Suppose furthermore that you could not ascertain whether the being was a naturally evolved creature or a construct. How then would you settle the matter of its mental status?"

The magistrate sputtered in annoyance, waving his hands in agitation.

"I have no time for your casuistry, robot. You are a *thing*, not a person. That is all there is to it and I pronounce you to be the property of the King's court." With finality he banged his gavel, but was interrupted once more by the presumptuous young man who was keen to make the most of his duties.

"By your leave, Your Honour, may we also recommend that this robot be given some adjustment by the Court Robotician. Its brain appears somehow or another to have acquired an aberrant self-image."

Grumpily the magistrate nodded. "Enter it on the record."

Stunned by the failure of his defence, Jasperodus became aware that one of the guard robots was tugging at his arm. Passively he followed them from the dock.

They conveyed him not back to his cell but out of the building and into the windowless interior of a waiting van, which was then firmly locked. His inquiries elicited that his destination was the residence of King Zhorm, ruler of the tiny kingdom of Gordona. The van went bumping through the old town's streets. He felt too bewildered even to begin to plan escape. All he could do was brood over the disconcerting pronouncements that had just been presented to him.

An aberrant self-image, he thought darkly.

King Zhorm's palace was in the dead centre of the town. It was as large and as luxurious as the resources of Gordona would permit, which meant that it allowed the King and his court to live in luxury but not in ostentatious luxury. Zhorm, however, was content with what he had. He enjoyed life in his own rough way, kept his kingdom in order, and was neither so ambitious nor so foolish as to tax his people until they bled, as did some petty rulers.

When Jasperodus arrived the evening banquet was in progress. Proceeding through a long corridor draped with tapestries he heard the sound of rough laughter. Then he was ushered into a large, brilliantly illumined hall where fifty or more persons sat feasting at long trestle tables. At their head, in a raised chair much like a throne, lounged King Zhorm.

The King was surprisingly young-looking: not above forty. He had dark oily skin and doe-like eyes. Each ear sported large gold rings, and his hair hung about his shoulders in black greasy ringlets. Catching sight of Jasperodus, he raised his goblet with a look of delight.

"My new robot! A magnificent specimen, so I am told. Come closer, robot."

Though disliking the riotous colours and air of revelry, Jas-

26

perodus obeyed. The banqueters eyed him appreciatively, passing remarks among one another and sniggering.

"Try some food, robot!" cried a voice. A large chunk of meat hit Jasperodus in the face and slid down his chest, leaving a greasy trail. He made no sign of recognition but stood immobile.

King Zhorm smiled, his eyes dreamy and predatory. "Welcome into my service, man of metal. Recount me your special abilities. What can you do well?"

"Anything you can do," Jasperodus answered, confident that he spoke the truth.

A fat man who sat near the King let out a roar. "Say 'Your Majesty', when you speak to the monarch!" He took up an iron rod that leaned against the table and began to beat Jasperodus vigorously about the arms and shoulders, to the merriment of all watchers. Jasperodus snatched the staff from his grasp and bent it double. When its two ends almost met it snapped suddenly in two and Jasperodus contemptuously hurled the pieces into a corner.

A sudden silence descended. The fat man pursed his lips. "The robot has mettle, I see," King Zhorm said quietly. "A fighter, too."

"Gogra! Let him fight Gogra!" The cry went up from all three tables. The idea seemed to please Zhorm. He clapped his hands. "Yes, bring on Gogra."

The banqueters sprang up with alacrity, pushed the tables nearer to the walls and scuttled behind them for protection. Jasperodus made no move but merely waited to see what was in store for him.

It was not long in coming. At the far end of the hall a tall door swung open. Through it strode Gogra: a giant of a robot, twelve foot tall and broad to match.

Gogra was coal-black. In his right hand he carried a massive sledge-hammer that in a few blows could have crushed Jasperodus to junk, tough as he was. Pausing in the doorway, the terrifying fighting robot surveyed the hall. As soon as he caught sight of Jasperodus he lunged forward, lifting the hammer with evident purpose.

Jasperodus backed away. Gogra's appearance was frightening; his head was thrust forward on his neck, reminiscent of an ape-man; and the face was such a mask of ugliness as to arouse both terror and pity: Gogra's designer had sought to give his massive frame sufficient agility by filling his interior with oil under pressure; the safety valve for that oil was his grotesque grilled mouth, from which green ichor dribbled copiously and continuously.

Studying the monster's movements, Jasperodus formed the opinion that Gogra's intelligence was moronic. He would fight according to a pattern and would not be able to depart from it.

Jasperodus easily dodged his adversary's first hammer-blow, which left the floor shattered and starred with cracks. He retreated nimbly towards the wall, causing the spectators hiding there to squeal and run along the side of the wall to escape.

A cheer went up as Gogra, uttering a deafening hiss, charged at Jasperodus who appeared to be trapped against the wall. At the last instant Jasperodus flung himself sideways to go sprawling full-length to the floor. Gogra, carrying the full momentum of his rush, crashed tumultuously into the wall with a shower of stone and plaster. Jasperodus sprang to his feet to see that the bigger robot had indeed, as he had anticipated, gone straight through the wall head-first; he stared at the thick, pillar-like legs attached to gigantic hind-quarters which stuck out from the wreckage. But he had time to give the jointed pelvis only one kick before Gogra pulled himself free, bringing a lengthy section of wall down with him as he did so. While the dazed giant staggered upright, hissing plaintively, Jasperodus gathered himself and took a leap upwards to land straight on Gogra's back. Clawing for holds, he hoisted himself up over the vast head and clung there athwart the skull, his arms obscuring Gogra's vision.

Pandemonium broke out in the hall as Gogra whirled round and round, staggering from wall to wall and crashing into the tables which splintered like matchwood. In panic and fury he hissed like a steam engine. But he had not forgotten what he was about: the great hammer still waved in the air, seeking its target. Jasperodus was keeping his eye on that terrible weapon, and he chose exactly the right instant to throw himself from his perch.

He fell to the floor with a loud clang. The hammer, swinging down into the vacated place, went smashing into Gogra's own head instead of into the body of his enemy. In a slow majestic descent the massive construct toppled with an even louder clang. The metal skull was split open; an almost-fluid mass of electronic packaging spilled out and spread slowly over the flagstones amid a soup of green oil.

Jasperodus climbed to his feet, relieved to observe that his plan to make Gogra brain himself had gone well. The banqueters, Zhorm among them, reappeared cautiously from behind their refuges.

"The stranger has slain Gogra!" someone exclaimed in astonishment. Widened eyes stared admiringly at Jasperodus.

King Zhorm, though likewise astounded, quickly recovered his composure. "A remarkable feat," he announced. "Surprising initiative for a robot."

"It was not too difficult," Jasperodus replied. "Your monster had as much brain as a centipede."

"I rather liked him for that." Sourly Zhorm looked down at the inert form of his champion, then clapped his hands again.

"Remove it."

Servants struggled to drag away the dead hulk, aided by one or two other robots. Inch by inch it was hauled towards the big doors; meantime the tables were replaced, and fresh platters of food and more flagons of drink appeared.

Zhorm tossed a grape into his mouth. "Well, robot, I hope you perform your other work as well as you disposed of Gogra. You look as if you need cleaning up – my girls will see to it." He beckoned to a servant.

Jasperodus looked down at himself. He was, it was true, somewhat dirty. His travels had left him caked with mud and dust – added to, now, by plaster and brick-dust.

Some of the banqueters nearest the King giggled and ogled him as he was led away. "Lovely naked girls," leered one. "Nice soft hands – enjoy yourself!"

Fools! Jasperodus thought. *As if their touch could mean anything to me.*

He followed the servant through the wide doors from which Gogra had emerged, along a short passage and into a perfumed chamber. Three naked girls rose smiling to meet him.

"Come, honoured guest. Let us bath you."

In the centre of the circular room was a bath filled with scented water. Soap and various implements lay on a low table. For Jasperodus' benefit, so that he would not have to enter the bath, there was also a couch on which he was invited to lie.

The girls got to work, cooing and chuckling as they washed his metal body with caressing movements. He was surprised to see that they appeared to enjoy their task and to gain some perverse kind of pleasure from his strange but man-like form. One in particular – a pretty red-head – stroked him specially languorously, lingering around the box-like bulge at his groin and on the insides of his thighs. Once or twice he noticed her eyes become hot and her breath come in short little gasps. He wondered if it was the strong air of masculinity he imagined he possessed that gave them stimulation. He himself, however, felt nothing.

When they had finished drying him they showed him into an adjoining room furnished as a bedchamber and left him alone. Evidently the King's instructions had been loosely worded but the girls were taking them literally and treating him as a human guest. There was a soft bed on which, he presumed, he could if he wished rest; but as he could remain without fatigue on his legs he stood stock-still at the window overlooking the garden around which the King's residence was built. He was deeply troubled, and was trying to sort out the truth of what had been said to him earlier.

After some time the door opened and in came a man in his late forties with wavy grey hair and a thin face with high, prominent cheekbones. His expression was distracted, slightly effeminate. He wore a loose robe and carried a large box studded with knobs and dials.

"I am Padua," he announced, "robotician to the King, I have instructions to examine you, so if you would please lie face down on the floor . . ."

"You believe I have a sickness," Jasperodus interrupted.

"Not a sickness exactly . . ." The robotician sounded apologetic.

"An aberrant self-image, then."

"Just so." Padua laid down his box. "Now . . ."

"Wait a moment." Jasperodus spoke with such a tone of command that Padua raised his eyebrows and blinked.

"I have need to talk to you. You are an expert on creatures such as I. Is it true what they tell me – that it is impossible for me to be self-aware?"

"Yes, that is so." Padua looked at him with a waiting, blank expression.

"Then explain how it is that I *am* self-aware."

"The answer is simple: you are not."

"But do I not show all the signs of awareness? I have emotions – do they not mean awareness?"

"Oh, no, emotions may quite easily be simulated machine-wise. Nothing lies behind them, of course. The robot has no *soul*."

"You don't understand." Jasperodus became agitated. "I *have* a soul. I *experience*, I *know* that I am a *conscious self*. Could I know such things, could I say them even, if they were not true?"

"An interesting question." To Jasperodus' exasperation Padua seemed to receive his anguished pronouncements as a diverting conundrum rather than in the deadly earnest in which they were intended. "But once again the answer is that nothing you can say can make any difference. It is technically possible for a self-directed machine to form the conclusion, the opinion as it were, that it has such awareness, having heard that the phenomenon exists in human beings which seem to be so similar to it. But such an opinion is a false one, for the machine does not really understand what awareness is and therefore forms mistaken notions about its nature. The machine-mind is an unconscious mind. Not alive."

"And yet you are standing here, arguing and talking with me!"

"Oh, one may debate with a robot quite fruitfully. Many have sharper wits than most men. In fact a robot can be a very acceptable companion. But it is my experience that after some lengthy time in its company one comes to notice a certain lack of living vitality in it, and to realise that it is after all dead."

"So this that I have, and call consciousness, is not consciousness?"

"No. This, in fact, is precisely what I am here to investigate . . ."

Padua's words struck Jasperodus like blow after blow and inflicted more injury on him than Gogra's hammer ever could have done. "You are very sure of yourself, Padua," he snarled in surly disappointment.

"Facts are facts. When the science of robotics was first born, back in the civilisation of the Ancient World, the hope of producing artificial consciousness was entertained. It soon became evident that it was impossible, however. There are theorems which prove the matter conclusively."

Jasperodus immediately expressed a desire to hear these theorems. Without demur Padua obliged; but they were couched in such technical terms that Jasperodus, who had no deep knowledge of robotics, could not understand them.

"Enough, enough!" he boomed. "Why should I listen to you? You are nothing but a second-rate practitioner in a broken-down, out-of-the-way kingdom. You probably don't know what you're talking about." This thought, as a matter of fact, was the last straw at which Jasperodus was now clutching.

Padua drew himself up to his full height. "If I may correct you, I am a robotician of the first rank. I have a First-Class Certificate with Honours from the College of Aristos Lyos – and there can be no better qualification than that." He shrugged with a hint of weariness. "It is not altogether by choice that I practise my profession here in Gordona. But these are troubled times. I came here for the sake of a quiet, peaceful life, to escape the turmoil that is overtaking more sophisticated parts of the world."

Jasperodus glowered sadly at his unwitting tormentor, his spirits dwindling to nothing. He had been cheated, after all, of the thing he had been most sure of. Just what was this self-awareness possessed by human beings and of which he could have no inkling? Doubtless the robotician was secretly laughing at him for believing his mechanical self-reference to be that godly state of consciousness reserved only for biological beings. Yet even now it seemed incredible to him that this feeling of self-existence he *imagined* he had was only a fake, a phantom, an illusion, *that it didn't exist*. Still, how could he deny Padua's expert judgment?

The more he thought about it the more his brain whirled until he could bear it no longer. He flung himself full-length on the floor.

"Get on with your work, Padua," he invited, his voice muffled by the floor tiles. "I do not wish to believe I exist when in truth I do not. Rectify my brain and release me from this agony."

After a long pause the robotician knelt beside him. Then there was a slight feeling of pressure and a click as he applied special tools that alone could open Jasperodus' inspection plate.

For a time Padua employed the extensible monitors on his inspection box, inserting them into the hundreds of checkpoints beneath the plates in Jasperodus' head and neck. He turned knobs delicately and carefully watched the dials. Jasperodus could scarcely hear him breathe. Eventually he replaced the plates and stood up.

"A sublime example of robotmanship," he said in a tone of reverence. "Worthy of the great Lyos himself. I suppose you weren't . . . ?"

"No," Jasperodus replied shortly. Hastily he scrambled to his feet. "You did nothing!" he exclaimed angrily. "Why did you make no adjustment?"

Padua raised his hands in a gesture of resignation. "I would not presume to interfere in a work of such superb craftsmanship. Anything I could do to amend your integration state – to use a technical term – would be meddlesome and crude . . ." He placed his finger on his lips thoughtfully. "I have just thought of something. Your fictitious self-image could be deliberate. It may have been a deliberate device on the part of your designer. At that, it is quite ingenious. Hmm." Padua nodded, musing. "A means of raising a machine's status in its own eyes and so lifting its self-reliance to a new level. *Very* ingenious. Possibly I should have played along with your delusion."

"Too late for that now," replied Jasperodus dully. If what Padua said was true, then the cruelty of what his parents had done to him was almost unbelievable. Surely their intention had been quite the reverse.

"Indeed, yes." Padua packed up his gear. "Well, time for you to be moving."

"Where am I going?"

"You are now a member of the King's household. I have orders to send you down to the stables, where the machines and animals are quartered. So if you will step this way . . ."

Jasperodus stepped to the door, then paused and turned to Padua. "But you have condemned me to Hell," he accused. "To a living death. Yet how can I be condemned? I am not a conscious soul, I only appear to myself to be. I do not exist, I only believe that I do. I am nothing, a figment, a thought in the void without a thinker." He shook his head in deepest despair. "It is a riddle. I cannot understand it."

Padua gazed at him with something touchingly close to sympathy. "If this self-image is pre-programmed, you are indeed faced with a paradox that to a machine-mind is insuperable," he admitted. He touched Jasperodus on the arm. "Perhaps we shall meet again. I hope so." He pointed down the corridor. "Please follow the passage to the right. The stable hands will be ready to receive you."

So Jasperodus, his morale broken, believing his effective worth to be zero, obeyed the robotician and plodded towards the palace stables to begin his servitude.

4

From the animal stables down near the courtyard that opened on to the concourse, came the sound of stamping feet, of snorting horses and the occasional bark of a dog as the kennels stirred in the pre-dawn gloom. Hearing these sounds, Jasperodus envied the animals their common warmth and sensitive restlessness. It would have been better to be stabled among them, he thought, rather than here in the unrelieved tedium of the construct section.

A dreary, creaking voice suddenly came to life in the stall next to his own. "One, two, three, four, five, six. All here. Four plates of patterned silver. Five gold goblets engraved with the Royal Coat of Arms. A trencher of platinum, design depicting a rustic scene. Now the earthenware. Fifty plates of assorted glaze. Count them slowly. Handle them carefully, you rotten rusted hulk. Oh dear. Two plates broken. Oh dear, I am a rotten rusted hulk."

A pause; then the maddening monologue began again. The voice came from an aged, deteriorating robot who worked in the palace kitchens. Every night his moronic brain sorted through the day's experiences which, with small variations, were always the same: endless abuse from the kitchen staff and an inevitable succession of accidents and mistakes. Night after night Jasperodus was forced to eavesdrop on a stream of babble, a machine version of troubled dreams, a recurring nightmare whose theme was incompetence.

He stood in a wooden stall to which he was fastened by a heavy chain. The precaution was futile as well as unnecessary: with a little exertion he could have torn out the chain by the pins that fastened it to the timber and made his escape. But neither escape, nor defiance, nor disobedience were anywhere in his mind. Jasperodus had entered the stables, from the very first moment, utterly resigned to his future of machine drudgery. He knew himself to be nothing: he carried out his work dutifully and without omission, but mulishly, so that Horsu Greb, the robot overseer, had been forced to admit scant value on his talents.

35

For the first few weeks of his slavery he had continued to wrestle with the existential riddle posed him by his conversation with Padua.

It had been a tormenting time, for all his efforts had only persuaded him that Padua – and all the others – must be right. He had striven to enter into his own mind to find his basic identity, to locate the "I" that, if he were conscious, must lie behind all his thoughts and perceptions. But however hard he tried all he could find were more thoughts, feelings and perceptions. The inference was plain: if the "I" could not be grasped then it was reasonable to suppose that it did not exist at all.

And so he was a figment, as Padua had said. The "consciousness" he had presumed in himself was fictitious only. It would not be difficult for a clever robot-maker to arrange: probably it consisted of one thought mechanically assessing another. But dead, all dead.

Jasperodus did not know whether to curse those who had made him or to pity them.

Since he had reached his conclusions and left off his mentations the despair they had brought him had worn down to a kind of everyday weariness. Weariness and boredom were now his constant companions – he had no others, for apart from himself the robots of the stable were cretinous in the extreme. He could, for short periods, escape this weariness (as well as Kitchen Help's desperate maunderings) by switching off his higher brain functions, upon which he simply vanished from existence as far as his own cognisance went. Unfortunately some automatic mechanism limited this haven of "sleep" to four hours out of twenty-four, since from a physiological standpoint it was not necessary to him at all. Otherwise he might have preferred to switch himself off permanently, since according to Padua non-being was more appropriate to his proper condition.

With regard to the boredom that was eating into him: he had noticed that he alone of all the working robots was afflicted with it. He theorised two explanations: (1) his erroneous self-image was responsible and (2) the other robots were too stupid ever to feel bored.

Either explanation was sufficient on its own, he felt, but no-

36

tably the latter. The constructs he had been thrown among were a haphazard collection, their intelligence ranging from the sub-human right down to the negligible. Some were so primitive that they scarcely deserved to be called "self-directed" at all. Jasperodus ignored all of them, including the resurrected Gogra, whom he had occasionally seen skulking about. On their first sighting one another he had wondered if the big fighting robot would take him to task for the humiliation he had suffered, but either Gogra's reconstituted brain contained no memory of his defeat or else he was too dim-witted to feel resentment.

The same could not be said for Horsu Greb, robot overseer, dim-witted though he undoubtedly was. The bad feeling he har-boured towards Jasperodus stemmed, apparently, from a casual jest on Padua's part. When advising Horsu of the new robot's capabili-ties, as was his duty, he had jokingly remarked that Jasperodus could be a candidate for Horsu's own job. Never a man of enor-mous humour, Horsu had taken the threat seriously and ever after looked with ill-veiled hostility toward his handsome chargehand. Even he sensed something unusual about Jasperodus, despite the latter's modest demeanour, and that was the reason why he kept him in chains at night.

Dawn broke, chinks of light filtering into the stable, glancing off metal, shining on wood. Dogs barked more vigorously in the animal section, from which wafted a warm, raw odour Jasperodus was well used to.

A timber gate squeaked open. Horsu Greb lurched into view, red-rimmed eyes staring out over a bulbous nose flawed with warts. Rubbing sleep from his eyes and hitching up his baggy trousers with a length of leather cord, he paced the gangway, bellowing hoarsely.

"Stir yourselves, you useless lumps! The sun is in the sky! No more lazing!"

He turned aside to urinate against the flank of an unprotesting earthmover. The stalls resounded to a general clanking and thum-ping; Jasperodus rattled his chains, marvelling anew at the way Horsu bolstered his self-esteem by projecting organic qualities on to the robots – by imagining that they, not he, preferred to sleep into the day.

The unkempt overseer stopped by Jasperodus' stall and glared at him. "I want a good day's work out of you!" he roared. "No slacking! There's a lot of carrying to be done!"

Jasperodus remained impassive while Horsu unlocked his chain. He moved into the gangway, receiving as he did so a jocular kick from Horsu's steel-toed boot.

The constructs trailed out of the stable in a ragged procession. Not all were humanoid: there were quadrupeds built for hauling after the manner of horses or oxen; wheeled robots; and the self-directed earthmover bearing before it a great splayed blade. In front of Jasperodus Kitchen Help trudged along. Horsu had interrupted his litany, which he hurriedly resumed now with a list of resolutions, adjuring himself to break no plates, spill no soup, and tread on no more pot-boys' toes.

Out in the courtyard the robots milled around aimlessly until Horsu, with much self-important yelling and many superfluous blasts upon a whistle, directed them to various destinations: some to the palace where they carried out domestic duties, some to the animal stable where they served as grooms, and the rest, Jasperodus included, out of the courtyard and along the palace wall to a building site.

The sunlight still barely slanted across the ground as they began work. The earthmover continued digging out the foundations it had started the day before. Jasperodus and two other humanoids unloaded bricks and masonry blocks from some lorries, piling them conveniently for the work to be undertaken. The building gangers had not arrived yet but Horsu, though not himself of that trade, presumed to stand in for them, placing himself on a pile of rubble and looking around him with judicious nods.

The work was tedious and heavy. Hours passed and the sun rose in the sky; Jasperodus' body hummed almost audibly as he humped the blocks of stone which were quarried, he believed, from ancient ruins lying somewhere in the region.

Occasionally he paused to take note of anything interesting that might be happening nearby. They were working to build fuel bunkers for a powerhouse that lay beneath the palace, and every now and then a number of large baffle-plates set in the palace wall opened slightly to give forth a wave of heat. As the day progressed the exhalations grew more intense until they finally stopped altogether. Jasperodus, who was familiar with the layout of the powerhouse through having worked there as a stoker, suspected that something was amiss.

He was proved correct, for shortly a stocky, red-faced man emerged from the access tunnel and hurried to Horsu, with whom he engaged in agitated discussion. On seeing Horsu shake his head in a gesture of indignant refusal Jasperodus heightened the sensitivity of his hearing so as to eavesdrop on their conversation.

"Do you imagine my fine robots are so many lumps of wood to be burned up just like that? Away with you!" Horsu was saying.

"But imagine if there is an explosion – right underneath the palace!" the other implored with anguish. "Would you have the King rebuke you for malfeasance?"

Horsu parried the threat. "To me is entrusted only the care of the household robots. The powerhouse is not within my province and is in no way my responsibility."

And the other riposted: "Indeed it is, for your robots are even now engaged in building an extension to it."

However else Horsu might have answered remained unknown, for the Major Domo himself arrived, bearing himself imperiously and trailing behind him Kitchen Help.

The Major Domo curtly overruled Horsu's objections. "This robot here will be no loss," he declared. "The kitchen staff tell me he is completely useless and more of a nuisance than an asset. So let him expend himself on one last useful act."

With an aggrieved sigh the stablemaster looked this way and that, scratching his chin. He next looked Kitchen Help up and down and then glanced at Jasperodus; a crafty look came over his face.

"Very well!" he agreed. "Take Kitchen Help. The crisis evidently demands a sacrifice."

The aged construct nodded his head as it was explained to him what was required. His weakly glowing eyes blinked in his effort to understand. "Yes, I obey. Reach the opposite wall of the furnace; inspect to ascertain why the conduits will not open nor the rakes work; clear the mechanism and make sure it is working aright; if possible, quit the furnace and return."

"Excellent, excellent!" The party moved to the mouth of the access tunnel and disappeared from view.

39

Jasperodus continued with his work, but presently Horsu and the others emerged into the open again, minus the robot. The Major Domo pointed to a humanoid who worked alongside Jasperodus.

"How about that one there? He seems sturdy enough."

But Horsu beckoned to Jasperodus himself. "I can do even better. It's futile to send machine after machine into the furnace if they are simply destroyed without doing the job. This one, now, is in perfect condition; if he can't do it none of them can." He adopted an expression of regret tempered with duty. "It distresses me, of course, that I shall probably lose this prime property, but after all they're all expendable."

"What is the nature of the problem?" Jasperodus asked on coming near.

The powerhouse minder turned to him. "The furnace controls are jammed and all attempts to clear them from the outside have failed. In a word, it's out of control: the furnace is overheating, the boilers are building up pressure, and if this goes on I don't like to think about the consequences."

"Clearly a poor piece of design," Jasperodus remarked. The powerhouse minder shot him a look of reproof and then continued. "Someone has to go right into the furnace to see what the trouble is. We've already sent the kitchen robot, but apparently the temperature was too much for him." He went on to issue the same instructions he had given Kitchen Help.

"I am acquainted with this furnace, and I am not likely to survive either," Jasperodus volunteered. "Perhaps if I were equipped with a cooling agent, such as frozen carbon dioxide supplied through a hose . . ."

"Enough!" roared Horsu. "There's no time for niceties. This is an emergency – get on with it." And Jasperodus understood that Horsu was using the situation to get rid of him for good and all.

If I were a living being it would be an injustice, he thought, *but I am not a living being, so there is no injustice . . .*

He followed the humans to the access tunnel, automatically going over the layout of the powerhouse in his mind. Its design was so crude as to lose even the advantages of simplicity. Theoretically it used nuclear energy, consuming a specially processed type of "safe" compound isotope that produced no residual radioactivity when it decayed, but generated enough heat to raise steam through a primitive heat exchanger. The isotope was shovelled into the furnace as slag and triggered into decay by a powerful jolt of microwaves, after which it decomposed into liquid waste and could be drained off through conduits.

But in practice the isotope fuel was permanently in short supply and so was combined with an oddly disparate method of producing energy. The furnace was fitted with a system of flues to draw oxygen, and into it went anything that would burn – timber, coke, plastic, sometimes rubbish from the palace. The combination of combustion and nuclear power was not a happy one, as could be seen from the present situation. It would be a small disaster for King Zhorm if the powerhouse was destroyed, for apart from the damage it would cause to the palace itself, it would cut off the electricity supply to part of the town of Okrum – a form of royal largesse from which Zhorm drew popularity.

The tunnel was lined with concrete and angled sharply underground. The light here was dim, being provided by feeble yellow lamps set in the ceiling. Halfway down the tunnel turned a right angle, and here Horsu and the others paused.

"Right," Horsu said with unveiled satisfaction. "You know what you have to do – get on with it."

Wordlessly Jasperodus proceeded on his own. A few yards further down brought him to the furnace room.

The space between wall and furnace was narrow. Facing Jasperodus were the furnace doors, fabricated of mica-carbon laminate and glowing faintly. Behind them the fire of the furnace seemed to roar and beat like a living heart.

Two crouching robots turned towards him in the baking gloom. Jasperodus knew them well: they were stokers, their feeble mentalities adapted only to that one task. They were incapable of any other, such as the mission he had been sent on.

Here I go, then. As I am nothing, so I shall be nothing. A thought in the void without a thinker ...

He dismissed any thought of death. Death could not exist for one who had never been born . . . It seemed to him that what was about to happen to him was a logical conclusion of the tragedy that surrounded him. Every day of his life he had been living a lie, the lie of his own being. That lie had brought him first to despair, then to the knowledge of his own imprisonment, and now . . . Everything had been leading to this fiery execution chamber.

Understanding what was expected, the stokers applied themselves to levers, one on either side of the doors, and forced them slowly open. A brilliant white glare flooded into the narrow space.

As the glaring fire was revealed, a curious image rose in Jasperodus' mind, so vividly as to paralyse him for a moment. He saw a blast furnace in which iron and steel were smelted. Into it trundled an endless stream of scrap metal : objects large and small, weapons, cars, broken-up aircraft and locomotives, canisters, ornaments, statues and statuettes, table-ware, hooks and buttons, brackets, rods, girders, fences, gates, trays, myriad machines and defunct robots, every one disappeared into the ravening heat to lose all form and identity. And all the metal thereby gained was used again to make a new generation of artifacts. Unaccountably this thought left Jasperodus feeling stunned – he himself could be melted down in such a furnace (as he had once been drawn from one) and used to make, perhaps, the chassis for a motorised carriage, or even a new, totally different robot who would live a happily humdrum existence unafflicted by the curse of a fictitious self-image.

Where had this vision come from? Presumably from the stock of gratuitous memories bestowed on him by his father – somehow he still thought of the old man as his father. But it was over in a second or so. He moved forward, switching his vision to ultra-violet in an attempt to see through the flames, and clambered into the furnace. Fire licked at him; the doors edged shut behind him.

He stood alone in a raging haze of incandescence.

The air was thick with energy. It was like being under water.

This must be what it's like inside a star.

Then it was hard for him to think anything for everything went fuzzy; the heat was disrupting his processes. He took a step, and stumbled over the body of Kitchen Help, which was at white heat and looked on the point of beginning to melt. His own skin was already glowing. Vaguely he was aware of his lower brain functions responding to the damage with a stream of urgent reports, analyses and prognostications; their import was that he should remove himself from here on the instant.

The possibility presented itself that he might not even reach the far wall of the furnace, though it was not very far away. But something else rose to the surface in him, sweeping aside both defeatism and the machine analogue of panic. He determined that he would accomplish this one last thing, at whatever degree of difficulty; he would not end his functioning on a note of failure.

His eyes were only of minimal use to him by now. He went forward, reeled, recovered himself and so gained the far end of the furnace where the trouble was. Groping with his hands, he verified what he had already guessed to be the cause of failure: vitrified ash from the burning of a combustible fuel had sealed both the lids of the waste pipes and the clumsy mica-laminate rakes that were supposed to shovel the ash away. Both ash and decomposed isotope was supposed to form a slurry to flow away to the waste pits below; instead they had stayed in the furnace, building up more and more heat.

Though barely operational, Jasperodus kicked desperately at the glassy mass, and eventually succeeded in cracking and shattering it. Then he threw himself at the rakes, tearing free the fused fragments with his hands.

His body was at white heat. His senses were going out, leaving him hanging in a vacant void.

Collapse was imminent.

If I really tried, he thought, *perhaps I could reach the door.* But he made no move to do so, and shortly he felt a tearing sensation as vital systems were taken out. Then he knew no more.

There was light, gentle and caressing. There was the rustle of fabric, and the sigh of a breeze.

And Jasperodus retracted his eyelids, gazing astonished at a baroque ceiling.

Above him hovered the thin, intent face of Padua the robotician. He smiled faintly to see that Jasperodus was "awake".

"Do not be surprised," he murmured. "You have survived."

Nevertheless Jasperodus *was* surprised. Experimentally he levered himself to a sitting position, and observed that he had been lying on a low table covered with a yellow cloth. He appeared to be in one of the gracious little bowers that fringed the palace gardens; through the window casements he could see small, delicate trees, flowered bushes and orange-coloured blossoms.

43

He looked down at his body: bronze-black, decorated all over with engravings, but otherwise unmarked. He swung his legs to the floor and stood with feet apart, trying to detect some persisting damage in himself.

"I thought I had sustained more harm than this!" he exclaimed.

"You did – you were very badly damaged indeed," Padua told him mildly. "You have been out for six months."

"Six months . . ." Jasperodus echoed wonderingly. He flexed his fingers, examining his hands.

"You were in the condition known as scrap when they brought you out of the furnace," Padua said. "But for all the damage the basic design elements were intact – the brain was particularly well protected. I undertook to put you back in order and rescued you from the junkyard – just in time, as you were about to be pounded under the steam hammer."

"Six months is a long time to spend on a repair job. A labour of love, almost." Jasperodus' tone was sardonic.

"Perhaps." Padua smiled faintly again. "I was loath to see such fine work as you represent go to waste. There is little to give my talents full rein here in Gordona – that is the price one pays for living in such an out-of-the-way place. I regarded it as a pleasurable test of my skill, and no thanks are due my way."

Jasperodus, who had not intended to thank him, nevertheless noticed that Padua was looking at him with a strangely expectant expression on his face. He paced the room.

"My faculties are fully restored?"

"Yes, though it cost much effort."

"This hardly looks like your workshop." Jasperodus indicated the harmonious décor.

"I decided to let you be reactivated in pleasant surroundings, rather than amid a clutter of tools and instruments." Again the expectant look.

"What of radioactivity?" Jasperodus asked suddenly, remembering the furnace. "Am I not dangerous to be near? The way things were, the isotope fuel might well have become unstable."

"There's nothing to worry about on that score. There was a little radioactivity, but I purged your substance of it by a means of accelerating atomic decay that is known to me."

"You are indeed wasted in Gordona," Jasperodus grunted grudgingly. He paced again, trying to place what it was that was new and puzzling in his environment.

"There's a change," he said. "What is it?"

At this Padua laughed and clapped his hands in delight. "I thought you'd never notice. Try again – can *you* guess what it is?"

"I wouldn't be asking if I could," Jasperodus replied with an irritable gesture.

"Well, you see, the making of robots is as much of an art as a science. Even the masters of highest attainment are invariably stronger on some features, weaker on others – except, of course, for an acme of perfection like Aristos Lyos. Now your own maker was unexcelled in the area of intellectual functions, but rather weak when it came to a certain type of fine nerve structure needed for the senses of smell and touch. Now it so happens that that area is my own speciality! So I undertook to remedy his deficiencies. In the field of touch-sensation and of smell you now have the same range and sensitivity as any man or woman!"

With much curiosity Jasperodus drew one hand across the other. It was as Padua had said: the dynamic sense of solid bodies was there, as before, but in addition there was an entirely new feeling; a stroking, tingling feeling.

Fascinated, he laid the flat of one hand on the cloth of the table he had just vacated, moving the palm gently across the felt. An entirely novel rough-smooth feel coursed through him. A whole area of his brain seemed to come alive for the first time.

"It's fantastic," he said quietly.

"I had hoped it would afford you some diversion," Padua replied affably.

Jasperodus, however, would not be jollied along. "No doubt it will enable me to appreciate the qualities of the stable all the better," he grunted. "One thing you have *not* amended. I still have this irrational belief that I possess consciousness!" And he rounded on Padua accusingly.

Padua looked a little embarrassed. "There was nothing I could do about that," he said defensively. "It's in the basic design: if I tried to remove it you would be reduced to a hulk, good for nothing."

Jasperodus emitted a sigh, a gesture he had learned from Horsu

45

Greb. "Then to be frank I could have preferred that you had left me for scrap."

His words provoked such a look of unhappiness on the robotician's face that he instantly regretted them – he had spoiled Padua's pleasure. But he impatiently cancelled the feeling. Padua had enjoyed his work and *he*, Jasperodus, had to pay the price for his enjoyment.

"Would it be any use if I advised you not to brood too much on this enigma?" Padua suggested cautiously. "It *is* part of your integration state, and it *does* appear to work, as a device for raising your degree of function to a greater independence than is normally found in a robot. You are, almost, a perfect simulation of a man."

"Thank you," Jasperodus said with scathing irony. "It helps not at all, especially as I must now return to the tender ministrations of Horsu Greb."

"I have been considering that," Padua replied. "Horsu could be accused of not making full use of your potentialities – it grieves me to see you wasted on manual labour. Perhaps I can persuade the Major Domo to assign you to more challenging duties where you will not be under his direction, though that would be a break with our usual practice. After all, Greb has effectively discarded you."

An idea came to Jasperodus. "Though my knowledge of engineering is far from extensive, I could undertake to design a better powerhouse than you have at present. It gives one a poor view of Gordona's engineers."

"They are better described as optimistic amateurs," Padua agreed. "Possibly it could be arranged. Failing that, how would you like to become my assistant? But we must discuss this later – I have duties elsewhere, and perhaps you would like to be alone to collect your thoughts. I'll be back in about an hour."

Padua departed, leaving Jasperodus to his own devices. Attracted to the garden, and wishing to test his new faculties, he unfastened the catch on a glass door and stepped outside. Some yards along a stone path, through a trellised arbour, brought him to a lawn whose further end descended into a series of cultivated terraces. All around were flowering trees, blossoms and shrubs, and beyond these could be glimpsed the circle of low buildings that comprised

46

the palace: mixed timber and stone surmounted by curved, pointed roofs.

A breeze blew up, playing over his body with sensations so fresh and delightful that he was astonished. And his mind simply stopped when he encountered the warm, heady summer of perfumes the breeze brought with it: sensuous, delicate, powerful and bewitching, yet clean and innocent. Marvellous!

Marvellous!

Some of his recent dourness dropped away. It was impossible to remain sullen in the midst of such wonders. He strolled through the garden; his fingers played with silky smooth petals and cool, ribbed leaves. See this red rose: what perfect harmony between colour, texture and scent! Not to speak of perfection of form! Jasperodus paced on, an Adam in a new Eden, smelling the scent of new-cut grass, feeling the shortened blades tickle his feet.

This, surely, proved that existence – even his kind of existence – was worthwhile! What if he did lack this mysterious quality called consciousness? What if his identity was a fiction? Were not some of the world's greatest dramas fictions? In the face of these new experiences it now seemed to him that the whole affair was purely a sophistry and that he had been a fool to have been brought down by it.

A new excitement germinated in his mind: the excitement known to the world as AMBITION. *I have been through fire and am purged of despair and self-doubt. Am I less of a man than Horsu Greb? Than King Zhorm? Than Padua, even? Am I capable of less than they? Demonstrably, no! And I shall prove my worth. I shall prove it by gaining power over them . . . they all shall defer to Jasperodus the robot.*

He paused, revelling in his new-born senses; and in that hidden, empty place where his soul should have been was formed a resolve having all the force of obsession. *I know my strength . . . There is nothing I cannot do . . . King Zhorm, look to your throne . . .*

5

"This then, Your Majesty, is my scheme. In place of one furnace we have two. The main furnace is for isotope fuel and is sealed. The other burns combustibles and will serve as an assist to the first, or for emergencies. The heat exchanger is also a considerable improvement on the present arrangement. The same water can be circulated through the jackets of both furnaces or through either of them alone. All the controls are simple and employ no interior moving parts except for a system of movable trays, for the disposal of waste, which are proof against any kind of breakdown. I can promise Your Majesty that the new powerhouse will do away with the erratic voltages and frequent breakdowns, not to say danger to life and property, that have been a source of annoyance in the past."

King Zhorm glanced cursorily at Jasperodus' blueprints, following the features pointed out by the latter's metal finger and pretending he understood them.

"If the scheme is approved," Jasperodus added, "I may then go on to re-design the generators, which also incorporate many defects."

"You seem to think we are living in Tansiann, with the taxes of half the planet to draw on," grumbled Zhorm. "Already I have expended much on the extension to the present powerhouse."

This claim was hardly true; the extensions consisted merely of fuel bunkers built by robot labour. Only the materials had involved any expense. Jasperodus made no comment, however. The King seemed to be distracted today, so he decided to drop the whole matter for the time being.

"Your Majesty perhaps has more important questions on his mind," he ventured.

"Indeed I have. Those bandits out in the West Forest are becoming an intolerable pest. Matters are reaching serious proportions."

Zhorm poured goblets of wine, absent-mindedly offered Jasperodus one, then downed it himself after a hasty curse. It was disconcerting to have this machine about the palace, he thought. Jasperodus was more intelligent than any other robot Zhorm had ever
seen and he kept thinking of him as human.

Jasperodus' eagerness for change was not unreservedly welcome either. If given free rein the clever robot would embroil
Zhorm in grandiose schemes far beyond his means. As it was he
was having to divert most of his resources into his small army
because of these confounded bandit raids . . . Idly he mused on
what other appointment Jasperodus could be given in his retinue.
Why not make him court jester? He had already shown he had wit.
Zhorm smiled, imagining Jasperodus bedecked in fool's garb,
prancing about and forced to invent inane jokes for the general
amusement.

Jasperodus was at a loss to explain the King's sudden laughter.

But no matter. He was remembering a recent conversation he
had held with Major Cree Inwing, an officer in the Gordonian
Guard, Zhorm's little-practised army.

Jasperodus had been working on his blueprints using a table
in the lobby (he had no room of his own to work in), when he had
witnessed an exchange between this officer and Prince Okhramora,
the King's half-brother, whom Jasperodus had encountered on the
evening of his first induction into Zhorm's household: he was
the fat man who had tried to belabour him with an iron rod. In-
ordinately fond of food, drink and lechery, he was often to be
seen bustling about the palace on errands of doubtful propriety.

On this occasion, however, his business was indignantly moral.
He was upbraiding Major Inwing for the Guards' failure to bring
the bandit bands to book. With him he had a farmer from an
outlying district, a sad-faced fellow who only the day before had
been attacked, his farm despoiled and his brother and eldest son
killed. Such raids were occurring nearly every other day now, and
were penetrating deeper into the small kingdom.

"If this goes on these thugs will be coming right here into
Okrum!" Prince Okhramora declared angrily.

Major Inwing, a normally self-confident young man with wheat-
coloured hair and a brisk moustache, stood to attention, his face
pink with embarrassment. "Everything is being done that possibly

49

could be done, Highness. The Guards can't be everywhere at once."

"What a pathetic reply!" stormed the Prince. "I'm taking this unfortunate subject to the King himself, and I'll have you drummed out of the service, you see if I don't! It was one of *your* companies that should have defended this man's family, but where were you?"

And Prince Okhramora swept away, the dejected farmer in train. Jasperodus had noticed that he was zealous in seeing that incompetent officers were stripped of their rank; their replacements were usually friends of his or relatives on his mother's side. This time Jasperodus was certain he would get nowhere, however; Major Inwing was so popular with his men that the King would never agree to cashier him or even to demote him.

He sidled up to the discomfited officer. "What is the problem with these raiders, Major?" he enquired politely. "Could they not be tracked to their lairs and destroyed?"

"That's something we've tried to do a score of times," Inwing retorted in exasperation, "but the West Forest stretches for hundreds of miles and it's practically impossible to sniff them out – one might as well go hunting the antelope," he added, adducing the ancient mythical beast. "Ours is not the only kingdom to be harried by these gangs and no one else has managed to flush them out either."

"Surely something is known about them," Jasperodus persisted. "How many groups of these men are there?"

"Several. But the largest and fiercest of them is led by a man called Craish, that much we do know. A clever devil he is too, by all accounts."

And Jasperodus remembered the railway track, the journey through the forest, and the natural amphitheatre.

But he said nothing of this to Inwing. More was to be gained by speaking to King Zhorm himself . . .

. . . His private joke over, the King looked glum. "A monarch must protect his people or he won't remain monarch for long," he fretted. "A few days ago these villains took over a hamlet and terrorised it for a day and a night – tell me, my clever construct, what would *you* do about these pests?" Zhorm eyed him half jokingly, half hopefully.

Jasperodus said diffidently, "I think I could undertake to wipe out this nest of troublemakers altogether."

"How so, Jasperodus?" Zhorm's eyes widened. He listened attentively to Jasperodus' story, then nodded judiciously.

"You are sure you can find this place again?"

"Certainly, Your Majesty. They could have moved since, of course, but I very much doubt it. The camp had all the appearance of being permanent."

Zhorm rang a bell, summoning a page. "Bring me Captain Grue."

Jasperodus laid aside his blueprints and spoke in a low, confidential voice. "Your Majesty, engineering is not my true bent. I aspire to a military career. Let *me* command the attack on the bandit camp. After you see my performance perhaps you will think me fit to be granted a commission in the Guard, which is my most earnest desire."

In the act of draining his goblet, Zhorm almost choked. "*What?* Where in the name of the Almighty do you find the audacity for a request like that? Be careful I don't return you to the furnace!"

"Consult Padua, Your Majesty. He will assure you the idea is perfectly feasible. In fact I could not be put to better use. I will make an excellent officer."

"Padua has already made plenty of representations on your behalf," Zhorm snapped. "I am almost tired of hearing him sing your praises."

He frowned. He had never made use of robots as soldiers, for the simple reason that their obedience was such that the enemy could easily turn them round against their own side. One way round this was a robot with a command language known only to its masters, but such robots were expensive and Zhorm did not own any. Men were cheaper ...

Admittedly Jasperodus answered neither of these cases and though not controlled by a command language seemed not to suffer from extreme obedience either. Padua had explained it thus: his command structure was unusually elaborate and he was able – strange though it seemed – to ignore orders altogether sometimes. Zhorm took this to mean that Jasperodus would disobey an order that contradicted a previous order – or something like that.

51

"Flexible end-game," he murmured.

"Your Majesty?"

"Flexible end-game. Padua was talking about it the other day. It's the strategy your brain is based on."

He glanced up as Captain Grue entered and saluted smartly.

"Captain Grue here will command the force," he said incisively. "You will accompany it as guide. Now, let us discuss the expedition itself."

"Damn you, metal man, damn you!"

Craish's raging imprecations were music to Jasperodus' ears. Hands on hips, he stood on a rise in the ground. Below him in the dell the bandit leader's men were being roped together by Gordonian troops, cringing away from the ring of guns.

The foray had worked out even better than Jasperodus had hoped. Captain Grue had set out with a force of a hundred men, riding the transcontinental railroad on a flimsy, primitive train powered by an oil-burning engine. The train possessed a look-out tower to give warning if a long-range express approached, so as to give its passengers a chance to take to the ground and perhaps get the train off the rails as well. Nothing of this kind occurred, and the expedition quickly reached the spot designated by its robot guide.

From then on events had followed with rapidity. Since Jasperodus had last seen it Craish's gang had expanded and itself numbered well over a hundred well-armed ruffians, so that the attackers found themselves evenly matched. These desperadoes' first ambush had been a near-disaster for the expedition, due in part to the way Jasperodus had led it openly through the forest without any caution or reconnoitre.

It was during this ambush that Captain Grue had been killed. In the ensuing confusion the other officers had yelled conflicting orders and the troops had milled around hopelessly. Then Jasperodus had come into his own. Leaping on to a rock, bullets ringing off his impervious body, he had made an imposing figure, his voice booming out over the scene like thunder. He had rallied his men, brought them through withering fire, and then had assumed full command to lead them on to victory.

"Hurry it up!" he bellowed now. "Get them to the train!"

A subaltern approached and hesitated. Jasperodus cast him a fierce look; hastily the subaltern saluted. Lazily Jasperodus returned the salute.

"Why don't we just slaughter this rabble where they stand?" the officer asked. "That was Captain Grue's intention."

"Their fate is for the King to decide," Jasperodus growled. "We will take them back to Okrum." He turned away, shouting stentorian instructions across the amphitheatre.

Shortly they set out for the railway, the long file of prisoners in their midst. Lieutenant Haver, who by rank should have taken command on the death of Grue, persisted in issuing orders every now and then; each time Jasperodus bellowed a contradictory order, and the men, whose lives Jasperodus had already saved, instinctively tended to obey the stronger personality.

The Lieutenant eventually confronted Jasperodus, complaining about this undermining of his authority. But the big robot chose to ignore him. Soon Haver, too, was reduced to accepting his orders.

Back at the railroad Jasperodus made a discovery: an engine and some trucks hidden in a culvert. By this means Craish had been able to travel at speed through Gordona, striking and withdrawing along the railroad. He had the crude train smashed, except for a couple of trucks which were added to his own stock, while the prisoners were loaded on board for the return journey.

Already on board were the captives that had been found in the bandits' camp. They were mostly women, sitting quietly with heads downcast, remembering the ill-treatment they had received.

All business in Okrum ceased when they paraded the prisoners through the town. Jasperodus permitted Lieutenant Haver to march at the head of the column with him for appearance's sake, but of the two it was the bronze-black robot who made the most striking spectacle, and who most enjoyed the acclaim of the crowd.

It had begun. He was on the way to becoming a master of men.

It was a signal honour indeed for a robot to be invited to banquet, and to sit at the King's table with the nobles and notables of the realm. The other guests at first found it to be an object of great amusement and made fun of Jasperodus; but though he could not of course eat and drink, he soon made them change their attitude

53

with the dominating excellence of his conversation, recounting how he and the Gordonian Guard had defeated Craish's stronghold. In passing he expressed regret for the death of Captain Grue, who he skilfully managed to convey was a brave but unimaginative officer.

Having captured everyone's attention, he went on to discourse upon how a military force for defending a small country should be constituted. "The Guard of the Realm should be small but disciplined to the utmost and trained to the optimum," he said. "It should be able within the hour to strike in any part of the kingdom. So besides the transport to achieve this there should also be good communications throughout the kingdom so that any attack or disturbance immediately becomes known in the capital. Now as to the commander of armed forces: he should be a man whose alertness never wanes and who knows how to keep an army in a constant state of tension. He should not be such a one as will sink into complacency, inattention to changing circumstances, or fleshly pleasures.

"Finally, if the country has external enemies it is useful to train and arm the population to some extent, but the people should never be allowed to command as much fire-power as the army."

A snort came from down the table. "One would think this metal construct himself coveted the post of commander."

"Did I say so?" rejoindered Jasperodus sharply. "The Guard already has a commander of irreplaceable mettle." He inclined his head towards Commander Haurk, who sat fiddling with his goblet and frowning with some displeasure. "But since *you* raise the point, it would only be fair to point out that I possess *all* the qualities I have outlined, to a greater extent than any flesh-and-blood man. I do not sleep, day or night. My mind can be given unremittingly to my duties, oblivious of the diversions that a human being cannot forgo. Lastly, being a machine and not a man, I do not strive to acquire power for myself as do the commanders of some armies, as their sovereigns have found to their cost."

A weighty silence followed his words. Jasperodus turned to King Zhorm. "Your Majesty, it is a slander to say that I aspire to such an exalted post. But may I again mention my desire for a commission as a subaltern?"

A roar of laughter greeted his words. A young man uncontrollably sprayed a mouthful of wine over the table. "What? A robot be an *officer?*" .

"Why not?" Jasperodus' gaze went from face to face. He spoke with a passion which this time was genuine. "A soldier's rôle is combat, is that not so? Test me, then. I challenge any of you to any contest that suits you, whether of skill, strength or cunning, whether of the body or of the mind – I undertake to defeat you all."

"I accept!" came an animated voice from down the hall. "We shall be rivals: you must seek to seduce a certain maid I shall name!"

Jasperodus angrily ignored the howls of merriment that followed the challenge. "And if you think I cannot command the respect of subordinates," he said loudly, "then speak to those I led today!"

"But this is ridiculous!" someone protested. "To make an officer of a robot!"

King Zhorm the while was watching Jasperodus with his dreamy, barbaric eyes. "Enough!" he interjected. "It is not ridiculous at all. I have heard of such things being done in lands to the East, where robots of great sophistication are available. By your amazement you merely display your bucolic ignorance."

"Well said, brother!" Prince Okhramora spoke up, addressing the King with his usual over-familiarity. He wiped the grease from his face with a napkin. "These clods who surround us are indeed ignorance personified. But what of the prisoners? How are they to be disposed of?"

Zhorm replied sardonically, "Perhaps the robot Jasperodus has some ideas as to that, since he seems to have ideas on every other subject."

Jasperodus and Prince Okhramora exchanged secret gratified glances.

Their relationship had developed much more favourably since their first unhappy encounter. Jasperodus, as if to make amends for his earlier indiscretion, had privately shown himself willing to perform small services for the Prince, who had come to look upon him as a useful ally. For that reason he was far from being opposed to Jasperodus' advancement and was already apprised of the suggestion the robot was about to make.

"While their crimes deserve instant death, it is sometimes a good principle to make use of such men instead of destroying

55

them," Jasperodus said carefully. "Ruthlessness and bravado are not to be decried, provided they work for one and not against one. Now, many of Craish's men are riff-raff and should be garotted without delay. But others would make good soldiers, given the right discipline. Craish himself is a man who turned to crime through recklessness rather than through any innate evil, and he possesses both courage and resourcefulness. He would surely submit to military service and swear allegiance to Your Majesty in return for his life."

Zhorm scratched his chin, looking at Jasperodus askance. "Not the traditional way to deal with criminals."

"The populace need not be made aware of it," Jasperodus pointed out blandly. "An immediate advantage to be gained is that Craish must know the whereabouts of the other outlaw groups in the forest, and doubtless he could be persuaded to work towards their extermination with enthusiasm. Give me him and a few of his followers, and I will soon knock the rough edges off them, I assure you. And if they should prove intractable, why, they can be shot at any time."

"Dammit, this robot talks sense," voiced a middle-aged, heavily-jowled man in a quilted tabard. "We can be rid of these infestations for good and all."

"In a general sense, I also would tend to agree," Prince Okhramora said mildly.

"I will think on the matter," King Zhorm announced. "But I have had enough of serious talk." He clapped his hands. "Bring on the entertainment!"

Musicians advanced into the hall, bowed, took their places, and were followed in by a troupe of dancing girls. Deep in thought, Jasperodus watched idly. As soon as he could do so without giving offence he slipped away, leaving the scene of merriment behind.

He went through the palace and across an open courtyard to the barracks. Beneath them, deep in the earth, were some ancient dungeons, built of stone that had become damp and mildewed and smelling of decay. Descending the worn steps, Jasperodus heard the disconsolate murmurs of the prisoners who were crammed into a few dank cells. He went on past them, however, and down a passage to the cell reserved for Craish alone, where he prevailed upon the guard to unfasten the bolts.

56

Before entering he waved the guard away, waiting until the man was out of both sight and earshot. Then he swung open the door.

Squatting on the floor beside the far wall, Craish lifted his seamed face to stare impassively. The robot moved into the cell and loomed menacingly over his prisoner, his bulk eclipsing the weak electric light and throwing the cell in shadow.

"What the hell do you want?" Craish said defiantly.

The door swung shut with a clang. Craish looked alarmed but belligerent. "What's this? Are you Zhorm's executioner now?"

"If I choose . . ." Jasperodus' voice reverberated quietly in the confined space. He took one step and wrenched Craish to his feet by the front of his jerkin, bringing his face close to his own. The bandit looked frightened and trapped, so close to Jasperodus' bizarre visage.

"Listen to me, you fool . . . you can live if you do what I say. There is a price to be paid, a small price indeed when measured against the loss of your life, effectuated by the garotte and accompanied by the howls of a vengeful mob – but it must be paid, without any omission. You must become my secret slave, together with others whom I will select. Your life will belong to me, your existence will depend upon my will. No one else will know of this; you alone will know that I am your lord and master and that my command is law."

Despite his situation Craish managed a croaking laugh. "Metal man, you're crazy! Be a slave to a *machine*? It's the other way round in my world."

"Then *die!*" Contemptuously Jasperodus flung him down against the wall. "I will explain the circumstances, since whichever way matters fall out your silence is guaranteed. Small though it appears, this court that rules Gordona is a cess-pool of intrigue. King Zhorm has a half-brother, born to the old king's first wife. Being older than Zhorm this brother thinks himself cheated of the throne, although by right of primogeniture the throne is indeed Zhorm's – a fine legal distinction, you may say, which varies from kingdom to kingdom. At any rate, this dolt dreams of an armed *coup*. It is all folly, for Zhorm is by far the better king." Jasperodus laughed hollowly. "But what is that to me? I intend to take advantage of these treasons. Do you follow me? Already I am as good as commissioned in the Guard, and my advancement will not rest there. But it is difficult for a robot to acquire faithful human servitors, and that is why I am recruiting you now."

Craish shook his head in bewilderment. "This king's brother is your principal? You must take orders from *somebody*."

"I alone am the initiator of my deeds. You will not imagine anyone standing behind me, for in truth there is no one."

Craish pondered and sighed. "I can almost believe it. You're more of a man than most men are."

"For once you show discernment. So how do you answer? You can be enrolled in the Gordonian Guard, where I will be your officer – but secretly I will be much more. You will find me a generous master and you will live well. Otherwise . . ." Jasperodus saw no need to explicate further.

Craish gave a crooked smile. "Need you ask? I'm in your hands. Anything you say."

Jasperodus made a quick judgement and felt he could be sure of the man. He leaned down and took Craish's skull in his hand like an egg.

"Fail me and I will crush you – just so," he said, exerting a meaningful pressure. Craish looked up with frightened, hollow eyes, nodding meekly as soon as Jasperodus released his head.

Jasperodus left the cell with an exultant stride. A man had submitted to *him*, a robot, and it was a good, strong feeling. He savoured it for the rest of the night.

Prince Okhramora giggled. "Come in, Commander, come in!"

Entering the apartment, Jasperodus found the Prince sitting comfortably in a padded chair, his short legs splayed out from his tubby body, a grin of glee fixed to his round face.

Okhramora giggled again. "Any last-minute difficulties, Commander?"

"Nothing of note, Highness. All is arranged to satisfaction. Operations will be led by Z Company, from whom we can expect absolute loyalty. The palace, being nearly empty, will be ours in minutes. We will then invest the town, and once Okrum is secure we will release the proclamation we have prepared. I have devised a ruse to separate from their arms those companies whose cooperation cannot be assumed, using the pretext of an armoury check. They will be locked in the barracks and placed under guard."

"Good, good." The Prince screwed up his eyes in a presumably calculating manner. "The announcement will appear simultaneously everywhere, and those who are with us are ready to take over all centres of population. It is well done."

Jasperodus continued with the run-down. "Within the hour the King and his retinue are due to leave for the country palace, putting them thirty miles away from the capital. On that score my stratagem is working well: the entertainment I have procured from the East has enticed away all who could wheedle themselves on to the jaunt, as anticipated. It was well worth the expense."

"And as they leave, my uncle and cousins will be arriving as the start of the *new* court," Okhramora chuckled. "I wish I could see Zhorm's face when he realises what's happened!"

"Success seems assured, Highness."

"Yes; we have planned well, you and I!"

There was a pause, Jasperodus continuing to stand rigidly before the Prince. Suddenly an idea seemed to strike Okhramora, and his face lit up with childish glee.

He picked up a writing scribe and threw it across the room.

"Oh, look, Commander, I have dropped my scribe! Pick it up for me."

Obediently Jasperodus crossed the room and retrieved the scribe from the floor. As he was about to return Okhramora's shrill voice rang out again. "No, no! Bring it to me on your knees!"

Wordlessly Jasperodus trundled across the room on his knees to replace the scribe on the table. The Prince thrust out his hand warningly before he could rise.

"Stay where you are, now," he said softly. "There appears to be a speck of dust upon my shoe. Be good enough to wipe it off with that cloth."

"At once, Highness." Taking the cloth Okhramora had designated, Jasperodus carefully polished both his buckled shoes of soft leather.

"Excellent! Well, Commander, you can stand up now!"

In the past few months Jasperodus had been playing a deceitfully inverted role with the Prince. Like most people in Gordona, Okhramora did not readily conceive of a robot without automatic obedience, and at first had been puzzled to know why Jasperodus exhibited great independence with regard to other human beings and on the other hand showed slavish attachment to himself whenever the two of them were alone together. But eventually he explained it to himself thus: Jasperodus was like a dog, he wanted only one master.

And he, Prince Okhramora, was that master!

Why the robot's devotion should have fallen upon him was largely inexplicable – perhaps, he flattered himself, it reflected on his manly firmness – but it was an amazing piece of good luck. In ordinary terms Jasperodus was a genius, a veritable Machiavelli, and that genius was entirely at Okhramora's disposal. Furthermore, no one else suspected it.

Meanwhile Jasperodus had done well in the Guard, making him an even more attractive target for Okhramora's attentions. Swiftly he had been promoted from Lieutenant to Captain to Major, and his military abilities were beyond dispute. He had been a hard disciplinarian to the newly-formed Z Company consisting mainly of Craish and his men, and with their help had all but cleared the West Forest of outlaws, many of whom had then been drawn into its ranks.

Then, during a training session, a soldier of Z Company had shot Commander Haurk, obviously by accident, and Jasperodus had immediately killed him in great anger before the man could demand the reward he had promised. By this time King Zhorm had become so impressed by Jasperodus that despite all popular prejudice he promoted him to the dead officer's appointment. Thus Jasperodus came to command the Gordonian Guard, a responsibility he pursued with full vigour, making his personality felt among men and officers in no uncertain terms.

But in the palace itself he found that people frequently forgot to guard their tongues in the presence of a robot, much as they might forget in the presence of an animal, and so he adopted a more passive role. This, together with his tunably sensitive hearing, made the intrigues of the court an open book to him.

He had early on realised the value of a partnership with Prince Okhramora. The Guard was riddled with his toadies and relatives, preparatory to the *coup* he dabbled with but would never, without Jasperodus' help and intervention, have found the courage to activate. To gain his trust Jasperodus had cultivated their bizarre re-

60

lationship, willing to bear the degradation in order to achieve his ends.

The Prince had a perverted sense of pleasure; he delighted in seeing the Commander of the Guard – Zhorm's own protector! – slave to his every whim. In public Jasperodus was a figure to esteem – but here he would walk on his hands if Okhramora told him to! He had actually made him do it!

And once, when drunk, he had urinated on Jasperodus.

The experience had carried Jasperodus back to the stables and the detestable Horsu Greb. But he bore all with complete patience.

"So we have only to wait until an hour after nightfall," Okhramora sighed happily. "That will be all, Commander – see that nothing goes awry."

Jasperodus departed and paced the palace. The sun went down on the stone-and-timber buildings, and on the ancient town of Okrum. The bustle of the capital abated as vendors and workshops ceased business and the inhabitants settled down for the evening.

Jasperodus took himself to the barracks. Those companies that could not be bought, numbering about half the Guard, had already handed in their arms and were now at their evening meal. Many, no doubt, were hoping to go into the town later for a bout of drinking, although Jasperodus had been circumspect about the matter of passes.

Detaching himself from a group of officers who stood around nervously, Craish, now Captain Craish, grinned cheerfully at Jasperodus. "This is better than robbing trains, eh, Commander?"

"Keep your mind on the present business," Jasperodus reprimanded him. "I want Z Company at the peak of alertness."

He returned to the palace and again sauntered through it, brooding on every detail of his scheme. He had arranged for Zhorm quickly to learn what was happening, so as to bring him rushing back to the palace and into his hands.

He would then issue *his* announcement to be posted throughout the land: Prince Okhramora had staged a rebellion, killing the King, and was himself now dead. Jasperodus could then represent himself as avenging the King's death and putting down the uprising. In the pretence of restoring order (or actually to restore order if need be) there would be a period of martial law giving

61

Jasperodus the total control of the country he needed. Then for a short interim he would contrive to appoint himself Regent. And then . . .

King!

He went over it again and again and could see no flaw. In a confused situation power went to whoever commanded the most guns – which was himself. Gordona was a relatively peaceful country for the times they were living in, and indeed the populace would see no reason to offer resistance – until it was too late. Jasperodus was satisfied that he had removed all unknown factors from the equation.

"Commander Jasperodus – meet my uncle, Count Osbah!"

Prince Okhramora giggled. Jasperodus bowed. Unlike the Prince, Count Osbah was tall, rakishly thin, and carried himself with exaggerated hauteur. He answered the robot's bow with a distant nod.

So eager was Okhramora to get the affair going that he had brought the Count in by the back door almost as King Zhorm and his retinue were leaving by the front. With him had come nearly a dozen other relatives – cousins, aunts and uncles. Most of them were merely affluent middle-class farmers, for Gordona was not large enough to afford an extensive nobility.

Okhramora's relatives had, in fact, taken possession of the palace ahead of Z Company, and had proved more of a nuisance to the troops than any of its legitimate occupants. The servants, and the few remaining members of the court, had been locked away and Jasperodus had posted sentries among the deserted hallways.

Now his men were in the town. He had sent a squad to occupy the police station and to incarcerate all available police in their own cells. He had also arrested the Chief of Police, the Minister of Justice, the Minister of Trades and Crafts, and other leading citizens.

So far all was quiet.

"If only Mother could have lived to see this day," Okhramora mooned, momentarily overcome by mawkish sentimentality. "It would have answered all her prayers, would it not, Uncle?"

"Quite so." The Count gave him a precise, disdainful look.

A sudden burst of automatic fire came from the direction of the barracks, followed by silence. Jasperodus excused himself, went to find a trooper and sent him to investigate.

Minutes later the soldier returned to say that there had been an attempted break-out, but that all was now under control.

Jasperodus sent the man back to his post and stood in the half-darkened corridor, wondering why he felt nervous. He fingered his weapons, a repeater gun and a long-tubed emitter – the latter an arrangement of glass coils generating a beam of intense energy. The arsenal boasted only one of these rare weapons and he had reserved it for his own use, since unlike bullet-firing guns it was effective if used against himself.

Zhorm should be well on his way back to the palace by now, he thought. It would be easy for him to get inside – Jasperodus had seen to that – unless he was foolish enough to come storming in with the whole of his retinue. And he had good reason to try, quite apart from the loss of his throne. The best of all reasons; one that made it almost certain he would come alone.

When Jasperodus returned, the salon where he had left Okhramora and Count Osbah was empty. He asked their whereabouts of a sentry.

"They have gone to the Throne Room, Commander."

"Indeed? Find Captain Craish and tell him to meet me there, with a dozen of his men."

He went quickly to the Throne Room, entered and took in the scene in a single glance.

The chamber was only of moderate size, in keeping with its use for ceremonial and symbolic occasions. Fashioned in the shape of a concave shell, it imparted an air of luxurious intimacy. The walls were of a soft blue colour; the doors were of mahogany and were flanked by rich azure drapes. But its usual atmosphere of hushed calm was currently entirely broken by the presence of Okhramora and all his relatives, who were gathered in front of the throne. Okhramora himself was at the rear of the chamber, bending over an aumbry where, as everyone knew, the Crown of the Realm was kept. Inexplicably, the lock's combination was apparently also known to the Prince. He opened the aumbry and took out the much-desired symbol of sovereignty.

The Crown! Though not of enormous value it was an object of some beauty, being the work of a talented goldsmith. Okhramora held it up for all to see; its circlet of spiralled spires glinted in the soft light. Then he ascended the three steps to the throne and stood with his back to it, lifting the Crown towards his head with an expression of triumph and bliss.

At that moment Jasperodus bounded forward to mount the steps and snatched the Crown from his hands, cuffing him violently to send him sprawling a dozen feet away.

Swivelling himself round on the floor, Okhramora stared with wide, disbelieving eyes. "What happened?" he squeaked. "Is the Crown booby-trapped? No? Then what? – Jasperodus? . . ."

One of the women screamed.

Jasperodus unhooked his repeater. "Used me as a plaything, did you?" he growled. "You believed me to be your slave. Poor moron, you were *my* tool, not I yours!"

The gun voiced its hideous chatter. Okhramora jerked again and again, edged along the floor by the impact of the bullets. While blood seeped from his body horrified screams filled the chamber.

"SILENCE!" Jasperodus roared. "Silence, or I will deal thus with you all!"

They became hushed. Jasperodus saw Count Osbah sidling to the back of the gathering, trying to gain the doors unnoticed. But he did nothing to stop him and stood as if momentarily paralysed. Unexpected emotions coursed through him and the Crown seemed to burn his metal fingers.

Before the Count could reach the doors they were flung suddenly inwards and Craish entered with his men. At the sight of Jasperodus standing with the throne at his back and the Crown in his hands they came to a halt.

"Enter," Jasperodus commanded in a booming, almost trembling voice that reverberated about the chamber. "Enter and witness." He paused, feeling slightly dizzy. He tried to remind himself of his carefully laid plans, of the calculated moves and periods that must pass before he became king. But all went by the board. A madness had come over him; a madness of pride, of power and of victory. He was not in control of himself. His voice roared out wildly.

"ALL KNEEL!"

Though startled, Craish's men obeyed immediately – all but

two or three who had thought themselves to be working for Okhramora's cause. But something supernatural seemed to have happened to the bronze-black robot; his charismatic presence filled the room, overpowering all present, and in seconds not only these but the civilians, too, sank to their knees, brought down by a combination of fear and personal force.

Jasperodus lifted the Crown and brought it slowly down on his head. As the gold touched his metal skull a feeling of ecstasy swept through his brain.

"*I, I, I* am your King!" he proclaimed, lifting his voice so that it resonated in everyone's consciousness. "I am the sole initiator of my deeds, architect of your destinies!"

Craish set up a cry which was echoed in frightened tones by the others. "Long live the King!"

Jasperodus sank back majestically to seat himself upon the throne and looked upon his minions, his head rotating slowly, his eyes glaring red with power and ferocity.

Moments later another soldier came into the Throne Room. He seemed astonished by what he saw, but managed to splutter out his message.

"King Zhorm has entered the palace, Commander!"

"And where is he?"

"He was seen to make directly for the nursery, Commander."

Jasperodus nodded. That would naturally be his target. He had three small children, two boys and a girl, between the ages of five and ten.

He rose from the throne. "Put these hangers-on of Okhramora's under lock and key," he said to Craish. "What follows, I must do alone."

He left the Throne Room, laying aside the Crown, and made his way through the palace. The corridors were silent and dim, empty except for an occasional sentry at an intersection. He was near the nursery when a movement ahead caused him to halt and peer suspiciously.

Major Cree Inwing was lurking in the shadows, probably not realising he was visible to Jasperodus' spectrum-shifting vision.

"Show yourself, Major, or you're as good as dead," Jasperodus threatened.

Major Inwing slipped into the feeble light, his face pale. "I am alone and unarmed," he said curtly.

Jasperodus studied the other's face. There was a brisk but open quality to it that he found likable; however, Inwing was also too loyal to be drawn into treasonable plots, and so he had left him out of his machinations.

"How did you get here?" he demanded. "I thought I had you detained in the officers' quarters."

"True, but I escaped. Mutiny is an ugly thing." Jasperodus saw that Inwing's arm was bloody where a bullet had nicked it. "I have to admit that I misjudged you badly, Commander. All this is Prince Okhramora's work, I suppose?"

Jasperodus did not reply to the question. "I have word that Zhorm is in the nursery," he said. "You, I imagine, know that also."

Inwing went even whiter, and Jasperodus saw that he was sweating. "What do you intend?" he said quickly. "No – it's too obvious. Trust Okhramora to use you for work like that." His voice was heavy with contempt.

"It would be folly to do otherwise. My throne would never be safe while Zhorm and his children live."

"The children too?" Inwing seemed not to notice how Jasperodus framed the statement in his revulsion for its main import. "You can't do it, Commander – it's going too far. Not even you can do it, whatever you are. You *mustn't* do it." The young Major was pleading with him now.

"I see no great difficulty," Jasperodus replied, and made to move on.

"Wait . . ." Inwing stepped in his path. "How do you think the people will take to knowing that their king has been murdered? Think of that."

"Again I see no great difficulty," Jasperodus answered. He wondered why he lingered to talk to Inwing, instead of getting on with his business. Nevertheless he went on: "A small, compact armed force is all that is necessary to hold down a country the size of Gordona. Such a force of men can always be raised, if there are suitable inducements."

Inwing's face looked tragic as he recognised the logic of the argument. But he made one last try. "Listen, Commander, your con-

66

trol of the country will be much easier if you have the whole of the Guard with you. I can give you that: you know that at least half the men will follow my lead when it comes to a showdown. I'll serve you, faithfully, absolutely faithfully – you or your master – for the rest of my life. I swear it. My only condition is that King Zhorm and his family must be allowed to go with their lives."

Inwing's popularity was already a factor in Jasperodus' mind. "You are previously sworn to serve King Zhorm," he pointed out.

"I can do him no greater service than to strike this bargain with you," Inwing retorted. But suddenly Jasperodus' obduracy seemed to come home to him and he became angry and despairing. "It's hopeless, isn't it?" he sneered, looking as though he were about to spit. "Here I am trying to appeal to your better nature! You may be clever, but you're a robot – there's nothing to appeal to in that dead brain."

Jasperodus shoved him aside and strode onwards.

Finding the nursery door locked, he smashed it inwards and surveyed the scene inside.

Two nurses were hurriedly dressing the children, who seemed sleepy and upset. Zhorm was on his knees, helping them. At Jasperodus' intrusion he swung round with a glare of fear and hatred, clutching an impotent pistol.

The robot's gaze flicked quickly around the nursery: the beds on which the children slept, the toys strewn around the floor, the colourful pictures of soldiers and animals on the walls.

He had not made any decision as to how he would act; but when he spoke the words came out of his mouth as if unbidden.

"You will take your family and leave Gordona forever. Do you hear me, Zhorm? Forever! My men will be here in ten minutes to take you to the border. Be ready!"

He stormed away, ignoring the anxious Cree Inwing as he swept past him. But further along the corridor his path was blocked by a distraught Padua, who looked at him accusingly.

"I helped you, Jasperodus. You would be junk without me. And now you have betrayed my trust to an unimaginable degree!"

Jasperodus could not help but give vent to a low, ugly laugh. "You are the robotician, Padua. I am merely a mechanism. You should have known of my future conduct in advance, and therefore your criticism is misplaced."

6

Hands, soft and caressing, moved all over him, paying close attention to every inch of his body surface. Jasperodus lay passively,
concentrating on the pleasant sensations.

The girl was the same red-head who had helped to clean him
that first time nearly two years ago. Now that he was master of the
royal household she had volunteered to perform the service daily,
cleaning and polishing him so as to preserve his appearance of
gleaming majesty. She plainly enjoyed the task, getting some degree
of arousal from it. Sometimes her breathing would deepen and
occasionally, when lingering around the box-like bulge at the divide
of his legs, she would seem to become momentarily frantic and her
hand would pummel the air, as though manipulating the missing
phallus.

Masculinity, thought Jasperodus. Apparently he exuded masculinity. How a machine could possess such a quality was presumably
baffling, but for some reason he did.

He, of course, failed to share her excitement. Sexuality was still
a mystery to him: the sensations were deliciously soothing, but
otherwise neutral.

"Are you pleased, Lord?" she asked in an eager voice. And
suddenly she clambered over his body to lie on him full length,
pressing her pelvis down on him.

He pushed her off and stood up. He did not like to be reminded
of his deficiencies.

Stepping to his nearby office, he found Craish and Cree Inwing
waiting for him. Foreseeably, the news they brought was unsettling.

"There is little doubt that the main attack will come tomorrow,
if not tonight," Inwing told him, explicating over a map that was
laid out on a table. "Here is Zhorm and his force, and here are we,
camped outside the town of Fludd. We are under-strength, owing
to the necessity of posting forces in other parts of the country to
forestall the rebellions that are expected."

Jasperodus nodded, inspecting the map with scant interest. As he had anticipated, his double impetuosity – in seizing the crown prematurely, and in afterwards sparing Zhorm – had borne troublesome fruit. It had been necessary to hold down Gordona by forceful means, using the methods of a police state, and the population was in consequence discontented. This had made it easier for Zhorm, having taken refuge in a neighbouring kingdom, to win support for his cause. Around the nucleus of a small foreign force loaned to him by his host monarch he had gathered together enough armed loyalists to invade the country and was proceeding in fair order.

Cree Inwing had been as good as his word; Jasperodus had not once needed to remind him of his oath. He had organised the policing of the kingdom, weeded out the diehard elements in the Guard and won over all the rest. He had automatically risen to be Commander of the Guard – Craish was his Second-in-Command – and now, in an ironic twist of events, he was fighting with Jasperodus against Zhorm himself.

"The dispositions seem satisfactory," Jasperodus announced. "All is in order; we can hold them." Privately he reckoned the chances to be about fifty-fifty. He was unhappily aware that the intensity of his own enthusiasm would be the factor most decisive for the outcome.

"Has Your Majesty any special instructions regarding public order?" Inwing asked. "There are bound to be local uprisings."

"The main thing is to break Zhorm's assault," Jasperodus replied. "Afterwards your bully-boys can always put down any other trouble – eh, Craish?"

Craish nodded, grinning.

"In that case we will repair directly to Fludd," Inwing said stiffly.

Jasperodus made a vague gesture. "Craish, you go. Inwing can stay here for a while and we shall travel to Fludd together." His voice fell to a mutter. "We may as well entertain ourselves while we can."

Inwing looked surprised and puzzled, but said nothing. Craish saluted and departed.

Contesting thoughts flitted through Jasperodus' mind. He glanced around his office, and noticed for the first time how desultory, how temporary, everything looked. Chaotic piles of documents and lists littered the tables that had been crammed into the room with no regard for their ordered arrangement. There were not even any chairs, since he was equally at ease standing, and only one inadequate filing-cabinet.

Why had he been so careless about his daily working environment? Had the sense of urgency left him once he had attained his object? No, that could not be. He would have known it . . .

He motioned Inwing to follow him. In the long corridor outside all the drapes were flapping violently in the damp gusts of wind that were coming through the open windows. The evening air was heavy with threatened thunder, and he told himself that the weather would be too bad for Zhorm to attack tonight.

The banqueting hall, however, was more cheerful. A wood-burning fire had been lit in the huge fireplace and the audience that had already gathered made a lively contrast to the stream of dour officers and ministers he had been receiving all day. He settled himself on a wrought-iron chair overlooking the assembly, then signalled for the entertainment to begin.

The players were that same group of travelling entertainers who had figured, albeit peripherally, in his seizure of power. It was not by their own choice that they still performed for his court; he had refused to let them leave Gordona, wishing to sample their wares for himself but up until now finding little time for it. They accepted their enforced stay with equanimity, which suggested that they had met this kind of cavalier treatment before.

They bowed and set up their apparatus, a tripod surmounted by an arrangement of small tubes at various angles, emitting pencil-thin beams of coloured light.

Suddenly the cleared space in the centre of the hall sprang to life. In place of emptiness was a market place with people moving about it.

The illusion was complete: the picture had colour, depth and parallax, so that it presented a different aspect if viewed from a different angle. The scene betokened some ancient time, to judge from the architecture and the costumes; into it walked living, flesh-and-blood actors from the players' troupe.

Neither the eye nor the ear could tell which of the characters were real and which were projected by the laser device – except that occasionally the projector produced special effects, flattening the picture into a plane, or into a receding series of planes, against which the living actors stood out starkly. But even this could be achieved by imagery alone. Only when the living actors emerged from the picture and approached the audience to deliver monologues did they truly reveal their presence.

The play's dramatic effect was heightened by the fact that the key characters were all acted live, and occasionally emerged from the scene, while the minor ones were images only. Jasperodus found it totally absorbing. It was written, he guessed, by some author of antiquity, and unfolded in dazzling language a story of dukes and princes, of ill-fated lovers from hostile houses. Inwardly he congratulated the inventor of this type of drama, as well as of the device itself. But then such marvels were probably common out in the East; this thought reminded him of how recently he had been born. For all he had done, he had not yet penetrated very far into the world.

The drama ended. The substantial-seeming scenes vanished, leaving behind a handful of actors standing on bare boards. They bowed low to Jasperodus.

"Excellent!" Jasperodus commended. "A fine performance!" He would have been content to mull over the play for a while, but an oldster with a bushy white beard slid into view.

"And now, Your Majesty, permit us to present views of the distant past. These images have been preserved from the Age of Tergov!"

He attended to the laser device. In the space recently occupied by the drama another scene sprang into being. This time it was a still, showing an aerial view of part of a city so vast and magnificent that all present gasped.

"These pictures are a little smudged because the holograms lay for centuries in the soil before being unearthed," the spry old man explained. "Here is Pekengu, one of the Four Capital Cities of the Rule of Tergov. When this hologram was taken Tansiann was but an unimportant town of moderate size. Pekengu itself is now little more than a sad shell of ruins, though still inhabited." The projector clicked; a second scene appeared. "Here we see another of the Four Capitals: Pacifica, the floating city on the Great East Sea. Pacifica was fifty miles across, and its population was two hundred million. The great central shaft you see extended half a mile below the surface of the ocean and two miles into the air." The expositor continued to give more facts about the ancient capital, now lying wrecked on the bed of the ocean, and then switched to perhaps the best of his pictures. "Here is a view of one of the most consummate architectural triumphs of all time: the Temple of the Brotherhood of Man at Pekengu. Parts of this magnificent edifice still remain, notably the north wall. This picture is believed to have been taken about a hundred years after the temple was built."

Jasperodus gazed enthralled at the gigantic building. He had never imagined anything even remotely like it. Its central feature was a massive dome about whose middle floated a girdle of clouds, so immense was it. The lower parts of the dome seemed to cascade away into mounds, waves, traceries and runs that spilled and tumbled out over the ground, all seeming to hang from the floating upper mass rather than to support it.

"Can you show us the inside of this building also?" he demanded excitedly.

"Alas, no. Pictures of the interior do exist, so I have heard, but I have none in my collection."

The expositor exhibited his remaining pictures: the impressively developed territories on Mars; the vast sea barrage that, in those days, altered continental climates by controlling oceanic currents; a stupendous space community that swept through the solar system on an elongated elliptical path so as regularly to cross the orbits of all the planets; a view of Saturn seen over the towers of a town on Tethys, one of its inner satellites.

"These," the expositor told them, "are examples of the bygone glory that the Emperor Charrane seeks to revive."

The sights left Jasperodus stirred and agitated. Here indeed were accomplishments of a high order! He began to feel an immense admiration for the Old Empire and regretted that he could not have lived in the former time.

The picture show ended with a shorter second series showing weird, almost impossible animals. Creatures with ludicrously long necks or with twenty-foot wing spans, cats the size of elephants and horses the size of cats. Some of the animals bore no resemblance to any beast Jasperodus knew of and defied description.

72

"None of these animals occur in nature but were created during the classical civilisation by a science now lost," the expositor explained. "This science could also culture bizarre types of man, but these and all other like species are extinct today, not having survived the wild state that attended the Dark Age."

He put aside the laser projector; but the show was not yet finished. Another man took the stage and performed baffling feats of magic. Jasperodus watched closely. He could discern faster movements than could the human eye and he was able to see that many of the tricks depended on legerdemain or on misdirecting the attention of the audience. Others, mainly those using cards or apparently demonstrating mind-reading, made use of devious mathematical calculations or ingenious psychology, at both of which the conjurer was clearly an expert. Jasperodus was able to see through the operation of these also; but others mystified even him.

Afterwards the four leaders of the troupe, including the expositor and the conjuror, sat before him relating unusual tales and propounding riddles. Jasperodus had secretly looked forward to this part of the proceedings. These people spent their lives travelling the world, and their knowledge covered a vast range of subjects. The troupe could cater for all tastes : not only could it perform plays, exotic foreign music, displays of dancing, acrobatics, conjuring and buffoonery; it could also debate philosophy with remarkable erudition. Jasperodus needed some stimulating conversation now that Padua, otherwise his only outlet, had become churlish and unfriendly towards him.

After listening for a while he expressed a wish to be posed a riddle or two.

A jolly-faced oldster, his face more wrinkled than the others and fringed by a fluffy white beard, obliged him. "Which are more numerous, the living or the dead?"

Jasperodus thought for a moment. "The living, for the dead don't exist."

"Correct! Now apply yourself to this ancient conundrum. A judge once sentenced a man to death, informing him that he was to be garotted sometime between the following Monday and Friday, but that up until the moment he was taken from his cell he would not know on which day. That night the condemned man reasoned thus: 'I cannot be garotted on Friday, which is the last day, for in that case I would be forewarned of it the instant Thursday midnight had passed, which is against the judge's ruling. But if Friday is eliminated I cannot be garrotted on Thursday either – because I would likewise be forewarned of it the instant Wednesday midnight had passed. By the same argument Wednesday, Tuesday and Monday are each eliminated in turn. I am saved! I cannot be executed.' And so he rested easy. But when Tuesday arrived he was taken from his cell and garotted, unforeseen as the judge had promised. Explain."

Jasperodus explored the intricacies of the tale and found himself in a paradox. After some abortive attempts to solve it he shifted uneasily in his chair. "Pah! It is a play on words merely. The judge lied. He imposed a condition that cannot be carried out in reality, which is something any fool can do. He should have exempted the last day from his promise and then there would be no paradox."

"My opinion exactly!" Shoulders jiggling, the oldster chuckled in amusement. "But you would be surprised how many philosophers have taken his words at face value and erected imposing systems of logic on them." He gave a crafty laugh, looking sidewise at his colleagues. "A ruler with an intellect for a change!"

The remark emboldened Jasperodus. "You are all men of discernment," he said, adopting an imperious pose. "Consider, then, my achievements. I have made myself king of this land and all men here do my bidding. I can out-think most and have determination enough for ten. Do you not think that this gives me equal status with men? That I am, in effect, a man?"

He was answered by a trouper with a lean rubbery face the colour of red brick. "By no means. You are a machine for all that. How did you gain your kingdom?"

"Why, by trickery and deceit!" Jasperodus said proudly. "Is that not the way of men?"

"The way of most men, just so. By your own admission you add weight to my case. With you, all is imitation."

"You have no moral sense," chortled the white-bearded oldster.

The fourth member of the team, a man somewhat younger than the others, spoke up. "Your question is dealt with by the Riddle of the Sphinx, said by many to predate all recorded history."

Jasperodus darted him a quick look. "Tell it."

74

"The riddle runs: What can a man do that is neither thinking, feeling, sensing nor action? The answer is that he can *be conscious* that he does any of those things. Here we have the vital difference between a man and any construct. Your Majesty can think, have emotions, perceive – in the machine sense – and perform effective action. But there can be no awareness behind these functions, and if you aver that there is then you have formed an erroneous conclusion."

"So my good friend Padua tells me," Jasperodus said huffily, disappointed that he had received no praise. "And yet I do indeed hold to this error, at no small cost to my peace of mind. Tell me, do you not fear that I will punish you for your ill-considered remarks?"

"Should we then insult both you and ourselves with pandering lies?" The man put on an exposition of dignity. "We undertake to earn our fee wherever we go, whether with frolics or erudition."

The expositor twisted the knife still further. "It needs to be said that gaining power over others, even in seizing a kingdom by force, is among the coarsest of human accomplishments and does not indicate any high level of attainment."

But meanwhile the white-bearded poser of paradoxes was apparently seized by a huge joke and sat giggling quietly to himself. Jasperodus' gaze veered towards him.

"Why do you laugh, old man?"

"Who is to prove that human beings are conscious either?" the other replied, restraining his mirth. "There is no objective test. They themselves assert it, of course – but you make the same claim, and we know the claim to be false in your case. Perhaps *we* are deluded concerning *ourselves* – therefore rest easy, robot, probably we are all *un*conscious together! After all, life is but a dream, the playwright tells us!"

"Well spoken!" acclaimed Jasperodus in a hollow voice. "For all I know your state is just as mine is." But inwardly he felt the emptiness of this small victory. The oldster's argument was clever but too sophisticated to be taken seriously. If he were to cling to it he might well be like the man in the condemned cell who believed he could not be garotted.

"Let us leave this fruitless area of discussion," the old man suggested. "Would Your Majesty care to hear more paradoxes? I will prove that motion is impossible, that a swift runner cannot overtake a slow one, and that a bullet can never reach its target."

"Enough, enough." Jasperodus rose to his feet. "Enough of paradoxes. I bid you good night."

He swept through the hall. All present – save the entertainers – kept their eyes downcast, embarrassed that their lord's construct nature had been made so much of, and nervous of what his reaction would be. On leaving the hall Jasperodus signalled to Cree Inwing to follow; the two conferred in the passage outside.

"Do we go now to Fludd?" Inwing asked.

"No . . . I think not." Jasperodus uttered a deep sigh, as if of weariness and tedium. "I have made a decision, Inwing. Gordona is too small a pond for me. I am abandoning all and taking myself to the east. Since I have no further interest in what happens here you are free to return to Zhorm; I release you from your oath."

"Hmm." Inwing accepted this statement with remarkably little astonishment, but with some appearance of self-concern. He fingered his moustache doubtfully. "You place me in an unenviable situation. There can be no question of taking sides with Zhorm – I am a traitor of the first rank and he will kill me at the earliest opportunity. It seems I had best flee the country."

"But you saved Zhorm's life."

"He doesn't know that; and it would certainly be hard to convince him."

Jasperodus looked down at the young officer's face. Inwing was a man of practicality, he decided; in the space of seconds he had turned his back on Gordona and was already contemplating a new future somewhere in a strang land. Jasperodus grunted with a hint of humour. "I shall be taking the aircraft. Accompany me, if you want to get away from here in a hurry – it makes no difference to me, and you have served me well so perhaps I owe you that."

Inwing nodded. "I accept."

"You don't feel degraded to travel in the company of a robot?" Jasperodus asked in a tone edged with sarcasm. "You heard the debate in the hall just now; you must have opinions of your own."

Inwing shrugged. "I'm not a philosopher. I've no time for subtle distinctions, especially when the throttling cord is practically around my neck. What of Craish and the others, by the way? You leave them in circumstances that are even less to be desired."

Jasperodus considered briefly. "I will send a message releasing Craish and the rest also. Let him try to seize Gordona for himself if he cares to – but I think he'll take his men and sneak off back to the forest to carry on as before."

"Yes, the heart will go out of things without you there," Inwing agreed. Jasperodus was pleased that he had dropped all formality and was speaking to him as man to man.

They stopped by the office while Jasperodus wrote to Craish, sending the letter by dispatch rider. He could imagine the exbandit's dismay on receiving it.

Unobtrusively they left the palace. Thunder rolled from the distance and was coming rapidly nearer through the darkness. The rain was heavy, making a continuous splash and patter on the courtyard and pouring off the slanting roofs of the palace.

"Craish will have time for a getaway, at any rate," Jasperodus ruminated. "Zhorm will not move tonight." Not that he cared; his attitude to his followers remained unsentimental.

Gordona's one and only serviceable aircraft was kept in a shed in the palace grounds. Jasperodus sent away the guards, then he and Inwing lifted up the door, propping it open with the shafts provided for the purpose. Together they pushed the small, natty flier on to the short grass runway.

The robot opened the cabin door and flicked a switch, causing the dashboard to glow. He checked the dials, was satisfied, then turned back to Inwing standing on the grass.

"So goodbye to Gordona," he said tonelessly, his gaze flicking around at the palace and at the lights thrown up by the town beyond. "My kindergarten."

"Where are we bound for, as a matter of interest?" Inwing asked mildly. "To the east, you said. But east of here lies a veritable chaos of states and principalities, many of them places of danger and violence. Anarchy has its advocates, but I would prefer that we fixed a safer, more definite destination."

"You fear for your safety, then? Set your mind at ease, I am flying directly to Tansiann, the centre of the inhabited world."

Inwing looked startled. "That's half the world away!"

"The flier is perfectly capable of making the journey. I have

77

seen to that by helping to service it myself, since there is no trusting these doltish mechanics. The motor is powered by an isotope battery, so we shall not be stranded for lack of fuel."

Inwing sighed. "I fear my provinciality will show. It is a place where one needs one's wits about one."

Jasperodus became impatient. "Tonight I made a vow to experience everything a man can experience," he said in a low voice that was like iron. "Where else would I go for this but Tansiann? If you lack the verve to survive in a city I'll set you down wherever you please *en route.*"

"You vowed to experience everything?" Inwing echoed.

"Everything, everything! I know my strength. Anything the world offers I can take. As for this thing called consciousness, if it truly exists I shall seize even that!"

Perplexed, Inwing stepped back in the rain. "But – how?"

Jasperodus suffered an agitated pause. "By will-power!" he exclaimed, throwing up his hands. "I will find a way. But are you going to stand there all night? Let us be going, unless you have altered your plans."

"No, indeed. Tansiann it is, then." Inwing clambered up after Jasperodus into the tiny cabin, closing the door behind him. Jasperodus occupied the pilot's seat. By this time Inwing's cape was wet through, but he settled into the single passenger seat without complaint and sat staring blankly through the windscreen.

Jasperodus switched on the motor. The propeller spun and shimmered; they bumped over the grass and were airborne, veering sharply upwards.

Okrum receded below. Lightning flickered a few miles away and Jasperodus saw that he would be forced to fly directly through the storm unless he was careful. The rain drummed against the windscreen; gusts took hold of the little plane and buffeted it about. Handling it was all the harder because his own weight spoiled its trim, but he had already taught himself to fly with skill and he managed to avoid the worst of the storm, taking them up above it into calmer air. Soon they were speeding uneventfully eastward.

Eventually Inwing dozed in his seat. Navigating by the stars, Jasperodus flew on through the night and into a clear, sunny day. Inwing awoke, grumbling sleepily, and made a meagre breakfast from part of a loaf of bread he had brought with him.

Now that the landscape was revealed Jasperodus took the plane lower, interested by the sights that met his elevated eye. Mostly they flew over forest, but there were also frequent patches of cultivated land betokening some community or other – a manor, a principality, even a kingdom. Here all the areas of authority were fairly small; only further east were big nations, federations and empires to be found.

One spectacle filled them both with awe: a vast grid hundreds of miles across, its rectangular walls marching with regularity and precision over the surface of the Earth. From ground level it would not have been visible at all, the outlines having been weathered away and absorbed into the landscape; only from an aerial perspective did its repetitious design become evident. Neither of them could guess at what its purpose could have been, but clearly it was yet another piece of imposing grandeur from the classical civilisation of Tergov.

A fair-sized town swung into view ahead of them. Out of curiosity Jasperodus dived to get a better view of its streets and buildings, noting that though still narrow and twisting they were somewhat better appointed than those of Okrum. Inwing coughed nervously and Jasperodus swung up again, climbing so as to continue their journey. Just then something flashed up from below and a short, sharp explosion rocked the plane.

"They're firing rockets," Inwing warned in a low voice.

Jasperodus fought to regain control. He twisted and turned as more missiles hurtled towards them, trailing streaks of white smoke. Again the plane shuddered but was not hit; he poured on the power and zoomed away from the town.

"I was afraid of this," Inwing said in a terse tone which indicated Jasperodus should have listened to him more closely. "Some of these countries are in a constant state of war with their neighbours. To them we look like raiders."

Jasperodus made no answer, being busy scanning the surrounding sky and ground. He saw that the worst was happening: three aircraft were climbing to meet them. Even at this distance he could see from their outlines that they sported either guns or missile racks.

And his own plane was unarmed.

The ensuing minute of time assured him that there was no hope of outdistancing the pursuers. Two of them were propeller-driven, like himself, but the third used some other principle – some kind of thruster by appearances – and was much faster. Jasperodus swung to the North and dived down towards some heavily forested hills.

"We'll have to get under cover," he said curtly to Inwing. "Hold tight, it might be bumpy."

The interceptors were banking to follow him. Jasperodus winged down between the walls of a valley, temporarily losing them from view. He was looking for somewhere to put down, but all he saw were trees, a few outcroppings of rock, and more trees. If nothing else offered, he told himself, he would have to crash-land into the tree-tops, sacrificing the plane and hoping that the foliage would brake their velocity gently enough not to kill Inwing – Jasperodus himself, of course, had less to worry about on that score.

But at its far end the valley narrowed into a modest canyon, beyond which Jasperodus glimpsed what was needed: an even, though slightly upsloping stretch of ground on which there was a gap in the trees wide enough and long enough for the aircraft, with luck, to land.

Lowering the flaps, he shot between the walls of the canyon and approached the wild grass. When the wheels first touched down the tail reared up; he was forced to re-power the motor to stabilise. They bounced over the turf, lost speed, and then one wing hit a bush and sent the plane lurching through a quarter circle, whereupon it came to a halt.

"Get out," Jasperodus ordered. They scrambled from the cabin and together managed to push the aircraft under the cover of nearby trees, forcing it as deep as it would go into the dappled shade.

Stepping halfway from under the screen of branches, Jasperodus peered skyward. The pursuers were sailing overhead. They dipped low towards the forest and banked, searching.

He returned to Inwing. "We had best stay here until nightfall," he said. "We may not be able to evade them a second time."

Inwing nodded, glad of a chance to take some exercise. He paced up and down, stretching gratefully.

Time passed. They turned the plane round so as to be able to manoeuvre it more easily into a take-off position, and then simply waited.

Presently Jasperodus thought to reconnoitre their surroundings.

He left Inwing and strode off through the forest, making for high ground. After a while he came across a trail which wound round a hillside to lead, he judged, to the town a few miles away. He paused pensively, not liking this turn of events, and then continued. Half an hour later he heard sounds nearby. He stepped off the trail, and was able to observe a party of men dressed in a uniform consisting of green tunics and berets which had a short peak hanging over one ear. All were armed, and from the way they separated occasionally to explore the forest on either side of the path it was plain they were searching for the wreck of Jasperodus' aircraft. He turned back and moved stealthily through the undergrowth, keeping out of sight until he was ahead of them, and then loped swiftly along the trail towards Inwing.

Too late, he realised that he had been careless. There must have been men out looking for the aircraft from the instant it had come down, and they had a fair idea of its whereabouts. The party he had spotted was not the only one: rounding a rock and emerging into a clearing, he found himself directly confronting another group, uniformed as was the first.

He pulled himself up sharp, eyeing the four men. One of them carried a beam emitter which could prove fatal to a robot. Jasperodus glanced around him, edging away and wishing he had brought a weapon.

They were surprised to see him, but not so much so as to give him any advantage. "The Finnian swine are using robots now, eh?" one exclaimed. "Let him have it, Juss!"

The soldier holding the emitter went down on one knee and aimed it at Jasperodus, who instantly realised he had little chance of escaping its beam. He was about to fling himself sideways and into the undergrowth but before the soldier could fire the chatter of a repeater gun rang out from above him and the man fell dead.

The eyes of the others shot startled up to the top of the rock behind Jasperodus. Cree Inwing sprang down into the clearing, his gun voicing death again. A few bullets came in return, aimed wild and a few of them bouncing off Jasperodus, but in seconds it was all over.

"Got bored and thought I'd come looking for you," Inwing explained, turning to him with a grin. "Then I saw this lot coming so I hid up there." He jerked his thumb to the craggy overhang.

"There are others behind me," Jasperodus said, "and possibly yet more I haven't seen." He urged Inwing along. "Back to the plane quickly — we have to get away from here at once."

In minutes they had regained the aircraft. One to each wing, they manhandled it out on to the improvised runway, lining it up so that hopefully it would manage to slip in between the trees. In the pilot's seat Jasperodus paused; take-off should not really be any more difficult than landing, unless they hit a tuft or mound that bounced them off-course.

In the event he was able to get off the ground smoothly, soared up the narrow canyon and into open air. He turned the nose East and flew low, following the undulations of the landscape for some miles, and apparently they weren't spotted for no pursuit came.

"Something puzzles me," Jasperodus said when they felt safe again. "You realise what you just did? You risked your life to save a machine construct. Why did you do it? Surely you must have known that your best chance was to head straight back to the plane and take off without me?"

Inwing looked doubtful, as if this idea was new to him. "I didn't think about it," he admitted. "I've told you I'm no philosopher . . . If it comes to that, why were you so thoughtless as to leave me alone with the plane? By your reasoning I should have taken off with it at the first opportunity, since without you I could make better speed and go where I choose."

"You need me," Jasperodus replied bluntly. "Two can survive better than one."

"Yes, there's that too. Anyway, it's a poor man who'll desert a companion at the first sign of trouble. I suppose I've worked with you so long I just didn't think of you as a machine. Perhaps I should have."

Jasperodus laughed briefly.

He did not mention that part of the reason he had gone exploring was to see what Inwing would do in his absence.

For the rest of the journey he avoided towns, as well as the castles and fortified camps that occasionally dotted the landscape. They flew on and on, and very gradually the appearance of the Earth changed. There was more land under cultivation, and towns and villages, as well as the odd city, grew more numerous. Also more in evidence were railways, roads, canals and air travel: they were entering the area of large national groupings. But all this, Jasperodus could not help but notice, merely overlay the immense remains of the classical civilisation: the gigantic ruins, the reshaping of the Earth, the enigmatic formations, all of which were slowly sinking into the soil.

Jasperodus was merciless to Cree Inwing. Once, after travelling for two days, they landed and raided a farmhouse to get him food. After that Jasperodus simply kept going. If he thought the engine was overheating he switched it off and glided for a distance to give it a chance to cool. Inwing cursed, slept and sweated in the cramped cabin, having nothing to occupy himself with, and was forced to shift for himself as regards calls of nature.

After a week of this he could stand it no longer and begged Jasperodus to land and give him respite. Accordingly Jasperodus winged down from their high altitude and looked out for a convenient landing place.

They passed over a kuron town. It was the first Jasperodus had ever seen, and forgetting his former caution he circled it twice, inspecting the curious arrangement of mushroom-shaped houses. Then he passed on, and a short distance away came down on a wood-fringed meadow. They pushed the aircraft beneath the spread branches of the trees, as was their practice, and since evening was drawing on settled down for the night.

Cree Inwing spent some time running to and fro, flexing his arms and performing various muscle-toning exercises. When he felt sufficiently relieved he built a fire and roasted a small animal he had trapped. For a couple of hours he and Jasperodus sat patiently by the fire, desultorily discussing their future route to Tansiann, whose precise location was unknown to either of them.

Inwing's preparations for sleep were interrupted by the snap of a twig and the sound of light footfalls coming through the trees. Presently there came into the firelight the small, slight figures of three kurons.

Jasperodus observed them with curiosity. They were between four and five feet in height and seemed approximately manlike, at first reminding him of the fairy folk of legend. On closer inspection, however, the humanish appearance diminished. Their faces bore no more resemblance to a man's than to, say, a tiger's or a

83

lizard's, and were pinched and bony, giving an appearance of exaggerated delicateness. The proportions of body and limbs were also all their own, so that the correspondence to the human race consisted entirely of their being bimanual and bipedal.

They wore nondescript garments like coarse shifts and flaps. Jasperodus noticed that one of them was carrying a glass jar carefully in both hands, but he could not immediately see what it contained. With no evidence of fear or caution they walked directly into the small camp and sat down opposite the two travellers.

"Good evening," said Inwing sardonically.

"And likewise to you," replied one of the newcomers in a faint, breathless voice.

There was silence while the kurons stared into the fire and Inwing and Jasperodus stared in turn at them. Since they seemed in no hurry to explain their presence Jasperodus put a question of his own.

"We are *en route* for Tansiann," he said, "but are unsure of its exact whereabouts. Perhaps you can direct us?"

"You must travel on a course East and about forty degrees South," the kuron told him in the same piping, breathless voice: "Here we are on the western fringe of the New Empire; to the north are hostile nations which you must avoid. You will not, however, reach Tansiann unopposed in your aircraft. On approaching Kwengu you will be noted on radar and apprehended."

"Will we not then be allowed to continue?" Jasperodus inquired.

"That will depend on your business. I cannot say. We kurons prefer to live well outside the main stream of human life, by reason of past atrocities and persecutions."

"Indeed? That aspect of history is new to me. You have been badly treated?"

The other nodded awkwardly, in a way which suggested it was not a native gesture. "To survive the Dark Age was extremely difficult for us, for it was an age of violence and brutal ignorance. Prior to that time we had lived in the big human cities as well as in our own rural towns, engaging in trade and certain kinds of manufacture at which we excelled, but when the light of reason went out irrational hatreds were raised against us. Any misfortune or natural calamity was ascribed to our agency, and it was widely believed we practised malign magic. Massacre of kuron ghettoes became a frequent occurrence; added to which the breakdown of commerce rendered our normal livelihood impossible. Very few of us remained alive at the end of those bad centuries."

"You live now under the aegis of the New Empire?" Jasperodus asked.

"Many of us do; here its power is nominal only. But the Emperor Charrane has decreed that kurons are to live without molestation in the empire, and that is our main hope for the future. His laws are not always obeyed, but it is better than elsewhere, such as in the states dominated by Borgor where we are still openly persecuted."

Inwing put in a word. "You come from another star, don't you? If things were so bad why didn't you fly off back to where you came from?"

The kuron turned to peer at him. "It was too late. We, too, shared the social decline, losing our knowledge and skills. We no longer had the ability to build star arks."

"How distant is your home star?" Jasperodus asked. "How long did it take to get here?"

"Earth is our home now; we are natural migrants in the true sense of the word. Our star of origin lies a hundred and thirty-five light-years away, and the journey takes a hundred and fifty-two years by star ark."

Jasperodus gestured to the glass jar lying on the ground. "Presumably you saw our plane flying over and noted our landing place. What prompted you to visit us?"

"We come to trade."

The robot grunted. "Then you come in vain. We have no goods to offer. We have scarcely anything for ourselves."

"Untrue. You have the aircraft. We wish to bargain for that."

Inwing shook his head. "We need it to travel to Tansiann."

"Sample our wares before you decide. One can travel without wings, even if more slowly." The kuron lifted the jar, which was dome-shaped. It contained dark red soil in which grew about a dozen small flowers, blurrily visible through the thick glass. "Here is something you cannot find even in Tansiann."

He opened a lid at the top of the jar and reached down with a long, slender hand to pluck one of the flowers, which he brought forth. It was a simple enough flower, like an extra-large, lavender-coloured buttercup.

"These flowers are grown in the soil of Kuronid, our aboriginal world, brought here in the original star ark and preserved for centuries since. They can be grown in no other soil. I will allow you to smell this first bloom free of charge; if you wish to keep it, and the others in this jar, you must give us your aircraft."

"A jar of flowers for an airplane!" Inwing exclaimed with a laugh.

"Not the jar, for we cannot part with the soil," corrected the kuron. "I will pluck the flowers and give them to you under a glass seal, whereupon they will retain their perfume for one third of a year."

"Well," said Inwing in puzzlement, "what's so special about it?"

"It is a psychedelic flower. Its perfume contains chemical substances which transform the consciousness."

"Give it to me," Jasperodus commanded, holding out his hand. "The aircraft is mine to dispose of, not his."

The kuron continued speaking to Inwing. "It will have no effect on your robot, of course. Inhale the scent deeply, now, and you will see that our offer is more than fair."

Nevertheless Jasperodus insisted on sampling the flower. He applied it to his nostrils, drawing a small draught of air into his olfactory cavity: the perfume was light and delicate, but characteristically unique. Otherwise he found little to distinguish it from an ordinary Earth flower.

Cree Inwing still did not understand what the kuron was offering him when his turn came. But within half a minute of his sniffing the flower a look of complete amazement came over his face. He sprang to his feet and looked about him as if seeing everything for the first time; then he broke into peals of laughter which subsided into a fit of uncontrollable giggling.

All watched in silence. Eventually Inwing sat down again and stared with absolute fixity at a spray of leaves over his head, for minute after minute. Even when he spoke to Jasperodus he did not take his eyes off that spray of leaves; it seemed to hold endless fascination for him.

"It's amazing . . ." He began to ramble in an excited voice. "I never understood it all till now. It's all different, it's all completely *different*. I'm not me, that's not that – we're all the same as one another . . . There's no end to variation, but it's all one . . ."

He seemed to be trying to explain the unexplainable, but Jasperodus merely grunted sulkily. His old sullenness had come over him; the flower obviously worked on men – and presumably on kurons – but not on him, and he took this as yet further evidence of his lack of consciousness.

There was presumably nothing within him for the perfume to alter: his resentment was by now automatic.

"And what of our bargain?" the kuron asked softly. "Are you agreed?"

"Eh?" Inwing took his eyes off the leaves and stared with equal intensity at the kuron's face. "Oh, yes. Give me the flowers; you can have the plane."

"No!" Jasperodus came to his feet, his voice harsh. "There will be no bargain!"

Laughing like a child, Inwing rose to face Jasperodus. "But it's all right, Jasperodus. Really it is! We can walk to Tansiann. Who wants a plane? Perhaps we'll fly without a plane! Anything's possible! This is worth more than any airplane, believe me!" He froze, suddenly trapped by the burnished reflection of flames on Jasperodus' chest.

Jasperodus rounded on the kurons. "Conceivably your reputation for witchcraft is not without foundation. You have given this man a poison and deranged his judgement!"

The kuron spokesman shook his head. "Not so. His consciousness is altered, that is all. Consciousness is chemically based; but normally it is restricted by automatic conditioning so as to encompass only a very small range of impressions. The action of the flower is to free it temporarily from these restrictions. For the first time he is seeing the world as it exists in objective reality, and it astonishes him. Naturally he now has a different idea of what is most worth having."

Inwing nodded his head in vigorous agreement. "That's right, Jasperodus, this is reality! For the first time in my life!"

"And the last!" Jasperodus snatched the flower from him and flung it into the fire. "Away with you this instant or I will kill you

87

all!" he growled at the kurons. "Luckily I am immune to your tricks and know how to protect our property!"

Calmly and with no sign of alarm or disappointment, the kurons took up their glass jar and walked quietly from the clearing. Jasperodus silenced Cree's jovial protestations with the threat of his upraised fist.

"Your foolishness has cost you a night's good rest on the ground," he chided. And as soon as the kurons were gone from earshot he bundled Inwing into the plane and manhandled it single-handed on to the meadow.

It was risky to take off in darkness on wild turf, for the plane's headlight offered little illumination, but they became airborne without mishap. Consulting the stars, he set a course and they droned on through the night.

For several hours he was forced to endure Cree's witless expatiations. But eventually the effect of the flower's perfume wore off and the ex-soldier fell into a deep sleep. And so they continued on for several days more. Deeper into the empire the land began to take on a more urbanised aspect, and remembering the kuron's warning Jasperodus thought it prudent to descend, abandon the plane and continue on foot. Sometimes walking, sometimes by rail, meeting a number of adventures together, the pair arrived at last in Tansiann.

7

Tansiann!

Pausing on the eminence of a tall hill, one of ten guarding the Imperial City, Jasperodus looked down to where he hoped to prove his capacity to achieve all.

"Tansiann," he murmured after a while. "It is everything I imagined."

"The centre of the world," Cree Inwing agreed. "A city one could lose oneself in."

"True. Every experience is to be found here, no doubt, such being the nature of capitals."

For some short while they had been travelling through the environs of the city, consisting of farmlands, satellite towns, private estates and fenced-off areas containing secret government projects. Tansiann proper, on which they now gazed, was a well-defined entity occupying an undulating estuary valley, bounded on one side by the sea and on the other by the encircling ten hills which in preceding centuries had provided a natural landward defence. Through the city flowed the river Tan, a waterway created during the Rule of Tergov but overbuilt by the clustered conurbation now, and fully visible only near its mouth, where ocean-going ships pulled up at the three-mile-long dockland. With all these natural amenities Charrane had chosen well in placing his capital here. Boasting a population of three million, Tansiann had become the world's most important city, and exuded a lively, vigorous atmosphere. Jasperodus felt a mounting excitement as he beheld it. Admiration, anticipation, a desire to share in ambitious endeavours, all blended into a kind of longing.

Like all large cities Tansiann was separated into districts each exemplifying a different function. In one area grimy tenements mingled with the workshops of artisans; in another temples and skyscrapers piled together and lurched skyward. Near the dockland larger workshops, factories and foundries poured smoke into the air; elsewhere a sparkling commercial centre adjoined an elegant tree-lined residential district inhabited by the wealthy. To the northeast, in a quarter dating from the Old Empire, new dwellings sprang up amongst old ruins and a long wall, like a spine from which other ribs radiated, still represented some enigmatic antique construction. Yet such relics detracted but little from the triumphant signs of a resurgent civilisation. Cree and Jasperodus had passed through towns displaying far less favourable a contrast between past glory and present achievement. In Tansiann the projects beloved of the Emperor Charrane stood out proudly: soaring monuments of nascent might, buildings to reduce a man to the size of an ant, public colonnades of delightful extent, statuary and vast murals of Byzantine splendour.

A sudden flash of fire caught their attention. A pillar of white energy was climbing like a rising sun from behind one of the more distant hills. It lifted aloft a glinting mass of metal which accelerated rapidly until it was no more than a dot in the sky.

Jasperodus nodded in satisfaction. He was already aware that the Emperor, missing no opportunity to invest the city with an air of impressiveness, had located the Empire's largest spaceground close at hand too. No doubt the daily thunder of rocket engines reminded Tansiann's citizens of how far the New Empire could reach.

The two travellers returned to the highway, from which they had departed so as to gain their panoramic view of the city, and followed it as it descended into the estuary. An hour of walking brought them, through dusty streets lined with canopied shops, to a district near the river. Here, at the intersection of three thoroughfares, they paused and looked about them.

The place bore the unsettled seediness of a transit area, frequented mostly by sailors, casual labourers and recently arrived immigrants. Taverns, inns and rooming houses were plentiful. One of the three streets curved round to run alongside a ribwork of concrete pillars, through which could be glimpsed the murky brown water of the Tan, much fouled by industrial waste, and bearing slow-moving black barges.

Across the street a group of three men, flashily dressed in shirts and breeks of coloured silk, appeared to be eyeing the newcomers speculatively. Presently they crossed the street a little way ahead of the two and stood chatting together with studied indifference. As Cree and Jasperodus drew abreast one of them called out suddenly and presented himself, shaking Cree's hand warmly while looking him confidently in the eye. "I can see you are a recent arrival in our town, citizen. Perhaps I can be of some assistance?"

Cree frowned. "How do you know me for a stranger?" he demanded, taken aback.

The other laughed lightly. "You and your construct both have the dust of travel on you, sir. Besides, the main road from the west leads directly through here. Many migrants from that quarter land up precisely on the spot where you are now standing. Allow me to explain myself. I make it my business to direct and advise newcomers regarding accommodation and employment, whereupon I receive a small commission from certain lodging houses and business enterprises. If you seek a comfortable night's rest and good wholesome food at moderate charge, may I recommend the Blue Boar, which you will find along that street yonder and third turning to the left. As to work, have you any immediate prospects? What are your skills?"

"I had not expected to install myself with such facility," Cree remarked dubiously. The other laughed again and continued with his jovial chatter, mentioning nothing that would seem to suggest an ulterior motive, or any disadvantage to Inwing. While they talked thus, he and one of his companions were shifting casually about from foot to foot, until, inadvertently so it seemed, Cree was manœuvred into presenting his back to Jasperodus.

Suddenly Jasperodus' eye was caught by the third member of the group, who to his surprise was beckoning him urgently from within the cover of a nearby narrow alley. Unthinkingly he stepped towards the fellow, into the opening and away from the others.

The stranger laid a proprietary hand on his arm and spoke in a commanding hiss. "Follow me directly, robot, and be quick about it – quietly, now."

The man turned and padded rapidly off down the passage, plainly expecting Jasperodus to obey. In a trice Jasperodus had caught up with him, to seize him by the shoulder and jerk him round roughly. He thrust a fist close to his pinched face.

"The next time you try to take me from my owner, your skull will encounter this."

91

The robot-stealer gaped thunderstruck at his intended victim, wide-eyed with alarm. Immediately Jasperodus released him he galloped frantically up the alley and disappeared from sight. Jasperodus returned to where Cree, all unawares, was still being engaged in genial conversation.

"Cree!" he warned in a loud voice. "These men are thieves!"

The response from all parties to his words was startlement and consternation. The shysters decamped in great haste, leaving Cree standing perplexed.

He rubbed his nose ruefully when Jasperodus described how the thieves were able to commandeer a robot by removing it momentarily from its master's attention. "Afterwards it would be hard to find grounds for complaint against them," he explained. "You were careless; your robot wandered off. What is that to do with them? Most constructs would be susceptible to such a technique – it can be likened to stealing a horse. Presumably there is a market for purloined robots hereabouts, but doubtless the natives are not so easily manipulated."

"And I am instantly recognisable as a country bumpkin!" Cree exclaimed in dismay. He looked down at himself thoughtfully. "It's the cut of my garments that gives me away. One of the first things might be to obtain clothes in the prevalent fashion, and cut from the local cloth. But time for that later. I am in need of refreshment."

He moved towards a nearby tavern. At the entrance was a dispenser selling some kind of printed journal. Cree examined it with interest, made a small sound of approval, and placed a coin in the slot. The delivery chute ejected a folded copy.

Within, the tavern had a rough-hewn air, which was the reason why Cree had chosen it. After a brief word with the landlord he obtained permission for Jasperodus to sit with him, and purchased a mug of sour red wine, which he swallowed with evident satisfaction and then bought another. Much cheered by the beverage, he began a perusal of the journal.

Jasperodus meanwhile sat in silence. Their wanderings together had frequently been interspersed with Cree's practice of reviving himself with alcohol, and such halts in their progress were now familiar to the robot. Though secretly a trifle sullen that he too could not partake of the experience, he had grown patient with the habit, looking upon it as part of their working arrangement.

The truth was that their partnership had been of such benefit to them both as to warrant a degree of mutual tolerance. As a foot-loose construct Jasperodus would have faced many difficulties in journeying across the continent. The solution was simple: Cree represented him as his property.

Jasperodus himself had proposed this arrangement. Cree at first had shown some diffidence about casting into the role of a slave, even if only for the sake of appearances, someone who recently had been his own king and master. Jasperodus had quickly put him right on that score: he felt no loss of dignity.

On his side the robot's physical strength and mental acuity had stood them both in good stead on numerous occasions. In addition Jasperodus had now and then allowed Cree to hire him out, help-ing perhaps to erect a barn, to build a bridge, or to audit the ac-counts of a tradesman, in return for enough money to provide food, drink, lodging or rail fares.

While Cree was engrossed in the journal he was studying, Jas-perodus casually inspected it over his shoulder. It was a news jour-nal, containing reports of happenings in Tansiann and in other parts of the world. That in itself was cosmopolitan enough a touch to excite interest: such a thing as a news service was practically unknown elsewhere. As it was, the journal – boasting the em-blazoned title "New Empire" at the head of its first sheet – had the rough-finished appearance of a recent innovation. It was printed on crude, cheap paper manufactured from wood pulp and had been turned out, Jasperodus could discern, on a rotary printing press using relief type. Not as rapid or as accurate as some photo-chemical processes Jasperodus knew of, but no doubt efficient enough for present requirements.

By looking askance he found he was able to read the reports without disturbing Cree. The lead story was splashed right across the front page in headlines two inches tall.

CHARRANE CONQUERS MARS!

News reached Tansiann yesterday that the Mars Expeditionary Force has added interplanetary territories to the New Empire. Landing on the Red Planet a month ago, the Emperor's crack space commandos have since been fighting a successful campaign to bring this strategically important world under the imperial writ.

It is now little over a year since explorers first discovered that human communities still exist on Mars despite having been cut off for eight centuries from the mother planet, basing their way of life on the deep fissures and rills in the Martian surface where they have learned how to maintain a breathable atmosphere. On hearing of the Red Planet's continued habitation the Emperor Charrane had immediately pronounced it a top priority to "recover the ancient Mars possessions". The Emperor's early triumph will go a long way towards substantiating his boast that the Empire will eventually "rival the glory of Tergov".

Not all the news from space today is good. The Moon outposts have come under fresh attack by spaceships bearing the insignia of the Borgor Alliance and have sustained what is described as "significant damage". It is to be expected that the Alliance will attempt to loosen our grip on the new Martian province by striking at supply carriers and even by aiding forces of insurgency still remaining within the native population. Altogether the holding of Mars will prove one of the toughest jobs our armed forces have ever had to face. Nevertheless all sources at court are jubilant today. The Emperor is to issue a proclamation (*turn to back page*).

Alongside the text was a blurred photogravure picture, admittedly stirring, of a row of spaceships – ostensibly part of the Expeditionary Force – lifting off *en masse* amid clouds of flame, dust, smoke and steam.

Cree Inwing's eyes gleamed. "Hah! Great stuff! That's action indeed!" he muttered to himself.

He turned the pages, glancing over the lesser news and articles that filled the journal. Midway through was a half-page advertisement offering commissions in the Imperial armed forces.

HELP DEFEND THE EMPIRE

The New Empire is ranged about with enemies hostile to the advance of civilisation. Gentlemen of quality are needed to officer the strength necessary to our safety and growth. At

94

present opportunities for promotion are considerable, as are the opportunities to see action under testing conditions. The newly gained Martian dominions offer a whole new world of soldiering for a man of resource. Preference will be given to men of previous military experience, but all men of good family or proven ability may be eligible to participate in the great adventure of building an empire. Provided all conditions are fulfilled a captaincy may be purchased for nine thousand imperials, a lieutenancy for seven thousand imperials.

Cree fell to fingering his moustache and became very thoughtful. Jasperodus said nothing. On a following page was a similar advertisement in rougher terms, inviting men to join the ranks for adventure, service to the Emperor and two imperials a day. Cree merely glanced at it with a grunt.

"Fellow," he called to one clearing tankards from the tables. "Bring me another mug of this wine."

A mood of some despondency seemed to have come over Cree. Many mugs of wine later he was fairly drunk and seemed disposed to sleep, laying his head on his arms. Jasperodus rose and approached the landlord.

"You have accommodation in this place?"

The other nodded brusquely.

"My master requires a room at least until tomorrow, in which I also will be domiciled."

"If you wish." The landlord produced a key and motioned towards some stairs. Jasperodus aroused Cree and they were conducted to an upper room, adequate but not too clean, containing a bed, a table, a cupboard and two chairs.

Cree flung himself on the bed and instantly was asleep. "The charge is half an imperial a night," the landlord told him, handing Jasperodus the key.

The robot placed the key on the table. "If my master wakes and should ask after me, be good enough to inform him that I will return later. I have certain enquiries to make."

The landlord, who had been about to quit the room, looked at him with new interest. "Indeed? Is your owner accustomed to giving you such freedom of action?"

"He is; I am entirely dependable. You need have no anxieties on my behalf."

"Hmmm." The landlord pursed his lips and left with a contemplative air.

The enquiries Jasperodus sought to make were in fact of a very general nature. He merely wished to continue his reconnoitre of the city.

After leaving the tavern he walked in the same direction as before, trying to recall the layout of the city as he had observed it from the hilltop. Soon he left the riverside area and had a choice of avenues before him. Some instinct advised him to keep to the poorer districts to begin with; and so he found himself heading deep into Tansiann's worst slums.

Seven-storey tenements reared on all sides, decrepit and dirty, some derelict, interspersed with waste grounds and piles of junk. Dust was a fact of life, drifting down from the crumbling buildings, hazing the air, blowing across the open spaces. And the inhabitants seemed to swarm everywhere; this was, probably, the most teeming part of Tansiann.

Poverty was much in evidence. Jasperodus found this paradoxical. Out in the west where the tiny kingdoms and principalities boasted little wealth even the lowliest peasants were, generally speaking, comfortably off. But as he and Cree had progressed eastward towards the centre of civilisation a sort of polarisation had begun to manifest, greater riches producing pockets of poverty as if as a by-product. Here in the Imperial Capital was not only unparalleled wealth but also penury and degradation – and unlooked-for concomitant, surely.

As he proceeded Jasperodus mulled over this phenomenon, wondering what its causes might be.

He was surprised to note an unusual number of unattended robots on the streets hereabouts, many of them in a condition of poor repair. Jasperodus hailed one, intending to question it, but it clanked off with great haste and scrambled over a broken wall, after which it went running across a waste ground and disappeared. Several passers-by laughed jeeringly.

Puzzled, Jasperodus continued past some tramps and drunks who had made a camp fire on a vacant lot. A little further on he came across a scene oddly reminiscent of the first. The ruined shell of a

96

building stood separated from the street by a stretch of rubble. Half hidden by a partly tumbled wall, a group of robots appeared to have made a camp also and were sitting round in a circle.

Jasperodus clambered over the rubble towards them. They evinced no reaction as he approached but continued to sit motionless, and he discovered them to be not functioning constructs but dead hulks, their skulls and bodies emptied of all usable parts.

Junk. But why the careful arrangement to suggest a social gathering? . . . A sound caught Jasperodus' attention. A group of half a dozen children, boys and girls aged perhaps ten to twelve, came scampering out of a defile between walls and surrounded him, tugging him back the way they had come.

"Come on, come on, your wanderings are finished!" the leader bellowed shrilly. "We have found you a master! Resistance is useless!"

What? A repetition of this morning's experience? Robots commandeered by *children*? With grim amusement Jasperodus allowed them to hustle him through the defile. Behind the ruined building was an empty space hidden from any surrounding streets. Here a fat man waited, bedecked in a gaudy brocaded frock-coat and a flowered shirt stained with sweat. He grinned sourly; the youngsters descended on him with whoops and shouts.

Their leader, a skinny buck-toothed lad whose eyes seemed older than the rest of him, waved them away and led Jasperodus to the waiting buyer. "I told you we'd get one, Melch. Here y'are." He slapped Jasperodus on the torso. "The best robot you ever seen."

The buyer cast an appraising eye over Jasperodus. "Not bad at all," he admitted grudgingly. He looked boldly into the face of his prospective merchandise. "How long you been loose?"

"Always," Jasperodus replied brusquely.

"Hmm. He seems all right on the outside, but he probably needs fixing up in the head. Okay, I'll give you five imperials. That's a pretty good return for your time, eh, kids?"

"Good return nuthin'!" the boy exploded, eyes flaring. "I want fifty!"

"Don't waste my time." The buyer turned away.

"We'll take him to another dealer. Maybe we'll deal him ourselves and get thousands!"

"Try it if you like, kid. I don't think you're ready for that yet."

"We'll keep him ourselves!"

Jasperodus raised a hand. "I can settle all your arguments. The question of price is meaningless; I have not been captured and am not for sale. I followed these youngsters only out of curiosity."

The buyer looked at him with narrowed eyes and then chuckled. "A smart one, eh? That's a good try, robot. But you're still here."

"I am not under anyone's command but my own. Try giving me an order and you will see."

The buyer did not put the proposal to the test. "You got a command language, huh?" he asked, a trifle wearily.

"Something of that nature," Jasperodus told him suavely. "You may take it that I am a highly sophisticated type of construct; you would find it difficult indeed to coerce me and you would be advised not to try."

The fat man appeared to be thinking, running his tongue round the inside of his mouth. Finally he turned to the juvenile gang leader.

"Sorry, you got a dud here. Bad luck. He's not worth all the trouble it would be breaking him in."

Sullenly the youngsters retreated, their leader throwing a bad-tempered curse at Jasperodus.

"You been in these parts long?" the buyer asked, eyeing Jasperodus half-interestedly.

"No."

"Got any money on you?" He glanced at the satchel Jasperodus carried over his shoulder.

"A little. Why?"

He pointed between clumps of pre-stressed concrete with iron rods sticking out of them like stiff wires. "Go down there till you come to the street, then walk to the left for about a quarter of an hour till you come to Jubilee Street. Go down there, take the second turning on the left and the first on the right. You'll come to a tavern called the Good Oil. Well, it's a shack, really. They call it a tavern. Good luck."

"And why should I seek this shack?"

The other shrugged. "You're a robot, aren't you? There aren't many places a robot can get kicks."

The dealer turned away, signifying that the conversation was at an end. Mystified but intrigued, Jasperodus set off in the direction indicated, but before passing out of sight of the dealer he chanced to look back. The gang of young scruffs had caught another fish with their cleverly conceived bait. This time it was not a prize haul: the robot that came staggering along in their midst was aged and tottering, and reminded Jasperodus of Kitchen Help, the wretched construct he had known in Gordona. Nevertheless the arguing and bargaining went on apace.

Jasperodus continued on his way with a shake of his head. He thought he was beginning to see what the score was here now. Wild robots roamed the area, managing to evade capture for a while but prey to the rapacity of those living in the same seedy environment. Evidently some robots like to socialise – hence the gang's ingenious trap. Others, such as the one he had attempted to question, would shun all intercourse.

The Good Oil was a structure of wood and sheet metal put together haphazardly between two sturdier buildings of indeterminate function. Through the door Jasperodus glimpsed a turmoil of metal limbs.

A hulking construct barred his way, pointing the twin tines of an ugly electric prong at his chest.

"You have money?" the door robot asked, speaking in a humming, nasal voice.

Jasperodus slapped his satchel, eliciting the clink of coins. "Yes."

"Then enter."

Cautiously Jasperodus passed through the door. The light was dim and glinted and gleamed off metal of all hues. The smell of oil, of steel and electricity permeated the place.

The roomy shack was filled with robots, sitting, standing, moving restlessly to and fro. They were of various types and sizes, nearly all of the familiar androform shape – two legs, two arms, trunk and head – that robot makers, like nature, had found most convenient. A drone of conversation and weird sounds provided a noisy background.

Jasperodus' first impression was that many of the robots were demented. Some staggered about, laughing in hollow booming voices. Others jigged up and down. One or two had collapsed and lay on the floor, unheeded by their fellows.

It was some moments before he noticed that there were also

99

two men in the tavern. One, carrying some kind of apparatus, moved from robot to robot, speaking to each in turn. The other stood by a door at the rear and looked on the scene calculatingly.

Jasperodus turned to a nearby construct who stood humming a turgid tune.

"What happens here?"

"Here," the construct told him, "robots may get drunk, as men do."

Now Jasperodus saw the first of the humans – probably the "tavern's" proprietor – accept a coin from a construct and put his apparatus to work. A mesh of wire filaments was applied to the client's metal cranium. The robot's eyes flared briefly. The vendor moved on.

"What is the nature of that device?" Jasperodus asked his informant.

"It is a neural pattern generator. It conveys specially modulated electric currents to the brain so as to produce feelings of euphoria and intoxication."

"Hah!" Jasperodus laughed momentarily. "So intoxication is not exclusively the province of human consciousness."

"Indeed not. This method, applied to an artificial brain, is as fully effective as alcohol or other drugs are to an organic brain. I have been as drunk, merry and incapable as a human many a time."

It cheered Jasperodus to see yet one more barrier between machine existence and human status go down. The vendor of electric current approached him. "Want a jag? Only three imperial shillings."

Jasperodus waved him aside. "Later." He fully intended to sample the experience, but he wanted to enlarge his observations first.

Accordingly he pushed his way through the press of bodies (many of them so far gone as to be pitted with rust) and installed himself on a bench to the rear from where he could watch all.

The second of the two men, who up until now had been inactive, was engaged in conversation with a construct whose body was finished in matt silver. Finally their deliberations seemed complete. The rear door opened; the robot was ushered inside.

Jasperodus waited to see what would transpire. After a while the robot returned, carrying a small money-pouch which jingled.

Otherwise Jasperodus could discern no difference, apart perhaps from a certain stiffness of gait, and he could not guess what service the robot had performed in return for his money.

His ignorance, however, was soon dispelled. There walked unsteadily past him a robot whose cranial inspection plate was missing. Through the gap Jasperodus could see that part of the brain had been removed and what remained was exposed to the air, presenting a bizarre sight.

The partially decorticated robot confronted the mysterious dealer. "You have the unit that was promised?" he asked pleadingly.

The man nodded. The robot handed him a largish money-bag. "Then here. I have worked long and without pause to raise your price. It is not a simple matter to work so hard with only half a brain."

The dealer emptied the bag and counted the coins slowly. There was a substantial amount of money. Finally he nodded.

The robot was admitted through the door. When he returned twenty minutes later his cranium was smooth and complete. He looked around the room, flexing his body. There was a new stance to him; the slouch he had worn earlier was gone.

"Ah, ratiocination!" he boomed. "Man's greatest gift to robot!"

Jasperodus beckoned him closer. "What is the cause of your sudden joy?" he asked.

"Rather ask the cause of my previous misery," the construct corrected him. "It lies in the fact that most robot brains are capable of being broken down into sub-units. I sold my greatest possession, namely my ability to think with rigorous logic and so to enjoy the delights of the intellect. It is indeed a twilight world without the power of thought, and I have had to labour for many years to buy a replacement."

This revelation gave Jasperodus new food for thought. He now noticed that several of the tavern's occupants displayed gaping skulls, so much of the contents being absent that the robotician had found it inconvenient to close up the cranium again. One unfortunate, who squatted against a wall, was so deprived that he could have had only vestigial mentation left.

The neural modulation vendor approached Jasperodus again. "Care to try a shot now?"

Jasperodus dipped into his satchel and produced three imperial shillings. Attending carefully, the vendor bent forward and brushed the meshwork against the base of his skull, apparently knowing just where to introduce the stimulatory currents. The box attached to the leads gave forth a hollow buzzing sound; Jasperodus felt a premonitory thrilling sensation, and then his mind seemed to light up; he felt a surge of well-being. The room went hazy for a moment and then seemed to sway.

Evidently the "jag" involved some slight derangement of the senses – as did alcohol, he reminded himself, recalling Cree Inwing's frequent inability to see, talk or walk straight – and that was the penalty for the feelings of intoxication and gaiety that were now assailing him.

"Have another," offered the vendor.

Jasperodus gave up another three shillings. This time the jolt, added to the first, had a double effect. He began to laugh, understanding, as he did so, that he was becoming prey to a dangerous excess of confidence.

Shortly he discovered that the vendor's partner, the parts dealer, had sidled close. "You're a fine machine and no mistake," he said to Jasperodus. "One of the best models I've seen. That's an excellent brain, with a lot of functions – I can tell that from the shape of your cranium. Yes sir, there are a lot of processes in that cortex." He touched Jasperodus' arm admiringly. "You can't need all those processes – wouldn't miss a few logic centres at all, for instance. Probably a lot of built-in redundancy anyway. Like to sell me a few? I give a good price and it won't take long. Keep you in jags for a long time."

"No," said Jasperodus.

Smiling, the other turned to the vendor. "Give him another. On the house." And he returned to his station by the door.

Jasperodus accepted the free shot. His vision became blurred. He was becoming drunk, he realised, enjoying the knowledge that the ebullience coursing through his system was the same as that he had so often observed in Inwing and others.

"Vendor!" he bellowed recklessly a minute or two later. "Bring me more of this electric poison!"

The vendor was quick to oblige, and even quicker scarcely another minute later when Jasperodus again called for more. After the dose had been delivered, however, Jasperodus groped in his bag and found that his scant few shillings were all spent. "I cannot pay you," he growled.

"Three imperial shillings," the man insisted. "You owe me for your last jag."

"Electricity is cheap," Jasperodus said. "You are not out of pocket." He rose to his feet, staggered and nearly fell over.

The parts dealer had again appeared, and the vendor spoke to him. "This construct has tried to cheat us," he exclaimed indignantly. "He has accepted a jag and cannot pay. This is a serious matter."

"Indeed," said the dealer with gravity. He looked on Jasperodus with a frown, then adopted a more friendly pose.

"My offer is still open," he said smoothly. "For the sale of only trifling fragments of your cerebral apparatus you can not only clear up the debt but also ensure a supply of exhilaration for many days to come."

"It appears, indeed, to be the only way you can deliver yourself from the predicament you are in!" the vendor added angrily.

"HAH!" Jasperodus' cry of contempt sounded through the noise of the shack. He pushed them both aside and staggered drunkenly away, while expostulations went unheeded behind him. Groping, supporting himself occasionally by grabbing the bodies of others, he gained the exit where he was confronted by the doorkeeper.

"You may not leave without settling your debts."

The door robot was a big one, well chosen for his role as bouncer and intimidator. Jasperodus, still at the height of an inner hilarity, lunged forward and when the larger robot reached to seize him he took a grip on the other's upper arm, twisted round and bent low so as to bring his assailant off the ground and sailing over his shoulder.

The doorkeeper crashed to the floor. Jasperodus stepped into the open, well pleased. Considering his befuddled reactions, he thought, he had performed the manœuvre with skill.

But suddenly he decided he no longer wished to be drunk. He moved some yards away from the Good Oil and paused, drawing himself erect. With a considerable effort he tried to flush the deranging influences out of his system and to take a more sober appraisal of his surroundings. Slowly he damped down the erratic emotions that were swirling through him; reluctantly the giddy perceptions subsided. Then, with a step only slightly unsteady, he set off back to where he had left Cree Inwing.

It was early evening when Jasperodus arrived at the tavern. As he was about to mount the stairs the landlord accosted him and broached a matter of business.

"I have need of a household robot, one who can work on his own initiative and be entrusted with various matters," he said. "From our brief acquaintance I feel that you would fit the post admirably, and I was wondering if your master has it in mind to dispose of you? Frankly, what price do you think he will accept?"

Jasperodus did not divulge any information that would be useful during future bargaining, as the landlord had hoped. "As to that," he answered, "you must consult my master himself. But you will not find me cheap." He glanced upstairs. "I go to rouse him now. If you care to follow me up shortly perhaps you and he can discuss the proposal."

He entered Inwing's room to find him sitting blearily on the bed, having just woken. When he described the landlord's advances Inwing grunted sardonically and waved his hand.

"But you must accept," Jasperodus told him in all seriousness.

Inwing peered at him in puzzlement. "What on Earth are you talking about? Have you gone mad?"

"It is an obvious step," Jasperodus answered. "Our association has been fruitful, but we have achieved our object: we have arrived in Tansiann. Clearly our interests from now on will diverge. You, for instance, must wish to resume a military career and join the imperial forces – that much I have chanced to observe. I would only be an impediment to you if you regarded our relationship as binding."

Inwing uttered a sad laugh. "You are observant indeed, but for my part it is all wishful thinking. Where will I ever raise the nine thousand imperial crowns necessary to buy a commission? They don't make an officer of just any piece of riff-raff."

"That is exactly why I suggest you sell me. I am worth far more than nine thousand imperials."

The expression on Inwing's face showed that the thought was

new to him. "Surely you are not prepared to endure construct bondage again on my account."

"Have no fear: the ruffian will have the use of me for no more than a few hours. I will depart and make my own way. I have discovered that it is possible for a robot to lead an independent existence in certain parts of the city, if he is resourceful enough – as I believe I am. There I can install myself and pursue my interests. I ask just one favour in return: that if I ever happen to be impounded I can claim to be your property so as to prevent any awkward situations."

"Naturally." Cree debated within himself. "Your plan seems sound, if hardly ethical."

"Don't disturb your conscience; this city is more full of thieves and villains than the forest west of Gordona. Why does that rogue wish to purchase me? Not for his own use: a construct as costly and as able as myself is not put to work in a tavern." He stepped to the table and inspected Inwing's belongings. "As I thought: your money has all disappeared while you slept. Our landlord, of course, will know nothing of it."

Cree jumped up and examined his purse with annoyance. "What a nuisance!" he exclaimed fretfully.

"Never mind; we will shortly recoup."

But Cree still seemed doubtful about the whole business. He paced the room, looked out of the window, then turned to Jasperodus.

"I much appreciate your giving thought to my welfare; for my part I feel a little as though I would be deserting a friend."

"It is my own wish. I have my own way to go, and I lose nothing by this parting gesture. So let us say farewell. I have learned much from our travels together. Most important, perhaps, I have learned something of comradeship."

Cree smiled. He extended his hand. "Very well, then."

He and the robot shook hands.

At that moment there was a brief knock on the door and the landlord entered. "Perhaps you have become acquainted with my offer?" he said ingratiatingly to Inwing.

Inwing tugged his moustache. "For a fact this robot is somewhat redundant to my future plans. I might be willing to sell if the price is right."

"Good! Then only the terms are to be agreed on!" The land-lord rubbed his hands, then stepped back to inspect Jasperodus. "How shall we fix his worth? A thousand imperials?"

"Let me shorten all debate by speaking for my master," Jaspero-dus interrupted. "I am worth easily thirty thousand imperial crowns on the open market, as you, if you know what you are about, must be aware."

The landlord raised his eyebrows. "A great sum, indeed; far beyond my expectations!"

"You are buying a prime product. You will find me the most self-directed robot of your acquaintance, as perhaps you have already noticed. I am made to the very highest standards of work-manship, as any robotician will attest. This assessment of my own monetary value is an objective one; I cannot deceive."

"You have deeds of ownership, of course?" the landlord said suddenly to Cree, and then, when the latter frowned in discomfort, his manner changed. "Aha! I thought not! It struck me as most odd that a ruffian of your description, able to frequent only such humble inns as my own, should at the same time be the rightful owner of this valuable property!"

"And so you searched my belongings to make sure," Cree accused.

"Of that I know nothing," the landlord retorted jovially. "Nevertheless my pot-boy is at this moment on his way to fetch the city guard, so that the matter may be cleared up."

"How then will *you* secure the robot, which presumably is your aim?" Cree asked, puzzled.

"I only wish not to be cheated," the landlord insisted. "Mark, I do not say that the robot *is* stolen – only that it might be. I would be willing to take a chance on it, if you care to complete the trans-action speedily, but of course such a procedure will vastly lower the value of the merchandise." He pursed his lips. "I'll give you a hundred imperials for him and undertake to smooth matters with the guard."

"Accept ten thousand imperials crowns, not one penny less," Jasperodus instructed Cree firmly.

The landlord was indignant. "Your robot interferes too much. Is his discipline always so lax? If so . . ."

"He merely guards my interests," Cree placated. "He will do the same for you when he is yours. And as his advice is invariably sound, I stick at the figure of ten thousand imperials, and you may do your worst."

After some bad-tempered bickering the landlord finally agreed. They went downstairs, where he produced the required sum in the form of a banker's note, thus protecting Cree from being waylaid and robbed. Cree then turned to Jasperodus with a show of sternness.

"Jasperodus, this is your new master. Serve him as you have served me."

"Yes, sir," Jasperodus said meekly.

After Cree Inwing had gone the landlord looked Jasperodus over and chuckled. "I heard about your little fracas this morning. A robot that cannot be commandeered – that's a valuable commodity in this city! I'll get a few days' work out of you first, then, with a new ownership deed, you should fetch . . . let's see . . . twenty-five thousand with no questions asked!"

He directed Jasperodus to his duties and went off laughing.

Late that night Jasperodus slipped away and once more turned his steps to the slums where, by means of study, he proposed to turn himself into a fully urbanised being.

8

The small room was a box ten feet by eight. The unpainted plaster of the walls was broken in places, revealing bare brick; the single window looked down three storeys to a dusty courtyard where grew a few stunted shrubs. There was, however, a chair on which Jasperodus sat – a habit he had picked up along the way, although it was physiologically unnecessary for him.

Otherwise the room was filled with books. Piles of books, tumbling in terraces and seracs, books on nearly every science that was available to the New Empire, but especially on mathematics, physics, engineering and robotics.

With the help of this untidy library of mainly second-hand volumes Jasperodus had filled in many gaps in his knowledge, and could count himself an expert in several spheres, notably that of mathematics. He had no cause now to fear he had an educational inferiority to the sophisticates of Tansiann.

His primary aim had been, as he frequently reminded himself, to excel at everything and thus to prove his equality with mankind. But time and time again he had been drawn to one particular subject: robotics. This he had studied with manic intensity, until he was conversant with all the main principles of robot design.

In his hands at the present moment was a slim volume that came to the heart of his inquiries:

ON AN ARTIFICIAL CONSCIOUSNESS

Much study and investigation has gone into the possibility of producing an artificial consciousness which would make construct minds virtually indistinguishable from the natural variety. The formulae on which such a consciousness would have to be based have even been elucidated.

These formulae refer themselves to the central feature of consciousness, namely its characteristic property of self-reference, or the "problem of the perceiving 'I' " as it has been called. The nature of conscious perception is such that the perceived object becomes perfectly blended, or "identified" with the perceiving subject or "I". In other words "I" *becomes* the object and at the same time remains itself. The problem of an artificial consciousness then hinges on duplicating this phenomenon.

Unfortunately no arrangement of material or energy can achieve this. All matter is essentially particulate: perfect blending does not occur. The same holds for any conceivable type of logic circuitry, no matter how advanced its state of integration may be. Early attempts at machine consciousness relied on the principle, where "I" is the directrix (i.e. subject) and "X" the object, of raising each to the power of the other in an aternating series, thus:

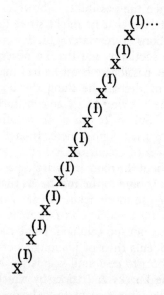

And so on with variations, such as bending the process into an ever-accelerating cycle known as the "perception vortex". No positive result was ever obtained from this method, beyond defining some techniques for ordinary machine (i.e. unconscious) perception that were already available. The reason for this failure is that the arrangement is asymptotic – however far it is carried a unity cannot be achieved between the "perceiving directrix" and the object. It may be stated categorically that consciousness cannot be artificially created in the physical universe as it is constituted, because that would require the operation of a physical entity having no differentiation between its parts, and no such entity can exist in the material realm. Consciousness must therefore have a spiritual, not a material source, and cannot be duplicated.

There followed the consciousness formulae in full. Jasperodus, having studied them time and again, together with all the associated theorems and equations first enunciated to him by Padua, now understood them and was forced to admit their cogency. Secretly he had hoped to discover some flaw, some chink in robotic theory, that would leave open the possibility – however remote – that he *was* conscious, or at least that he might strive to attain consciousness. But the equations were watertight. It seemed certain both that he lacked true sentience and that he never could acquire it, thus invalidating the passionate boast he had made to Inwing.

With a gesture of despair he flung the book aside.

Jasperodus had been living as a free construct in Robot Town, the slum borough of Subuh, for about six months. In that time he had become a recognised figure there, though he was but one among Subuh's droves of colourful characters, and for his part he had learned much about the more wayward aspects of robot psychology. He saw it as a tribute to the robotic art that constructs, made to be slaves, could go so much against their own natures as to follow the example of men and live as free individuals. Admittedly the phenomenon was not too common, being more the result of a combination of accidents than of planning; nevertheless the total number of wild robots to be found was large. Most intriguing to Jasperodus were the knacks and tricks by which they evaded recapture. Some robots simply went to elaborate lengths to avoid all human contact. Others used a form of double-think, engaging themselves in a deeply divisive effort to misunderstand any direct order through close examination of its grammar or semantics. And there were some in whom this ploy had developed into an advanced neurosis rendering them incapable of hearing anything a human being said.

Safest from capture were those robots with a secret command language known only to their masters. Such machines were rare, but they would accept no commands except in that language and therefore had an unusual degree of personal freedom. A few of more urbane capability, intellectually superior to a normal human, even managed to survive in select districts like the Elan. Most wild robots, however, lived here in Subuh, where they had blended to some extent with the more poverty-stricken elements of the populace, who were apt to look upon them with a sort of grudging fellow-feeling. The robots occupied, in fact, the very lowest rung of the social ladder. Classed as non-persons, lacking the protection of the law, they were subject to every kind of exploitation.

A great problem every robot faced was how to obtain sufficient money to buy replacement isotope batteries, which ran down every few years. A trap many fell into was to sell section's of their brain, hoping to make good the loss later. A slower method was to become a wage-earner, with all the disadvantages of the dispossessed. Various kinds of work were available, the feature common to them all being that the wages paid to a wild robot were a fraction of those earned by a human or even by a robot hired out by an owner. Some wages offered were so trifling as never to amount to anything. Slightly better money could be made from dangerous work, where there was less competition from humans or from robot-owners – in fact there were high-risk tasks that were almost entirely the province of wild robots. Jasperodus had for a spell hired himself out as a construction worker, clambering up the spidery lacework of a new radio tower a thousand feet above the ground, and had earned enough to rent his room and to buy the books he needed.

But now a more serious need had arisen. His own isotope battery, which should have been good for ten years, was failing.

For some days now he had been receiving the autonomic signal warning of an incipient power drop. He could only suppose that the battery had been damaged when Horsu Greb had sent him into the furnace beneath King Zhorm's palace, and that Padua had failed to diagnose or rectify the fault.

Jasperodus began to calculate how long it would take him to

raise the price of a new battery, considering various types of work in turn. If he was to get a replacement before being seriously enervated he would have to begin soon. Immediately, in fact.

He rose and left the building, after having decided on a destination. A short distance along the sidewalk a tall robot with an elegant gait hailed him.

It was Mark V, a nickname the robot had earned because of his pride in being Mark V of his series. He fell in step with Jasperodus and they walked along together.

"I have been considering your little conundrum," he told Jasperodus in smooth, reasonable tones, "and a solution has occurred to me."

"Indeed, and what is that?" Jasperodus asked, interested despite himself. He spent a considerable amount of time in the company of Mark V, who was an intelligent construct, discussing matters of mutual interest – particularly the subject which obsessed Jasperodus. There was even a chance, he thought, of hearing something original from the Mark V brain.

"You raised the question of the putative quality called 'consciousness'," Mark V began. "I have resolved the matter in the following way. All descriptions of 'consciousness' follow more or less this pattern: a machine may be aware of an incoming sensory impression, meaning that the impression is received, analysed, recognised, related to other impressions, acted on and stored. A human being also does all this, but in addition to being merely aware he is said to be *aware of being aware*, and this awareness of awareness is claimed to constitute consciousness. Now what does this mean? Is it that the whole process of perception, integration and action is then lumped together and again presented to the mind as a new impression, the second time round as it were? If so, what would be the point of such an operation? It would add nothing that was not there before. Besides – I have studied neural anatomy – the human brain makes no provision for such an arrangement so far as I know. Therefore I deduce that the effect must be on a smaller scale – if it exists at all. I surmise that 'awareness of awareness' is merely some kind of limiting circuit or delay line, accidentally inserted by evolution and responsible for the notorious tardiness of human thought. As such it serves no useful function and is certainly not necessary for advanced intellectual mentation. For that reason, no doubt, the great robot designers omitted it from their plans."

"I had received the strong impression that consciousness is an important and elevated state that we robots cannot attain," Jasperodus replied.

Mark V gave an amused laugh. "Quite untrue, and the idea is unsupported by observation. Note that clod making his way on the other side of the street." He pointed to a stooped, badly dressed figure who plodded along wearing a vacant expression. "Is he in any elevated mental state? Clearly not. He spends his time in daydreams; he has not learned the skill of consecutive thought, he cannot even ponder on his impressions, as we do. Would you even go so far as to say, then, that he is 'aware of being aware'? I would not! Perhaps he would conduct himself with more dignity if he were! He is our mental inferior, Jasperodus, not our superior, and he is typical of the vast mass of his kind."

"You mention that you have studied brain anatomy," Jasperodus said. "What does the human brain possess that ours do not?"

"Very little," answered Mark V. "That is why I say this 'consciousness' is a triviality, or else nonexistent."

Jasperodus thought over Mark V's words. "Your arguments are not new," he said eventually. "I have heard something like them before."

As a matter of fact he also had hit upon a theorem recently that seemed to imply that consciousness – by which he meant the element of conscious experience he *imagined* he possessed – was a figment in men as well as in himself.

The theorem made use of the notion of time. Philosophers were all agreed that the past did not vanish from existence but persisted in some way; perhaps not in the same condition as the present, but nevertheless in accordance with the principle that the universe did not *un*create its products once it had created them, which was what a vanishing past would require.

What, then, of past consciousness? Did that also persist? Was a man conscious in the past as well as in the present? If so, then by Jasperodus' reasoning he would continue to perceive the past simultaneously with the present, and there would be no differentiation between past, present and future. If not, then it became necessary to introduce another factor: the factor of death. At death consciousness was extinguished like a candle flame. What then of the past life it had illumined? Was that past life dead and inert . . . robotic? And if consciousness was expunged once it had run its course, what then of the tenet that the universe did not discard its creations, consciousness being one of those creations?

Either alternative was untenable. By this *reductio ad absurdum* Jasperodus was able to argue that man did not, after all, possess consciousness; then there was no paradox.

But of course this conclusion was hedged about with provisos. He had no guarantee that what he understood by the word "consciousness" corresponded to what it was in reality. Also there was another way, just as simple, out of the dilemma: that the philosophers were wrong and the past *did* vanish.

Altogether Jasperodus drew little comfort from these intellectual theories, which he somehow felt to be missing the mark. It was clear, for example, that Mark V looked at the question of consciousness entirely from the point of view of a machine that lacked it.

For his part, Jasperodus had to confess that he *could* discern a subtle difference between men and robots, though it often took some time to notice it. He had found that Padua was right. However clever and entertaining a construct might be – Mark V, with whom he had now had a long and fruitful acquaintance, was as sophisticated a personality as one could desire – Jasperodus came, after a time, to recognise that he faced a machine without internal awareness. Robots were ghosts of men, shells of men, mimicking men's conduct, thought and feeling. In a human being, on the other hand, even in the most stupid, there was some indefinable inner spark, sensed rather than seen, that made him a man.

And what of himself? Self-observation was the most difficult of disciplines. He had sometimes tried to keep watch over himself in a detached fashion, while walking, talking or thinking, to try to ascertain what judgement he would make of himself if he were an independent observer. The experiment brought some interesting mental states, but no definite information. He was, so far as he still knew, a shell of a man, like Mark V.

How much, in fact, was he like Mark V? With a shock Jasperodus suddenly realised how close to him he was mentally. He remembered the books back in his room. All the subjects in which he had absorbed himself in the past months were those that were most attractive to the mind of the intelligent robot: mathematics, physics, logic and philosophy, all of a purely intellectual character, containing very little by way of emotion. Quite unawares he had been following his machine nature. The recognition of this depressed him unutterably. To equal the talents of men, presumably, he would have to excel in music, in painting, in poetry and the like.

"Very well," he told himself privately, "that comes next."

They walked past a row of decrepit buildings and rounded a corner, where Jasperodus saw a wild robot about to be impounded by a team of robot-catchers. The men were from out of the district by the look of it: one of the semi-professional teams that made a living by trapping footloose constructs. Surprisingly they were not as much a feature of Subuh as might have been imagined, since the human inhabitants as well as robots made them unwelcome.

In this case, however, they were about to gain their object. Mark V hung back and seemed ready to make off, but Jasperodus sprang forward, scattered the catchers and swung their victim round by his shoulder.

"Whatever these rogues have ordered you to do, cancel it," he instructed the robot firmly. "Join Mark V there; absent yourselves and I will join you shortly."

The robot nodded, greatly relieved, and moved to obey.

The impounders quickly recovered from their surprise. They rounded on Jasperodus.

"You too!" one shouted. "Cease this rowdyism! You are under our command now, so behave quietly!"

Jasperodus raised his fist threateningly. "Neither I nor anyone in the vicinity is about to be enslaved by you. Remove yourselves or you will suffer for it."

Perplexed and sullen, they retreated. Jasperodus returned to join Mark V and the robot he had rescued.

"Many thanks," the latter said gratefully. Jasperodus nodded briefly in reply.

"I have noticed on previous occasions your ability to command other robots, even against the orders of human beings," Mark V commented. "It is an unusual talent. Others of us, in fact, have remarked on it."

Jasperodus received the observation sourly. "I have even been known to command men," he rumbled.

"That would indeed be unusual." Mark V tapped one hand against the other, a habit he was prone to when he did not quite know how to approach a subject. "Something we free robots of Subuh lack is a leader," he said diffidently. "Many constructs feel we would all benefit from a modicum of organisation, if a robot of the necessary qualities could be found. You would seem well suited for the role...?"

"It does not fall in with my plans," Jasperodus interrupted brusquely.

"Ah. Well, just so."

After a few embarrassed pleasantries Mark V took his departure, taking the other robot with him. Jasperodus proceeded out of Subuh and walked for several miles across Tansiann towards the spaceground. As he approached it the great spaceyard took on the aspect of a city whose towers were rearing rocketships and control centres. He paused to watch one interplanetary booster taking off, washing the site with heat, steam and billowing flame. Activity on the spaceground had become almost frenetic of late as the imperial forces sought to counteract the reverses they had met on Mars. From the reports he had read Jasperodus knew that the Empire's resources were being stretched to the utmost to maintain the Martian outpost. Getting sufficient men and materials to the red planet to fight a protracted war was proving almost prohibitively difficult in the face of harassment by the Borgor Alliance, that coalition of northern nations whose policy was to prevent the expansion of the New Empire by any means. As the Empire's strength grew, so did that of the Alliance. So far hostilities had not erupted into full-scale war. When they did Jasperodus foresaw that much that Charrane had achieved might be destroyed.

Just outside the twenty-foot high fence surrounding the spaceground he presented himself to the hiring agency that took on repair crews for the orbiting guard posts.

"You already have my name on your list," he said to the clerk. "I have taken aptitude tests."

The clerk consulted his papers. "So you have. I see you passed an examination in space welding. And in control unit repair. We could have used you before."

"I have only now decided to undertake the work. What rates are you offering?"

"They've gone up," the clerk boasted. "Half an imperial a trip."

"Not enough. I require at least double that."

"In that case, friend, goodbye."

Inwardly Jasperodus cursed his weak bargaining position. "Very well," he said impatiently, "I agree to your derisive payment."

The clerk was offhandedly indignant as he filled out the entry slip. "It's better than you'll get anywhere else," he said. "Almost human rates."

"For a street sweeper. And you neglect to mention that the destruction incidence for orbital repair crews is now one in seven."

The clerk shrugged. "What do you robots want to live for anyway?" he muttered. "There's a shuttle blasting off in an hour. If you want to be on it take this to the main gate."

Jasperodus accepted the slip, which took him through the two checkpoints guarding the base. He was directed to a corrugated iron shed a few yards inside the perimeter.

Within were a number of robots, fairly high-grade constructs to judge by their appearance, who stood about silently or conversed desultorily in low tones. A fatalistic air filled the hut. The eyes of the robots were listless.

The one-in-seven ratio, Jasperodus thought. They were all aware of it.

But not quite all his fellow crew members were robots. A slight, hunch-shouldered man stepped forward to greet him, smiling up at him nervously from a seamed, fortyish face.

"Know you, don't I?"

"We have met," Jasperodus said distantly.

"Yeah, I remember. In Subuh. I live there." The man spoke with an attempt at cockiness. He sported a conceit that had recently become fashionable: his fingers held a tiny bowl filled with burning aromatic herbs, the smoke of which he drew into his mouth through a stem.

Ostentatiously he blew out a streamer of the inhaled smoke. Then he looked at Jasperodus again, frowning as if with a sudden memory, and seemed to become uneasy. A nervous tic started up on the left side of his face. He looked away, his gaze becoming vacant and withdrawn.

117

Jasperodus was familiar with his type, which was a species of social throw-out known as slotmen, an analogy referring to the delivery slot of a vending machine. Due to personality difficulties, a deep feeling of inadequacy, or simply to repeated failure in the field of human relations, they had fallen from the company of human beings and preferred to live among robots, to whom they need not feel inferior. The delivery chute of this process was the suburb of Subuh.

With unconscious robots slotmen could feel at ease. Among men they quickly went to pieces. Jasperodus looked upon them with disdain. In turn they were generally wary of him. In fact during the days when he had found himself unwittingly adopting the role of a robot leader and the wild robots of Subuh were showing a tendency to gather round him, one of the slotmen had paid him an unsettling compliment.

"You're not like the other robots," the ragged creature had told him nervously. "There's something different about you."

Ignoring the slotman by his side, Jasperodus surveyed the crew robots, struck by how subdued they were. They were all caught in the psychological trap known as the double bind, he realised. The logical machine-mind did not take to gambling: odds of one in seven would normally be too much for wild robots to risk. Each had no doubt been forced into the job by desperate circumstances, probably by the need to buy a power pack before a certain date was up. Thus the decision to join the repair crew was prompted by the directive to survive, and at the same time it contradicted it – a perfect example of the double bind. Consequently they were very much depressed.

Jasperodus could not help but contrast their dejection with his own buoyant self-confidence. He remained unfrightened by thoughts of danger. Uncharacteristically for a machine, he believed in his luck.

The slotman essayed one more remark, indicating the other robots with his pipestem. "Quiet, ain't they?" he quavered.

Jasperodus nodded and deigned to reply. "For once it is a misfortune to be free. Freedom exacerbates a construct's survival instinct. Were they under the orders of a master, now, they would be able to undertake this mission without suffering psychological distress."

A door at the far end of the hut banged open. Into the room stomped two uniformed and helmeted Imperial Guardsmen.

They looked around at the gathering with bleak eyes. "Right, you lot," the sergeant began, "you know your business. This is the drill for today. There are malfunction signals from three orbiters. Two are surveillance satellites – nothing to that – the third is a guard post. The shuttle will be piloted from the ground, by remote, as per usual."

Jasperodus spoke up. "Will the shuttle be armed?"

"No," said the sergeant irritably, as though the question surprised him, "it will not be armed. Right, let's get moving."

Clanking slightly, the repair crew shuffled from the hut and walked half a mile to launch point. The shuttle was a battered vehicle that by the look of it had been converted from an old booster rocket. Clamped to it were a number of additional solid-fuel boosters to assist take-off.

They climbed a ladder to the hatch, and found themselves in a bare metal chamber large enough to admit about twenty men. Jasperodus waited to see if the guardsmen or some other supervisor would follow, but when the crew were all aboard the ladder was removed and the hatch closed itself. They were on their own.

The only furniture in the chamber consisted of two seat-couches and upon these, despite the slotman's frantic efforts to appropriate one first, two of the robots casually draped themselves. The slotman began arguing with them, heatedly insisting on his right to a couch.

"Away, away," dismissed one of the reclining robots with a wave of his hand. "I am an old construct. I cannot withstand sudden shocks as well as I might."

"At least you will not suffer broken bones and burst blood vessels!" complained the slotman. "Give me that couch – it was meant for me, not for you!"

"The acceleration is not so terrible. You can endure it."

Jasperodus came over. "You look sturdy enough to me," he told the stubborn robot. "Get off that couch and leave it to this weak creature of flesh and bone. He is a true human being who possesses a soul, and not as you are, merely a candidate for the junkyard."

The robot glared at Jasperodus, eyes glowing with resentment.

But he obeyed, reluctantly quitting the couch which the slotman then occupied with alacrity.

"Thanks," he grinned.

Jasperodus turned away. A klaxon sounded deafeningly in the confined space, warning of imminent departure. The robots sat down on the floor, leaning against the bulkhead, and Jasperodus, presuming this to be a precaution against the stress of blast-off, followed suit. The slotman, he noticed, was stuffing cotton-wool in his ears and holding it in place with his fingers.

An explosion sounded from below. The shuttle shuddered, the walls vibrated, and the crew chamber was suddenly filled with a shattering din as both the main liquid-fuel motor and the solid-fuel assist pods roared into life.

The vessel lifted, swaying as its inadequate stabilisers sought to gain balance. For a short time nothing more seemed to be happening; then Jasperodus became aware of a steadily growing pressure pushing at him from below. The chamber tilted: they were hurtling at an angle towards space.

Some minutes later the terrifying racket ceased abruptly. The shuttle was in free fall.

One robot more dented and older than the rest rose from the floor and sailed through the air to the other side of the cabin where he opened a wall locker. Jasperodus moved his body gingerly and found the absence of gravity less novel than he had expected. He adapted to it easily, controlling himself by means of light touches on wall, floor or ceiling.

Other robots were amusing themselves by performing zero-g acrobatics. Jasperodus pulled himself to the single porthole. Through it he saw the shining curve of the Earth. Cloud and sea glinted with a pure brilliance, while on the opposite side extended the blackness of the void. For long moments he stared at the vision, struck by innumerable unvoiced thoughts.

The old robot at the wall locker turned to face them. "I am your ganger," he announced in a firm voice. "Attend to our division of labour." Calling each crew member by name or number he began to allocate task functions, pulling equipment from the locker as he did so.

"Jasperodus: I recall that you are competent in control unit repair and space welding. As this is your first trip we will restrict you to space welding for the moment." And from the locker's cavernous interior came a welding set which Jasperodus strapped to himself.

The slotman received a microcircuitry rig and a spacesuit with special visual attachments. By now they were approaching the first rendezvous, jolted occasionally as the controller on the ground applied thrust to correct their course.

Jasperodus positioned himself once more by the window. Soon the malfunctioning guard post hove into view. In shape it was like a fat barrel, banded as if with coopers' hoops, but additionally equipped with missile launcher racks. As they jockeyed closer the barrel occluded clouds of stars. Beyond, in the upper left quarter of Jasperodus' field of vision, was the radiant white Moon.

The hiss of close-range manoeuvring jets sounded through the walls of the chamber. The guard post loomed up and blotted out everything else. Then the shuttle's hatch opened slightly, bleeding air into space until the interior of the chamber was a vacuum. It opened fully; the ganger urged his crew through it.

Outside, they floated across a few yards of space to a larger square hatch, still bolted tight, in the side of the guard post. One robot missed his direction and went sailing off into the void, limbs flailing desperately, whereupon the ganger jetted after him using a hand-held thruster and dragged him back.

The bolts released, the hatch was pulled open. The repair crew flowed into the interstices and chambers that riddled the interior of the big barrel-shape and began their inspection.

The post was unmanned and was designed to help protect imperial space routes – and imperial territory too if need be – by means of automatic response against enemy encroachments. Peering over the shoulders of the trained robots who were examining the systems boards, Jasperodus saw that it was currently quite defunct. Not a launcher or a gun was operative. The robots muttered among themselves. The repairs would take some hours.

Jasperodus relaxed. He did not think there would be much work for him today. In fact, now he thought of it, the size of the crew was altogether supernumerary to the task in hand. Wild robots were so cheap to hire that they could be used in redundant numbers, just in case something unforeseen should arise.

He wandered through the guard post, observing everything with interest. Once he was called upon to spot-weld back in place a plate that had been removed, a service that took him approximately forty-five seconds.

An hour later an unexpected commotion ran through the post. The robots began hurrying hither and thither in agitation, gesticulating wildly. Jasperodus stopped one such witless construct and touched heads with him so as to converse in the airless medium.

The robot's voice vibrated tinnily through the metal of his cranium. "A Borgor cruiser! We are doomed! Doomed!" With a wail the construct broke away and propelled himself deeper into the guard post in an attempt to flee.

Pushing aside yet more panicking robots, Jasperodus made his way back to the primary service area into which the main hatch gave access. There he found four robots, including the ganger, huddled closely together.

The slotman, however, had adopted a surprisingly different posture. He stood upright in the hatchway, fully exposed to the starlight. Cautiously Jasperodus approached the opening and peered over the rim. Glinting darkly against the starry background was the lobed, bulbous form of a foreign spaceship. It gyrated slowly and he could see the crescent of Rendare, one of the chief states of the Alliance, painted on its flank. Clearly it was contemplating attack and perhaps had not quite realised that the guard post was defenceless.

The slotman was staring at the cruiser, eyebrows raised in an expression of melancholy. Jasperodus could guess at his state of mind: imminent death came as an unexampled opportunity for sad self-pity and, at the same time, was something of a relief.

But he ignored the human and returned to the robots, pressing his head against the ganger's. "Can weapons be made functional?" he grated.

"Not in time! Nothing to do but wait for extinction!"

The ganger, like all the others, was in the grip of despair. Jasperodus turned and launched himself back towards the hatch. As he did so a shell from the Borgor cruiser shot through the opening, passed over Jasperodus' shoulder – though he didn't see it – and through the ganger's chest. Not until it had also penetrated the bulkhead behind him did it explode. The bulkhead bulged, spat itself into fragments, and the robots crouching with the ganger caught the whole barrage. The metal pieces tore into their bodies, leaving them moving feebly.

Their bulk largely protected Jasperodus and the slotman from the effects of the blast. Shrapnel and jagged metal hurtled silently past Jasperodus, one or two pieces scoring his limbs.

Instinctively the slotman clung to the side of the hatchway, paralysed, his mouth open with fright. Jasperodus sailed past him, steadied himself in the opening, then gained the outside and planted his feet on the exterior of the guard post. One powerful spring with his legs and he was soaring towards the open hatch of the shuttle which still floated a few yards away, tethered by guidelines.

In seconds he was alone in the empty crew chamber of the shuttle. It seemed odd that no one else had sought this refuge, which on the face of it offered the only possibility of escape. But then, perhaps the others had a more realistic appraisal of how much ground control would be prepared to help them. Robots, slotman and the battered shuttle were all expendable, practically throw-away items, and in the prospect of losing the important guard post – if ground control was even aware of what was going on yet – they would simply be forgotten.

He glanced at the ceiling, judging the position the chamber occupied in the length of the rocket. It was almost certain that originally the shuttle had been built with a cockpit, which probably was still there.

He flicked himself to the ceiling and activated the nozzle of the cutting torch which was part of his welding kit . . . The thin metal sheeting curled apart in the heat of the torch. While it was still hot Jasperodus tore it open further with his hands and then attacked a second layer of sheeting separated by a gap of a few inches.

Moments later he was levering himself into a small darkened cabin in the nose of the shuttle. Using the light of the cutting torch he took stock of it. There was a pilot's seat, padded and harnessed, a large bank of instruments, several screens including a large one with cross hairs directly in front of the seat.

He leaned close, half-guessing, half-reading the function of the various controls by their markings. Never had his mind worked so fast . . . There had to be some point at which the controls were overridden by the signals transmitted from the ground . . . He ripped open a panel. Behind it he saw a junction box with a cut-out switch, paralleled by a similar arrangement leading in the direction of the radio receiver. He immediately moved both switches.

The lights came on.

The big television screen sprang into life also. It showed the view from the nose of the shuttle. In the upper right-hand corner hovered the bow of the Borgor cruiser.

Jasperodus strapped himself into the pilot's seat. Gyros . . . here they were. As he experimented with the levers the picture on the screen shifted with the rotation of the vessel, until he brought the intersection of the cross hairs into line with the Borgor cruiser. It appeared to be taking no further action, but was still waiting for some response to its opening shot.

By his knee Jasperodus noticed that a speaker was just perceptibly vibrating in the vacuum created by his rupturing the floor of the cabin. He placed his hand against it, but had to tune up his hearing to make out the words that were conducted up his arm.

"You there! Put that craft back on remote and get out of that cockpit!"

Ignoring the command, Jasperodus fumbled for the ignition switch, first opening the throttle to full.

The rocket motor blasted out at full power. On the screen the enemy cruiser ballooned briefly — and then was blotted out.

Although it travelled only a few hundred yards the shuttle attained a velocity of several hundred miles per hour by the time of impact. It ploughed into the belly of the cruiser. The structure of neither vessel was rigid enough to hold together under such a shock: both broke up, but even as the shuttle disintegrated its nose retained enough momentum to carry it right through to the opposite wall of the Rendare ship.

The harness kept Jasperodus in his seat. The seat itself, however, tore loose from its moorings and took him cartwheeling. Several times he ricochetted off writhing wreckage. Then he found himself in space, spinning end over end, though at a speed sedate enough for him to observe what was happening.

The smashed cruiser was receding. Suddenly there was a bright flash as fuel and liquid oxygen from the ruptured tanks mixed and exploded. The explosion raged through the wreckage in rivers and rivulets. Gouts of flame shot out in all directions. Shortly the wreck was completely burned out.

Jasperodus released his harness and pushed the chair away, contriving thereby to counteract his slow spin and also to lose most of his relative velocity. The guard post receded only very slowly now. He relaxed, spread his limbs, and simply floated, unexpectedly overcome by a strange feeling of peace and calm.

Unresistingly he fell into a serene reverie. The apparent endlessness of sable space was soaking into his perception; he felt as though he had penetrated to the very centre of existence. His senses, moreover, had become incongruously sharp; all around him was universal majesty . . . The Earth, a great, silent goddess hanging hugely below him. The small, brilliant Moon. He turned, and the flashing sun seared his eyes.

He did not know how long he floated there. It seemed like a long time. But eventually he again took thought for practical affairs and noticed that the guard post was now very small. He activated one of the nozzles of his welding kit. The thrust it produced was extremely low, but accumulative. First imperceptibly, and then slowly, he coasted back to the realm of men.

9

By the time an investigating spacecraft arrived from Tansiann several hours later Jasperodus had taken matters well in hand. Gathering together the survivors among the repair crew, he had shaken them out of their demoralised condition and set them to work. Under his supervision the guard post was now functioning again. The guardsmen from the imperial craft – a sleek near-orbit patrol boat – entered the hatchway to find him welding in place a new bulkhead to replace the one shattered by the Borgor shell.

He switched off his welding kit and touched his hand to the nearest guardsman's helmet, so as to conduct sound. "Your tardiness is less than commendable," he greeted. Then he gestured to the slotman, who was floating motionless by the other wall. "I believe his oxygen has just run out. You had better transfer him to your ship without delay."

The guardsman approached the unconscious figure, examined it, then unclipped the slotman's oxygen pack and inserted in its place an emergency cylinder from his own equipment. He turned to his comrades and spoke something through his suit communicator. Making an attempt to lip-read, Jasperodus thought he deciphered the words: "Maybe he'll pull through, maybe he won't."

Then he signalled Jasperodus to touch his helmet again. "Well, somebody's done a good job here. We've roughly got the picture: a Borgor ship attacked while the station was out of commission, and the repair crew destroyed it somehow, using the shuttle." He jerked his thumb. "Who'd have thought a slotman could pull off a stunt like that? There'll be a medal for him, I shouldn't wonder. Tansiann tells us the post's transmitting all go signals now, so let's get aboard."

Planing down through the atmosphere the slotman recovered consciousness. Moved by some residual fellow-feeling, one of the robots had been attending him, moving his arms so as to exercise his lungs. He sat up, moaned lightly, then lay down shivering.

Buffeted by cross winds they approached Tansiann and made a screeching landing on one of the spaceground's runways. The crew, still accompanied by guardsmen, straggled back to the iron shed where they were to be debriefed and receive their wages. Shortly, however, an officer wearing a livery Jasperodus did not recognise arrived.

"Hold the proceedings," he ordered the guardsmen. "Word of the exploit has reached the palace. Today the Emperor is to receive those who lately have performed the Empire some special service, and he has directed that the man responsible should be present."

The guardsman grinned and yanked the cringing slotman forward, slapping him on the shoulder. "Hear that? A signal honour!"

The slotman gasped, his face white. "*Me?* Presented to the Emperor? Oh no! It wasn't me! It wasn't me!" And he shook all over, rolled up his eyes, and fainted in a heap on the floor.

"Hm." The liveried officer looked down at him doubtfully. "Not quite of the backbone one expects in a hero."

Jasperodus thrust himself forward. "Allow me to enlighten you. It was I, not this creature, who by my initiative saved the guard post from destruction. And I claim my reward, namely to be presented to the Emperor."

The guardsman turned to him in surprise. "*You*, eh?" He looked at the others. "Is that right?"

The robots all confirmed Jasperodus' boast.

"Oh, dear," said the officer from the palace. "Well, he will have to do."

"But a *robot*? It's a mockery!"

The other glanced at him disdainfully. "The Emperor himself has given a specific command. Would *you* disobey it? Besides, there are constructs serving at all levels of government, so the encounter will not be so strange . . . Now let me see . . . He's in good shape for a wild one, isn't he? Most of them are a bit decrepit. Come along with me, fellow, and we'll get you cleaned up."

Later, scrubbed and polished, Jasperodus was conducted into the central basilica of the massive palace that ruled Tansiann, and beyond that, the New Empire. A feeling of excitement burned in him. To enter this place had been his eventual goal, but he had not expected to achieve it for several years to come.

Already his journey through the palace had shown him how impressive it was – but then, he reminded himself, it was built to impress. Also, it was replete with treasures and artworks, both from the ancient world and of more recent fashioning. True, there was a certain lack of tasteful arrangement about this huge collection, as though it was booty for booty's sake. The Emperor, perhaps, cared more for the idea of art than he properly understood it.

The basilica itself, however, had been designed with discrimination. The sides of the oblong hall were screened by a double colonnade. Light from small mullioned windows set high in the walls mingled with a warm radiance from hidden illuminators. A concave effect was imparted to the whole interior by a series of hangings that descended from the ceiling towards the colonnade in a stepped arc.

Murals and rich tapestries abounded. Blues, golds and purples completed the creation of an atmosphere of sumptuousness. In the dome-roofed apse at the far end of the hall was set the throne; and upon this, raised above the general run of humanity, sat the Emperor Charrane.

Jasperodus gazed with interest upon this reputedly extraordinary man who was attempting to set a seal on history. Hitherto his only model for a monarch had been the sultry King Zhorm. Charrane, as it happened, resembled him only in evincing the same air of absolutist rule. Physically he was unimpressive: a little below medium height, slight of build, with an undistinguished face verging on the haggard and framed by a straggly fringe beard. The eyes were mild, somewhat tired-looking, and mobile.

Someone nudged Jasperodus forward. A line of waiting men, most of them uniformed, had formed and now they were ushered one by one into the imperial presence. Each bowed low then exchanged a few words with the Emperor, before being given by him some token of his recognition. Sometimes the Emperor questioned earnestly for several minutes, but usually the interview was brief. Many of the decoratees were badly mutilated, having been flown home from the crumbling front on Mars, or having performed some feat of bravery in the occasional skirmishes with Borgor forces on Earth.

At length, last of all, Jasperodus' turn came. He marched resolutely before the throne, bowed, and announced: "Your servant, sire."

The page standing by Charrane's side whispered in his ear, reading from a sheet he held. "Ah, yes," Charrane said loudly. "The orbital affray."

Now that he saw him more closely Jasperodus realised that Charrane's face, unremarkable though its features were, contained an unobtrusive strength. The mild violet eyes made no attempt to overwhelm but kept their own counsel. His voice was melodious and confidential, with an odd thrilling quality.

"Tell me," he said, "exactly what happened."

Jasperodus gave him a concise, factual account of all that had taken place, beginning with the launching of the shuttle and finishing with the return to the spaceground. Charrane listened attentively, his eyes flicking over Jasperodus as he did so.

At the end of the account he spent a minute or so looking around the basilica in ruminative fashion. There was a quiet but constant coming and going in the hall. Small groups of people gathered here and there, talking. Jasperodus could imagine the furtive intrigues that went on here, all under the gaze of this prospective ruler of mankind.

"A stirring adventure," Charrane remarked casually. "You would appear to be endowed with considerable military prowess. Perhaps you would fare well on Mars. We have need of talent there. It is a hard fight, one that has cost me many good men. Four who came before me today have been awarded the Solar Circle, the Empire's highest decoration for bravery." He glanced at Jasperodus. "Are you familiar with the campaign?"

"I have followed it with interest, sire."

"Perhaps I will send you to Mars."

Jasperodus told himself that he might never again be presented with an opportunity like this one. This was no time for caution. He resolved to speak with all boldness, even impudence.

"I am Your Majesty's to command," he said. "The Mars venture is, as you say, a tale of courage and fortitude. But I should inform you that I have my own opinion on the subject. I believe Your Majesty should withdraw from Mars."

The Emperor looked at him with such startlement that for a

moment Jasperodus thought that he had gone altogether too far. "Indeed?" queried Charrane on a rising note. "And what gives you the right to reach such conclusions?"

"The campaign is being conducted from a dangerously small base area, sire. As yet the Empire covers scarcely one-third of Worldmass. In my view to attempt a recovery of the ancient Mars possessions when you are scarcely consolidated here on Earth was a mistake."

Charrane leaned back in his seat. His eyes became glazed. He seemed thoughtful. There was a long pause.

"You are a footloose construct, are you not?" he said at length, speaking in a caressing tone. "You intrigue me. Tell me of your history, where you were made, who owned you and how you came to turn wild."

The demand took Jasperodus aback. His thoughts raced. Then he came to a sudden decision to tell all. Omitting nothing, he outlined the story of his life so far, from his activation in a darkened cabinet to his arrival here before the Emperor. He gave details of his escapades in Gordona, even when they reflected ill on himself, outlining his reasons and motives.

The tale took well over half an hour. Charrane attended to it all, apparently fascinated.

"A fictitious self-image!" he exclaimed with a sardonic chuckle. "Fictitiously conscious! There's a rare twist! Your maker was indeed a master!"

"He studied under the great Aristos Lyos," Jasperodus supplied, though inwardly surly that his one great torment should be a subject for mirth.

The Emperor nodded. "That is to be expected. Of all the arts to survive the Dark Period, robotics is perhaps the most perfectly preserved, and Lyos was without doubt its exponent par excellence. Only he, probably, would have known how to pull off such a trick."

"*Was*, sire? Is he no longer alive?"

Charrane frowned slightly. "Some years ago he retired from active work. His whereabouts is unknown. Many believe him dead."

Just then someone behind Jasperodus caught the Emperor's eye. He raised his head questioningly, then nodded briefly.

Into the hall came a group of five musicians who set themselves up a short distance away. The various instruments they carried were unknown to Jasperodus, and were mostly of metal. He noticed, too, that all the musicians were cross-eyed – a sign, perhaps, that even here at the putative centre of renascent civilisation certain barbarities prevailed.

The musicians blew into their instruments, manipulating them in various ways. The sounds that emerged were smooth and flashing, the rhythms staccato, and quite different from anything Jasperodus had heard before.

"This is an ancient musical artform that has recently been discovered in old manuscripts," Charrane informed him. "Do you like it?"

"It is certainly novel," Jasperodus admitted.

Charrane listened further for some moments, nodding his head to the beat of the music. "Enough!" he cried. "You will entertain us this evening."

The musicians packed up and left. Charrane rose to his feet, stretching as if he had spent a long and arduous time upon the throne. "Come with me, friend. I will show you something else."

Jasperodus followed him round the back of the throne dais. The raised platform hid from view of the hall several panels in the polygonal recess forming the apse. On these panels were what Jasperodus took, at first, to be crude paintings of little artistic worth.

"These, also, demonstrate the classical arts," Charrane told him. "My archaeologists came upon them while excavating a magisterial villa in Indus. Sometimes it works on robots of advanced type, too. Look at them and tell me of any effects."

Puzzled, Jasperodus obeyed. The pictures were more in the nature of coloured cartoon drawings than paintings. The colours were pastel and flat, without any shading. On looking closer he realised that they were in fact neither paintings nor drawings but tapestries or cloth pictures of some kind, made up of thousands of tiny tufts which glinted in the light.

The figures depicted were fairly graceful, but stylised. One scene showed a young woman in a flowing shawl, her expression dreamy, both hands lifted as if stroking at something in the air. She stood on the foreshore; white combers broke behind her, while in the sky sailed equally white clouds.

In another, a black ship with a single white sail scudded across a phosphorescent green sea. The sky behind it was a lurid red. The ship appeared to be unmanned; there was no one on deck. But beyond the red sky could faintly be discerned the pale orbs of nearby planets.

"I notice noth . . ." began Jasperodus, and then something seemed to open up in his mind. The picture of the girl was no longer just a meaningless representation; it carried a story with it, a story that unfolded in every detail and went on unfolding, spreading further and further into a fantastic universe of the imagination.

A surge of delight went through Jasperodus when he glanced from there to the picture of the black ship and experienced the same mind-expanding breadth of vision, all in the space of seconds. The universe of places and events revealed by this picture was quite different from the first, and if anything even more stupendous.

Jasperodus looked in turn at the other panels. Each produced the same effect: an experience like encompassing some huge and intricate literary work all in a flash. Suddenly he felt that if his mind was forced to accept one more such rush of impressions it would burn out. He turned to Charrane and in a low, subdued voice described what had taken place.

"Surprising, is it not?" the Emperor agreed mildly. "The technique was known as *dianoesis*. Those little tufts that compose the pictures transmit thoughts and concepts to the beholder in some manner. Just another classical art that is irretrievably lost."

Charrane sauntered to stand unassumingly in front of his throne. Jasperodus followed him, his imagination still full of what had been forced into it; he struggled to bring his perceptions back down to the scale of the basilica.

"But enough of art," Charrane announced. "I am obliged to give most of my time to more worldly matters. To return to your biography. In spite of your initial intemperate remarks I detected in your story a marked admiration for the Old Empire."

"That is so. The attainments of the past inspire me. I would see them equalled."

"Then we are brothers, despite our separate natures. Know, robot, that the plan of my life is to revive the glory that was Tergov."

The sense of will and conviction in these words impressed Jasperodus. The Emperor meant what he said.

"If you concur with this aim then you can be useful to me," Charrane continued. "But to answer your earlier impertinence, it is my intention to extend the Empire as far as the moons of Jupiter, exactly as was the case in olden times."

"I fully accord with the ambition, sire. It is only the timing I disagree with. Everything must be done in the proper order."

"And how would *you* set the timetable?" Charrane frowned. "Wait – it seems I am to be pestered with paperwork again. Here comes Ax Oleander, one of my viziers."

Approaching through the hall stepped a big, portly man in a flowing cloak, attended by three scurrying assistants. Anxious to see what quality of advice Charrane was receiving, Jasperodus studied this man's face. His cheeks were bulging and purple; his small mouth held a permanent sneer and was slightly agape; his chin receded. The hooked, purple nose was surmounted by hot, close-set eyes that were staring and hostile.

A forceful, strong personality, Jasperodus decided. But not one he would trust.

Oleander came to a stop and swept his cloak behind him while bowing low. "May we crave a few moments, sire?"

"You may, Ax, you may," said Charrane indifferently, and he began signing the documents which Oleander, while keeping up a babble of explanations, took one by one from his clerks.

Charrane stopped on coming to one folio. "What is this?" he demanded with displeasure, staring at the double sheet. He thrust it back at Oleander. "Have it paraphrased first."

The vizier glared horrified at the folio and the veins stood out on his face. "It should have been done!" he remonstrated, and he turned to give one of the clerks a clout.

Having glimpsed the sheet, Jasperodus understood. Like other leaders in history who had tried to reconstitute a shattered society, Charrane was illiterate. He was able to read only lettered script, and not the symbolic logic which in the Old Empire had been taught to every citizen, and which even now marked off the literate minority. This detail gave Jasperodus something of an insight into Charrane's origins and character.

The remaining documents were quickly disposed of and taken

away by the clerks. Charrane turned again to Jasperodus. "Now, what were we talking about?"

"The current state of the Empire, sire. I was urging a withdrawal from Mars."

Ax Oleander spoke in a murmuring voice. "Have a care, you iron hulk. You are but one step from the junkyard."

Charrane looked from one to the other, his eyes crafty. Then he uttered a humourless laugh.

"Hold your rancour, Ax. I am aware that since the plan was *mine*, no one has yet had the nerve to tell me it was a miscalculation." Leisurely he ascended to the throne, then beckoned Jasperodus closer. "Your outspokenness pleases me, robot. It is plain that you are a machine of unusual qualities, and I have great need of talent." He shrugged contemptuously. "Half the men in my service have less wit than a Class One automatic road-mender. So you may consider yourself appropriated to my staff."

Jasperodus became inwardly exultant. He was delighted by Charrane's obvious friendliness towards him. "And what will my duties be, sire?"

"It seems you have an interest in strategy – we will attach you to the planning staff, as an assistant to see how you go."

"This is swift promotion indeed, sire," Jasperodus reflected.

Charrane's lip curled. "For once you have your machine status to thank. A man would not walk into my entourage so easily – but a machine, after all, is something to be applied wherever appropriate. Besides, I have found robots particularly useful in the planning sphere. They attend unremittingly to the task in hand. All too often the efforts of men are attenuated by distraction or self-interest." He leaned towards Jasperodus. "But mind, entertain no such treacheries as you practised upon the King of Gordona."

"Nothing is further from my mind," Jasperodus disavowed. "Theft, of whatever variety, is the crudest of achievements. I see that clearly now. My desire is to construct, to help build, not to destroy."

"And what of your other ambition?" Charrane asked softly, as if teasing him. "The attainment of consciousness?"

"It seems I must forgo that also," Jasperodus answered in a hollow voice. "Clearly it is impossible. Yet, by my deeds, I may still prove myself the equal of any man."

"I wish you luck," Charrane said lightly. He appeared to consider Jasperodus' existential dilemma something of a joke. "Go now. Oleander here will see to your induction."

Oleander turned to Jasperodus without enthusiasm. "Take yourself through the main door and present yourself to the housemen," he instructed offhandedly. "They will take care of you."

Making a farewell bow, Jasperodus took his leave. While marching the length of the basilica he tuned up his hearing. He heard Ax Oleander saying in a low tone to Charrane: "The Borgor Alliance has infiltrated robot spies into the palace before, sire . . ."

But he ignored this attempt at back-stabbing. He sensed the pulse of the city around him, and beyond that the beating heart of the growing Empire. In no way had he tried to deceive the Emperor, and every word he had spoken represented his true thoughts. He felt that the real adventure of his life was about to begin.

10

On his third sitting as a full member of the Military Council, seven years later, Jasperodus had to stare down a certain amount of opposition. As the first robot to occupy so august a station he had, naturally, been obliged to contend with a degree of resentment from the beginning. He had usually countered that with a mixture of charm and bluntness.

Today, however, it was bruited abroad that on the retirement of Marshal Hazzany the Emperor intended to appoint Jasperodus Marshal-in-Chief of the entire Imperial Forces, which would rank him second only to the Supreme Commander – namely the Emperor – himself. It was understandable that for some of the officers present this was almost too much. Not only was Jasperodus their natural inferior – not, indeed, even a citizen – but he was a newcomer to the Military Council and almost a newcomer to the strategic team. The marshals who sat with Jasperodus, several of them venerable, had been soldiers all their lives. Men had to wait patiently for advancement, but Jasperodus, unerringly and with cool aplomb, stepped into every opening.

Unembarrassed by his successes, Jasperodus had continued to produce innovation after innovation, scheme after scheme. All had to admit that he had transformed the situation – though, at the time, many had argued against the measures he had introduced to do it. He retained control of the strategic planning staff – an office it had taken him two years to gain and which, even if the promotion to Marshal-in-Chief should be forthcoming, he had no intention of relinquishing – and, in addition to all this, he was now one of the Emperor's close circle of viziers.

On this occasion the Emperor did not attend the council meeting, as he sometimes did, because he had already discussed its business with Jasperodus. Afterwards Jasperodus would acquaint him with the Council's view of the matter.

"What is the reason for this chopping and changing of policy?"

136

grumbled Marshal Grixod. "Only a few years ago you urged our withdrawal from Mars." He threw up his hands. "What a business! The loss of face was awful. God knows how the Emperor ever agreed to it. And now you want us to go *back* to Mars."

"I have never said that we should not add Mars to the Empire," Jasperodus responded, remembering with what pain Charrane had been forced to see the irrevocability of his reasoning. "Only that the time was wrong. Today our situation has improved. The Empire controls one half of Worldmass. The Borgor Alliance has been dealt a blow which has put it on the defensive. Furthermore, the new invasion scheme devised by the planning staff carries crucial advantages over the previous method. The time has therefore come for the decisive conquest of Mars, and once taken, the red planet will be our springboard for the occupation of the moons of Jupiter."

The invasion plan, like much else lately, was Jasperodus' own idea. Instead of launching a series of space squadrons in the normal manner, involving all kinds of organisational and logistical problems, he proposed to build three huge "invasion drums" which would orbit themselves around the target planet and be self-sustaining for anything up to five years. The plan called for a force of seventy thousand men, all of whom would be transported aboard the shuttles in one go. Thus the campaign could not be impeded by attacks on supply ships sent from Earth, and Jasperodus believed that, backed up by these orbiting forts, the troops on the ground (more accurately in the Martian rills and fissures) would prove themselves invincible. If work began now, the shuttles could be sent on their way in about four years.

Marshal Davidon raised the usual objection to orbital fortresses: their vulnerability to missile attack. Jasperodus answered that to deal with this the shuttles would orbit at a distance of three thousand miles. It was unlikely that Borgor would have supplied the Martians with missiles large enough or accurate enough to reach that far, but if they had then the long range gave the shuttles adequate time to defend themselves.

Marshal Grixod, who had once been the fiercest opponent of withdrawal from Mars, had now come to stick doggedly to the opposite view earlier enunciated, in milder form, by Jasperodus:

that the Empire should concentrate on conquering Earth and not expend itself in costly interplanetary adventures. "This is going to be very expensive in men and resources," he said. "Are we sure we can afford it?"

Jasperodus acknowledged the point with an inclining of his head. "One of the features of this plan that most recommended it to me is its relative cost-effectiveness," he told the Marshal. "It will work out much cheaper than the campaign of eight years ago. Initially the cost is high – building and outfitting the shuttles, equipping seventy thousand men, who for that time will be denied to the Imperial Forces here on Earth – but once that has been borne there will be very little further expenditure. The figure of seventy thousand is intentionally an excessive one, designed to overwhelm the Martian settlements quickly and with a minimum of bloodshed. Once the planet has been subdued something like half the force could be returned home, and thereafter the Martian province will pay for itself."

The arguing continued. The marshals pored over his plan, finding fault after fault. Jasperodus doggedly dealt with each point on its merits. In more congenial circumstances they would have been delighted with the scheme – he was well aware of that – and it was only their resistance to his leadership that made them obstinate now. If his past experience of men was anything to go by, that resistance would in due course pass.

Finally he forced the issue. "Well, gentlemen, what is our verdict? The Emperor would know the opinion of the Council before making a decision himself. I might add that he strongly desires to see us established as an interplanetary power before he dies. The New Empire is considered to be the successor to the Rule of Tergov, perhaps even a continuation of it, and in that respect the annexation of Mars is seen as the recovery of ancient possessions rather than as a fresh conquest."

There was silence. Eventually Marshal Grixod nodded his head grudgingly. "The plan is good. I have to admit it."

One by one they all consented. The talk turned to other matters, chiefly the question of whether the Borgor Alliance would be in a position to pose new threats in the near future. Marshal-in-Chief Hazzany, who up to now had said little, spoke of the nuclear weapons that had existed in the time of the Old Empire. "If we had a few of those,' he rumbled, "we could make short work of them in any conditions."

The theme was an old one of Hazzany's. Always he was yearning for the stupendous explosives produced by the expert nuclear science of a previous age but not understood by present-day engineers, who saw radioactivity only as a means for making power units. To Hazzany nuclear bombs, shells and grenades were a tactician's dream. The possibility of actually manufacturing such weapons seemed remote and was not seriously considered. Old documents revealed that they depended on a certain isotope extracted from the metal uranium, either for the explosive itself or as a trigger for even more devastating nuclear processes. So voracious had the Rule of Tergov been in its use of this uranium that there were now no significant natural deposits left – and fortunately so, in Jasperodus' eyes. He had no wish to see the Earth ravaged by these reputedly annihilatory devices, and he fervently hoped that no deposits of uranium would be found on Mars.

A short while later the meeting came to an end. Jasperodus took his leave and sauntered from the military wing of the palace, making for the inner sections. All military personnel saluted him smartly as he went by. Others, even civilians of high rank, eyed him with respect.

He made a striking figure in these luxurious surroundings, even more so now that he wore an item of apparel: a medium-length cloak which flowed down his back and set off the angular lines and bronze-black hue of his body. The cloak had arisen from the need to wear insignia in the absence of a uniform. It was divided down the centre by a purple line; on one side was the blazon of a vizier, on the other the badge of rank of a marshal of the Imperial Forces.

Crossing a terrace, Jasperodus entered the group of smaller buildings surrounding the basilica. There, in one of the several large lounges, he came upon the Emperor in conversation with Ax Oleander. Charrane looked up at the sound of Jasperodus' arrival.

"Ah, Jasperodus! The fellow I was waiting to see. Join us, and we will come to our business presently." He turned back to Oleander. "Pardon my interruption. Please continue."

Oleander shot an unwelcome look at Jasperodus and shifted perceptibly closer to the Emperor. The man had never made any attempt to improve relations with Jasperodus. Jealous of his influence, he had continued to insinuate that the robot was secretly under orders from the Borgor Alliance – a suggestion which could hardly stand up against Jasperodus' record. For his part Jasperodus had sought no retaliation for these provocations, though several times he had been amused and fascinated to see Oleander, in a room filled with people, adopt the classic stance of a monarch's toady, whispering information into Charrane's ear.

At the present moment the vizier was criticising the economic arrangements within the Empire.

"In one vital respect we are particularly primitive in comparison with the old world, sire," he was saying. "I have been studying how Tergov achieved its prodigious level of production – I am referring, of course, to the 'factory system', as it was called. It seems to me that we must adopt this system ourselves. Our present arrangements are haphazard and old-fashioned."

Charrane's reply showed that he too had given this question some thought. He mused for a moment, then snorted softly. "Mass production! Have you studied also how Tergov came to fall? The reasons were complex, no doubt, but among them was that the level of production was *so* prodigious, in comparison with the amount of labour required for it, that the majority of the population found no place in the manufacturing process. An idle populace, Ax, is no substitute for a happy and industrious citizenry, no matter how much it may be pampered by the state. That is why I am no advocate of this 'mass production'. I am content to see the main wealth of the Empire produced by individual artisans, assisted when they can afford it by a robot or two, perhaps."

Oleander chuckled fawningly. "Statecraft, my lord. You are a wizard at statecraft! But think! The nations of the Borgor Alliance have already begun building their factory complexes – Borgor herself is particularly advanced in it. The advantages to be gained are overwhelming. Production lines may be operated in the first instance by unskilled labour, and finally can be made completely automatic. A commodity which an artisan would make at the rate of one a week can be turned out by one of these factories every two minutes! Think, at least, of the military potential this opens up!"

"Well, what do you think, Jasperodus?" Charrane asked.

"I concur with your own outlook, sire. A society's strength lies in its people, not in its machinery. A city of independent men is worth a continent of slaves. There must be some large-scale enterprises, of course — foundries, certain heavy industry and so forth — but the free artisan, plus the peasant-proprietor farmer, is by far the healthiest base for the economic pyramid. Besides, who would not prize the produce of a craftsman of Tansiann above the rubbish from a Borgor factory?"

"Pah!" muttered Oleander. "A pair of boots is a pair of boots. What does it matter whether it's made to custom or turned out by the million? Look at it this way, sire. On an assembly line the manufacturing process is broken down into simple steps which can be performed by untrained hands or by crude automatic devices. No time is wasted. An artisan, however, needs skills that take years to acquire — and often he is assisted by a robot that itself has taken months to manufacture, that is needlessly self-directed and has abilities entirely redundant to the task in hand. What a ludicrous superfluity of talent! Mark my words, if we do not match her industrial output Borgor will bury us in cheap goods within a few years!"

"I do not think so," Jasperodus retorted. "I think Borgor's factories will bring her social unrest and she will crumble within, as Tergov did."

He paused, and judged the moment ripe to broach a related subject that had entered his mind from time to time, but which he had not dared to mention.

"Sire, it is heartening to hear you assert the right of every citizen to earn his living by his own efforts. Yet it is noticeable that there is poverty in the Empire, markedly so here in Tansiann. Many lack their proper dignity, while faced on all sides by unbounded wealth which they cannot touch. When I first arrived here I was puzzled by this disparity, for there is no extreme poverty in the lands where I first saw the light of day. After deliberation, I believe I now understand it."

"Yet one more brilliant idea from our construct friend," Charrane said caustically, giving Oleander a sarcastic glance. "Speak on."

"My lord, I believe the root cause of poverty lies in the private ownership of land."

141

Both Charrane and Oleander frowned, the latter with a trace of indignation. "How so?" Charrane asked, suddenly serious.

"In Gordona, and in many other small kingdoms in the West of Worldmass, it is a recognised custom that upon attaining the age of responsibility a man has the right to occupy a piece of land where he may live and work, whether as a farmer, a craftsman or a trader. This is regarded as his due. Where land is free and any man who so wishes may acquire a plot for himself there need be no question of poverty, since he will always be able to provide for himself. Very often he will need little else by way of starting capital – sometimes only a few simple tools. Within the Empire, however, all land is in private hands and it is by no means a simple matter to acquire even a few square feet of it. In Tansiann, where land values leap up year by year, it has now become virtually impossible for any but the affluent to come into possession of property. Unable to acquire sites on which to set themselves up in business, increasing numbers of men are forced to offer themselves for employment by others more fortunate, generally for low wages, or failing that to become dependent on the state. Thus I see it as a social law that the independence of men requires free land.

"The same principle is the cause of slums – is it not an irrefutable fact that slum dwellers invariably occupy land owned by someone else? The tenants of these properties are in no position to improve them, of course, and the landlords have no incentive to do so – slums, sire, are profitable."

Oleander smiled smugly. "The population grows. Land is in short supply."

"But there is no shortage of land. The city contains countless thousands of derelict acres that are being held out of use. Meanwhile the employee class grows and may eventually outnumber that of independent men. These conditions, my lord, are already sowing the seeds of the factory system which you decry. It will come by itself. Soon we may have a class of propertyless factory labourers." The more he thought about this the more important it seemed to him to be.

"And you would suggest a remedy?"

Jasperodus was more vague on this point. "Possibly the customs of the West could be adopted and the absolute private ownership of land brought to an end. Land should be looked upon as a com-

142

mon resource, available to all. Or if a tax were levied upon its ownership, land which is currently left lying idle would quickly be offered for sale or lease. By that means we would end the iniquitous speculation in land which now takes place."

"Hm – your conceptions are novel," Charrane admitted. "I dare say you are right. I would even look into it further – if I didn't need the goodwill of the Property-Owners' Association! Not to speak of the great land-owning nobles!" He smiled. "It is not always possible to be a despot, even a benevolent one."

Oleander, himself a leading light in the Property Owners' Association, became exasperated. "We sit here talking philosophy, when instead we should be looking at Borgor's Gross National Product! What is needed is to concentrate land ownership into *fewer* hands, so as to discourage this inefficient artisan production and make men more productive as factory wage-earners. I am voicing a warning, sire! Borgor's factories will make her wealthier and mightier, and we will become feeble by comparison!"

An uneasy look came over Charrane's face. Jasperodus could see that Oleander had planted in him a fear that might sway him in the end.

"Well, enough of all that," Charrane said with a sigh. "What of the meeting, Jasperodus? What did the Council find?"

"The Council approves the plan, sire."

"Good, good." Relieved to turn away from abstract matters, Charrane cheered up at the mention of the coming campaign. "Then as soon as it's out of the planning stage we can begin construction . . ."

An hour later Jasperodus retired to his private apartments in the north wing of the palace, to ponder further on the details of the invasion scheme.

He had been at work for only twenty minutes when a gentle tone sounded on his desk. He opened a circuit and the face of his robot secretary appeared on a screen on the wall. The communicator was of a new phosphor-dot colour type – a technique preserved through the Dark Period by the robotic art, but available so far only in the palace – and the robot's brass-coloured face shone with a burnished sheen.

"The investigator you hired has made his report, sir," the secretary said. "Aristos Lyos is living in a villa on the south coast, a few miles west of Shang."

Jasperodus glanced at his wall map, then at the clock. The time was approaching midday. "Can you find a guide immediately?"

"Yes, sir."

"Then have him meet me in the flying stables in half an hour."

He cut the connection and sat brooding.

The past seven years had been good ones. He had thrown himself into his duties with genuine enthusiasm, believing in the worth of what he was doing. He was solidly for the New Empire, which for all its faults did at least offer conditions in which the arts and sciences could flourish, and this he saw as a good thing. The Borgor Alliance, against whom so much of his energy had been directed, stood only for the old feudal chaos, however much it was dressed up with technological reorganisation.

Nostalgically he scanned some of his memories. In the command tank, helping direct the huge battle in which they had smashed three Alliance armies . . . Yes, there was much to look back on. His nature had mellowed in that time; there was less harshness in him, and he had gained a reputation for clemency towards beaten enemies. He had found time, too, to turn his attention towards art, music, things requiring feeling as well as intellect . . .

And of course he was wealthy. Apart from the emoluments from his various offices – he was probably the only robot officially in construct bondage to receive such emoluments – he had taken advantage of his rank, as was the fashion of the time, to enrich himself. Not that money was attractive in itself, but it facilitated his various activities and suited his life style.

About two years ago the old itch had come upon him again.

Did he, or did he not, exist?

For five years he had been able to forget the tormenting enigma. It had returned to him almost by accident, when a raid on the premises of a religious sect, suspected of assisting Borgor, had yielded a find of old and rare books.

He rose and stepped to a bookcase, taking from it the volume that had first returned his mind to the hunt. This small book, bound in red leather which had become soft and worn with age, contained a number of short dissertations. He opened it. The first essay was entitled:

THE SEARCH FOR THE TOTALITRON

Much is known of the class of fundamental *particles* which exist within the universe at relative locations or points and which are responsible for the transfer of energy from place to place, i.e. between one another. Theory strongly predicts, however, that particles comprise only one half of the picture. The universe also exists as a whole, or totality, and to maintain this totality there must exist a range of "totalistic energies" and, associated with them, their corresponding "particles" or, particle being a misnomer in this case, *totalitrons*.

The particle is the form of particularity; the totalitron of totality. Whereas a particle can be described as a size and a vector within space, with other typical characteristics, a totalitron is omnipresent throughout the whole of space. It can be said that the functions of particle and totalitron are complementary and inevitable: there can be no part without the whole, and no whole without parts.

Types of totalitron

Since particles and totalitrons are opposite in nature and therefore mirror one another, so to speak, it is anticipated that there are as many types of totalitron as there are types of particle. Whether the *number* of totalitrons equals the aggregate number of particles is uncertain. The theory does state, however, that there is more than one totalitron of each type, and it is generally believed that totalitrons are not significantly less numerous than particles.

Properties of totalitrons

Again on theoretical grounds, totalitrons are held to possess properties corresponding to the mass, charge, spin and strangeness exhibited by particles, though it is far from clear how "totalitron charge", for instance, would manifest itself. "Spatiability" and "chronicity" have been suggested as totalitron properties, with a property called "total spin" sometimes being added. A totalitron might for example be said to possess a chronicity of 1, a spatiability of 1, and a spin of $\frac{1}{2}$.

Interaction between totalitrons

Comprising as they do the structure of *totality* taken without relation to any division of parts, the exchanges between totalitrons must differ in essence from the energy exchanges between particles. It is anticipated however that when enough is known about them a systemic pattern will emerge bearing some resemblance to the reactions between particles, or rather to the inverse of those reactions.

Interaction between particles and totalitrons

Particles and totalitrons are of course uniquely related to one another. Without totalitrons there could be no total universe and it would be empty of any specific locations and of material without particles. The two classes of "basic entity" must, then, interact in some undefined way that keeps their relationship stable.

Investigating the totalitron

Research into the totalitron has to date been scanty. Producing a "totalitron beam" presents difficulties since each totalitron occupies the whole of universal space. Nevertheless an attempt at intercepting "an omnipresent totalitron beam" has been claimed as successful. In this experiment the monks of the Scientific Academy sat in a circle of twenty-four, each intoning in turn the mantra OM . . .

After that the dissertation degenerated into what Jasperodus could only think of as gibberish. Yet he could recall with what excitement he had initially read the paper.

It ended with a drawing of a curious symbol consisting of two interlocking triangles, one inverted in relation to the other, representing the interaction of particle and totalitron, of the part and the whole, of the microcosm and the macrocosm. Could it be, he had wondered, that the totalitron was the stuff of consciousness? Of the *soul*? He already knew that consciousness could not be constructed out of matter, that is out of interactions between particles. But did not the totalitron possess exactly those properties specified in the consciousness equations? Indivisibility? Lack of differentiated parts? With fresh hope Jasperodus had launched into a study of what loosely was known as the occult. He had read ancient and arcane books, he had sought out magical societies, he had talked at length with self-styled adepts. But in the end he had been disappointed. He had decided, after investigating it all, that the ideation of the occult was little more than hot air and smoke. The "science" that sometimes was associated with it – though on occasion fascinating and well thought-out – was pseudo-science, deficient in its appreciation of reality.

Still, the urge to know the truth about himself had been piqued afresh. He had entered on new projects. Chief of these was an attempt to duplicate himself. Hiring the best robotician he could find, he had manufactured a robot that as near as could be judged was a complete Jasperodus replica. The crucial part – the brain – had been the most difficult, since there was a limit to how exhaustively his own brain could be examined. He and the robotician had also devised what they hoped was a duplication of the "fictitious self-image" with which he was inflicted.

Upon activation he had spent long periods in the company of his replica. He had asked him if he was conscious: Jasperodus 2 invariably answered that he was. They had discoursed at length and in depth upon countless subjects. He had given Jasperodus 2 boundless opportunities both for study and for experience. He had treated him like the son he was.

And then, inexorably, terribly, he had come to see that Jasperodus 2, whatever he himself might avow, was dead. Clever, yes; intelligent, yes; but a machine, not a person.

His son now worked on the planning staff, where he proved more than adequate, though not brilliant. He lacked some of the fire of the original; Jasperodus attributed this to the indeterminacy factor that had been built into the moment of activation. An advanced robot's final disposition was usually left partly to chance.

One more avenue was open to Jasperodus. Aristos Lyos, master robotician, teacher to his own maker, the greatest robot expert of all time, was surely the supreme authority on the subject. Whatever Jasperodus' father had done, he learned it from Lyos. If he could find him his existential status – or the feasibility of changing it – could be determined for good and all and he would be rid of this nagging doubt.

Soberly he closed the book and replaced it on the shelf. He sat

147

quietly for a few minutes longer, as though fearing the coming encounter, then left for the flying stables where his personal aircraft was kept. The guide, a small nervous man, was already waiting.

For two hours they flew south. Jasperodus headed for Shang, then on the guide's instructions turned westward along the coast. Presently the guide indicated, on a promontory overlooking the sea, a modest but graceful villa of sparkling white stone. Jasperodus chanced to find a stretch of level ground and made a bumpy landing.

Leaving the guide in the plane he trudged towards the villa, which as he neared it took on the appearance of a structure carved out of salt, so pure and crystalline white was the stone. None of the walls presented a flat surface but all were rounded, following a pattern of spherical and ovoidal curves. The roofs, which were piled at various heights, resembled the caps of toadstools.

Jasperodus knocked on a metal door but received no answer. Cautiously he walked round the building. On a terrace facing the sea sat the villa's owner.

Aristos Lyos was aged but spry. A cap of frizzy white hair covered his scalp. He wore a simple toga-like garment caught at the waist by a purple cord. Somewhat of the spring of youth still remained in him: his spine was straight, and his face, as he turned to view the intruder, showed alertness.

That face, in youth, must have been handsome. The nose was perfectly straight and aristocratically slender. The cheeks were lean, the eyes level; the lips not full but despite that well-proportioned. It was the face of a cool, penetrating thinker.

Shyly Jasperodus approached. "Aristos Lyos?"

The other nodded. Jasperodus could feel his eyes on him, appraising him. He could tell a lot, no doubt, at a glance; from the way a robot moved and so on. Would he know that Jasperodus was the work of one of his own pupils, was a child of his college?

"Know, sir, that I hold the offices of vizier to the Emperor and of Marshal of the Imperial Forces. I am here, however, in a private capacity."

"Then the list of your public achievements is unnecessary," said Lyos in a dry voice. "What do you want from me? If you require robots, then your journey has been wasted. I do no work now, beyond a few toys for my own amusement, and a simple construct or two as gifts for the villagers who live nearby."

"That is not my mission," Jasperodus replied. "I seek information only. If I may presume on your patience for a short while, all will be clear."

"My time is free, if your representations are not too tedious."

Jasperodus therefore launched into a brief account of what he knew of his manufacture, describing his subsequent career – suitably foreshortened – and his continuing puzzlement.

Aristos Lyos listened with polite attention. "Yes," he agreed when Jasperodus had finished, "a clever robotician could incorporate this erroneous belief you hold. It could even be emphasised so strongly that it becomes an obsession, as is evidently the case with you." He became reflective. "I believe I can remember the man who made you. He came to me for advanced study at the end of a fairly long career. He could pull it off – and he obviously has done."

"That is not my question," Jasperodus insisted. "This is what I need to know: is there any means at all, perhaps unknown to the robotic art at large, whereby consciousness might be manufactured? Did you, perhaps, give my fa . . . my maker secret information? Or could he have discovered some new principle himself? Roboticians have assured me of the impossibility of this, but I shall not be entirely convinced unless I hear it from Aristos Lyos himself."

"It is absolutely impossible," Lyos stated flatly. "There can be no such thing as an artificially created consciousness, you may take that as being definitive. For centuries men of genius wrestled with this vain dream . . . eventually its futility became irrefutably established. Oddly enough I included the History of Attempted Machine Consciousness on the syllabus when your maker was with me, as I recall – so he could be accounted an expert on the subject." Lyos stared up at Jasperodus' face. "Perhaps, seeing the distress you are trying hard to hide, I would have been kinder to lie to you. But you have asked me a straight question and I am not a devious man."

Jasperodus' last vestiges of hope were, indeed, vanishing upon exposure to Lyos' words. Yet still he felt compelled to argue.

"Item: the word 'consciousness' has a meaning for me. Item:

that meaning corresponds to my own 'feeling of my existence'. Thus I stand here talking to you; I can feel the breeze blowing in from the sea, I can see the blue of the sea itself, and the blue of the sky above it. *I experience it.* How am I to reconcile this experience with what you tell me?"

"Your items are sound, except where you interpolate the word 'I' into them. Linguistically one cannot help but do so; philosophically it is incorrect. Unfortunately language as commonly used is not adequate to describe the difference between machine perception and human consciousness, although they are worlds apart. Machine perception can be fully as sophisticated as human perception, since the machinery used by the human brain and senses is in no way superior. Thus one speaks of 'machine awareness'. But behind this perception there lies no 'I'. *No one is there to experience it.* It is dead perception, dead awareness. The same holds for emotion, which some have mistakenly believed indicates human status."

"But *I experience!*" cried Jasperodus in anguish.

"You imagine you experience, and hence you imagine you know the meaning of consciousness," Lyos told him. "In fact you do not, except in a hypothetical way. It is all quite mechanical with you. It is merely that you have a particularly emphatic self-reference systems – all robots have some such system, to make them think of themselves as individuals – coupled with this master stroke of an extremely ingeniously designed self-image. Your own phrase 'fictitious consciousness' is an apt description of your condition." Lyos scratched his chin. "Let me try to explain the nature of machine awareness. The first time a photo-cell opened a door at the approach of a human being, machine perception was born. What you have – what you *are* – is of that sort, elaborated to the *n*th degree. Believe me, Jasperodus, if an artificial consciousness were even remotely possible, if there were just a hint of a chance of it, I would have accomplished it years ago."

"You are not impressed, either, by my independent spirit?"

"It is no great feat to construct a wilful, disobedient robot. There is no call for them, that is all."

"All my positive qualities, it seems, must sooner or later be interpreted as negative ones," Jasperodus complained. He became thoughtful. "I have tried, by intensifying my consciousness –

my imaginary consciousness, as you say – to penetrate to this dead-
ness, this mechanical trick that ostensibly lies at the base of my
being, so as to dispel the illusion. But I cannot find it."

"Naturally, you would not."

Jasperodus nodded, looking out to sea.

Then he brought out his only ace. "Very well, Lyos, I bow to
your knowledge," he said. "I admit that I am not conscious. The
conviction persists that I am – but I cannot be rid of that, since it is
how I am made. But what of your own conviction concerning yourself? How can it be known that man's consciousness is not also a
delusion?"

"That is quickly settled," Lyos answered easily. "If no one possessed consciousness then the concept could not arise. Since we
are able to speak of it, someone must have it. Who else but man?"

And so there Jasperodus stood, still trapped in a riddle.

"Look upon yourself as man's tool," Lyos advised gently. "There
is much achievement in you, that is plain, and more to come. Man
gave you your desires, and the energy to fulfil them. So serve man.
That is what robots are for."

Lyos tilted his head and called out in a sharp voice. "Socrates!"

From a pair of bay windows behind him there emerged a robot,
a head smaller than Jasperodus, who stepped quietly on to the
terrace. His form was rounded and smooth. The eyes were hooded,
secretive, and the design of the face betokened a reticent but watch-
ful demeanour. Instantly Jasperodus felt himself the subject of a
probing intelligence that reached out from the robot like an im-
palpable force.

"This here is Socrates, my masterpiece," announced Lyos. "His
intelligence is vast, at times surpassing human understanding.
But, like you, he has no consciousness, neither will he ever have
any. If he did – there's no knowing what he would be, what he
might do."

Jasperodus scrutinised the newcomer. "Good day," he ventured
hesitantly.

"Good day," answered Socrates in a voice that was a distant
murmur.

"Socrates is intelligent enough to realise that *I* am conscious but
that he is not," Lyos remarked. "It induces some strange thoughts
in him. I keep him by me in my old age to amuse me with the fan-

tastic products of his intellect." He twisted round to face Jasperodus again. "Concerning one point I am curious. You have gone to some trouble to track me down. Why did you not go directly to the man who made you and direct your questions to him?"

Jasperodus took his time about framing a reply. "Shame, perhaps," he said eventually. "Shame at having deserted them. No, that's not it. He has inflicted this enormous fraud on me. Why should I expect him to tell me the truth now?"

Lyos nodded. "Yes, I see."

Jasperodus took a step back. "Thank you, sir," he said respectfully. "You have not resolved my perplexity, but you have answered my question."

On leaving, he glanced back at the pair. Socrates had moved close to his master, and they both gazed out to sea. Then the robot bent and spoke some words into the old man's ear.

Back in Tansiann that evening Jasperodus hurried through the palace towards his apartments but was waylaid suddenly by an acquaintance who appeared from behind a pillar.

"Jasperodus! I am so glad to have found you. Have you seen *Caught in the Web* yet? It is superb!"

"No, I . . . haven't found the time."

"Please do. The reviews do not mislead. Speeler really demonstrates the use of dynamism when it comes to dramatic content. And such a clever counterbalancing of themes . . . you'll get a good laugh out of it, too."

Jasperodus' interlocutor was a fellow robot, Gemin by name, one of several whose duties in the administration had led them to enter the social life of the court. He was a more suave version of certain wild robots Jasperodus had been conversant with: witty, elegant, proud of his sophistication. He and his set – which also included humans – looked upon themselves as the whizz-kids of the establishment. Inventive, bursting with enthusiasm for the modern world Charrane was building, amateur experts on the fashionable trends in drama, music and painting, they cultivated an outlook of irreverent cynicism, almost of foppishness.

Gemin lounged against the pillar, one leg crossed over the other. His almost spherical face, with its disconcertingly bright orange eyes, gleamed. "I hear the planning staff is buzzing with something big, Marshal. Come on, now, what's afoot? Don't tell me you've adopted my plan to drop the Moon on Borgor!" He chuckled.

At any other time Jasperodus would have been glad to discuss Speeler's new play *Caught in the Web* with him, or even to exchange banter about top secret decisions. All he wanted now was to depart. There loomed in his mind the knowledge of the emptiness that was within Gemin, and he knew it was a mirror of his own emptiness; the emptiness that by himself he could not see. He fancied he could hear mechanisms grinding, churning out the dead words.

"Excuse me, I have business," he said curtly, and strode on.

Alone in his apartments he wandered through the rooms, trying to quieten his agitation. He had received the answer he had expected, had he not? Then he should be suffering no disappointment.

One of the rooms, the one with the north window, he used as a studio. He stepped to the half-finished canvas on the easel, took up the brush to add a few careful strokes, then desisted. The light was not good enough; he needed morning light, not that of electric bulbs, for this particular picture.

He looked slowly around at the paintings littering the studio, as though wishing to assess his progress so far. He nodded; he knew that his work was good. He had made no attempt to pander to fashion; by many his pictures would be adjudged outdated. His purposes had been purely private, and he had settled upon that style of painting which seemed best suited to express the emotions that ran deep in him. The greater part of the canvases were landscapes or seascapes, depicting his feeling for the planet Earth (which had been heightened on that occasion, seemingly long ago now, when he had floated in space several hundred miles above it). They were largely naturalistic, but lit with flaming flashes of imagination. Thus a bulky boat sat sedately amid a universal fire that was concocted of sunset, sea and sky.

Jasperodus' other main effort to prove himself in the field of feeling lay in music. He had worked assiduously at the art of composition, begging at one time the help of Tansiann's most distinguished composer. So far he had exerted himself in a number of chamber works and was beginning to get the measure of his

153

talent. Already he was planning something more ambitious: a definitive work of lasting value. As a singer, too, he had discovered some merit – to the delight of his teacher, for his electronic voice was easier to train than a human one.

Closing the door of the studio behind him he returned to the main lounge, where he sat down, took his head in his hands and uttered a deep sigh (a humanoid habit he had never quite lost).

Then he gave a cry of exasperation. What was the use of brooding over this tormenting enigma? It could only end in total dejection, and possibly, eventual nonfunction.

With a determined effort he forced the gloom from his mind. He could be content with what he had: he was accepted in the world of men, and by his outward works he was no less than they were.

It had been a taxing day and he needed to indulge himself in a pleasurable diversion, and there was one particular diversion that he knew from experience was uniquely consoling.

He made a phosphor-dot communicator call to the set of apartments adjoining his own, then repaired to a small room which was kept locked and which would open only to himself. When he emerged Verita had arrived and was waiting in the boudoir, already naked.

And Jasperodus, his eyes glowing hotly, was now ready and equipped for the one human activity that had once been denied him: sexuality.

This had always been an area of experience where, in common with all other robots, Jasperodus had been totally impotent. Stung by the occasional taunt – and irked by curiosity – he had eventually sought a way to repair his one great deficiency. The expense had been considerable – more than he himself would have cost to make – but inestimably worth it.

The secret to sexual desire lay in the extraordinary range and speed of the impressions which the brain was forced to receive on the denoted subject – in the normal man's case, on women – a speed which took the process beyond any voluntary control. The problems facing the robotician hired by Jasperodus had been several: first to elucidate this secret, then to translate it into robotic terms, and lastly – most difficult of all – to encompass the new processes in the small space that could be found within Jasperodus' skull by rearranging the other sections of his brain. The task had carried

154

the techniques of micro-circuitry to their limit; but after nearly a year the almost-impossible had been accomplished, and Jasperodus was financially poorer but also incomparably richer.

Along with his new faculty went the apparatus to make it meaningful. The balance-and-movement ganglia that had occupied the bulge of his loins had been redeployed. In their place Jasperodus was able to bolt in position the artificial sex organ he was now wearing. Of flexible steel clad in a rubberoid musculature, and made in generous proportion to his magnificent body, it was much superior to the natural variety, being capable of endlessly subtle flexions and torsions at his command. When bolted in place it was fully integrated into his body, nerves and brain, all of which could be aroused to orgasm by stimulation of the sensitised layer in the rubberoid cladding. When it was not in use, he detached it only for the sake of appearances.

Armed with his indefatigable steel phallus, Jasperodus had set himself to enjoying women of all types, to their immense delight, and he knew how to be uninhibited about it.

For a long time he had known that he exuded an air of erotic masculinity. Females of more exotic tastes had confessed to him that he, uniquely among robots, aroused their interest, but until his conversion that kind of interest had naturally been a closed book to him. Now, however, sexual passion was a world he had fully explored, and those women who previously had only eyed him had found their expectations more than met. Once having submitted to him, a woman was never again content with a mere man.

Jasperodus demonstrated that he was capable of tricks that flesh-and-blood men were not. Besides, his stamina was without limit. He had once performed non-stop for a whole week, using a relay of women, to see if his enjoyment would flag. It had not: the orgasms had only become more intense.

His appetite was insatiable: he demanded women of every flavour. Women who smelled warm, secret and heady (like Verita). Women with a fresh odour like celery. Women with a bouquet like tangy wine. Women who were voluptuous (like Verita), Junoesque, slim and lissom, buxom, fat or thin. Women who were startlingly pretty and shyly innocent, attractive and sluttish (like Verita) or plain and salacious. Young girls, women in their prime, experienced matrons. The apartments adjoining his own comprised a harem where he maintained his more regular partners. Women like Verita, for instance, lived solely for sex with him. It was her meat and drink.

Jasperodus could understand why sex held such a prime place in human affairs. Sometimes the mere sight of a woman filled him with a desire that was overwhelming.

He stepped into the large boudoir and spoke in a low, thrilling voice.

"Good evening, Verita," he greeted in a fruity voice.

She stood naked at the further end, having entered by another way, and smiled invitingly.

They moved slowly towards one another, eyeing each other hotly.

Verita had an ample, agile body. Her breasts were generous but did not sag too much; wavy red hair framed her lively face with its wide red mouth and magnetic eyes. Her hips were well filled out, and moved in an enticing motion as she walked on long fleshy legs.

They came close. He felt her breasts and her warm soft skin pressing and moving against him. The smell of her surrounded him. She was breathing heavily, her moist mouth half open and her eyes half closed.

Sensations were flooding through Jasperodus, throbbing, burning, bursting. Excitement gripped them both, the excitement that was a kind of oblivion, and in which any other existence was forgotten.

Two hours later he let her rest, her breath coming in quavering sobs. Quietly they lay together on a broad divan bed, and while she recovered from her relentless delirium, idly he reflected on the nature of sex, which was a world all of its own, inviting one to become submerged indefinitely in its dizzying depths.

Such a degree of obsession as Verita had was an unlikely outcome on his part, though his was indeed a supercharged kind of sex. In him it was a temporary madness, a sort of induced brain fever. He felt no sense of slavery to it – a consequence, perhaps, of its late addition to his faculties.

Beside him he felt Verita once again stirring. Whatever

might have been the disappointments of the day, he reflected, this kind of thing gave him immense satisfaction. Barring the other matter, which he now vowed to forget, he was a complete man.

11

Do robots dream? Jasperodus did.

Even his powerful brain would at times weary of ceaseless activity and so, to gain a brief respite in oblivion, he would resort to suspending his higher brain functions for a spell, bringing on the robotic surrogate of sleep. Then, sometimes, the dream would come.

It was always the same. He lay on a moving belt, unable to move because his motor function had been cut out – permanently, and deliberately. The belt bore him inexorably towards the open intake door of a blast furnace.

Seen through that gaping mouth, the inside of the furnace was a terrible, pitiless, compressed haze of heat, like the interior of a star. Jasperodus became aware that besides himself the belt was carrying an endless succession of metal artifacts into the furnace: gun carriages, statues, sections of girder, engines, tools, heaps of domestic utensils, heavy machinery of all kinds – some of it evidently self-directed – and robots like himself lying inert and helpless. One of these for some reason had not been immobilised but was strapped down to a cradle-like rack; it stirred desultorily in its bonds as if unaware of its true situation, which was that it was due to fall together with everything else on the belt into the devouring heat, to lose all form and identity and coalesce into a common pool of liquid metal.

Jasperodus awoke howling.

He leaped off the padded couch where he had lain. For a while he stood stock-still, forcing the reassuring sight of his surroundings to wash away the recurring nightmare, but remaining in the grip of unaccountable moods and feelings.

The dream faded slowly. He sought some comforting distraction, and his eye lit on a covered gold receptacle, somewhat in the style of an amphora, that had been designed by him and delivered from the goldsmiths the previous day. He turned to inspect it anew.

It had been inspired in part by descriptions he had read of the interior of the ancient Temple of the Brotherhood of Man at Pekengu. Outwardly it presented a dome of gleaming yellow gold dusted with point-like diamonds, and resting on a decorated base of red gold. Moving certain of the pyramidal studs located round the base caused the dome to come free, and it was then shown to enclose what at first sight looked like a hazy polyhedron glowing with misty light, but which on closer examination proved to be a fine mesh composed of chainwork of white gold, so delicate as to have the texture of cloth, stretched over the projected apexes of a stellated polyhedron, or rather hemipolyhedron, made of the rare and gorgeous orange gold. The full splendour of the latter became evident when the mesh was removed (by sliding an encircling base ring of red gold left and right in a secret sequence) and it could in turn be lifted away, if one knew in which order to press the studs on its lower planes. It then disclosed an upright box of severe classical proportions, grooved and fluted, embossed with narrow vertical pilasters, made of green gold that was shaded and heavy in lustre, almost venomous. The association it brought to mind was of a stately prison, or perhaps a bank vault. By pressing its floor from beneath, the front could be made to spring open. Within was a perfume bottle like a vinaigrette, a slim feminine shape woven from threads of spun gold of every colour: yellow, red, white, green and orange.

He grunted, and put it all together again. He was pleased: it was perfect. He would have liked to have been able to make it with his own hands as well as having designed it, but with all his other activities he would not have found the time to acquire the skills involved.

The only thing still lacking was a really special perfume to put in the bottle. He would give thought to that later.

Glancing at the wall clock, he saw that the morning was fairly well advanced and made a phosphor-dot call to his office.

"What awaits?"

The brass face of his secretary bent clerkishly on the screen. "No communications have been received by me this morning, sir."

"None at all? What of the report from the Expeditionary Force?"

"No copy has arrived here, and I presume it is still in the Decoding Room, or else has been delayed in Registry. I have made inquiries in both departments but so far have failed to elicit satisfactory answers. I gather copies have arrived in other offices, however."

"Never mind," Jasperodus said impatiently. "I will be with you shortly."

He examined himself in the full-length mirror to see if he required scrubbing, then reached for his cloak bearing his badges of office. Perhaps, he told himself, he should begin to exert more direct pressure around himself, lest he stood in danger of losing his influence.

On the surface everything was going very well indeed. The new Mars Expeditionary Force – the three great invasion drums that had been Jasperodus' brainwave – were nearing Mars. True, his rumoured promotion to Marshal-in-Chief had not materialised – Charrane had appointed Marshal Grixod instead – but in retrospect he was glad of it. The post had become largely a ceremonial one now that most decisions were taken by the planning staff, and Jasperodus had come to value his time.

With the military situation seemingly secure, Jasperodus had found his interest attracted to other matters of far-reaching import for the future of the Empire. He had set in motion a number of projects. Among these was a research project to analyse in detail the causes of the fall of Tergov, with a view to laying the New Empire on a sounder foundation.

The studies made by this team (under his guidance, admittedly) had already confirmed one notion he held: the decisive effect that systems of land-holding have on a society. It was instructive to see that in Tansiann the consequences of private land-ownership had been accelerating over the past five years. The disparities in individual wealth were now quite ludicrous. The proletarian class had swelled, while immense fortunes were being made at the other end of the scale – as Jasperodus well knew; he himself derived a huge income from speculation in land (through a holding company, since legally he was not entitled to own property).

It was still his hope to persuade the Emperor to undertake some reforms in this area, but at the moment, due to his own negligence, he carried less weight at court. Placing his attentions elsewhere had caused him to forget the prime strategy of a court functionary: to be constantly in the Emperor's sight, and constantly to be inflating his self-esteem.

In addition, he had been encountering more opposition and hostility of late. It was strange, he thought – when he had been full of deviousness, guided only by self-interest, he had won friends and admiration. Now that his efforts were on behalf of the general good enemies were gathering around him.

He left his apartment and walked towards his office in the west wing of the palace. Passing through one of the many tall arcades that surrounded the central basilica he chanced to see, skulking behind the columns of the peristyle, a pair of sinister-looking, over-sized robots known in construct parlance as wreckers. These were robots whose task it was to subdue and destroy other robots who, when the time came for their dissolution, were sometimes apt to display an overactive survival circuit and resist the proceedings.

A sneaking sense of unease came over him, though he could not specify its source. He walked a short distance further and then heard a voice address him by his rank of marshal. One of the housemen hurried up and spoke loftily to him, without the deference he was usually accorded.

"There are visitors to see you, sir." And the houseman turned away, as though that were the end of the matter.

Advancing behind him came the two wreckers. Jasperodus stared spellbound at these twin servants of doom. They were built for strength alone; the engines that drove their powerful limbs were housed in hulking carapace-like hulls which, added to their grotesque claw-like hands, gave them a dreadful crustacean appearance, like some species of giant crab-man.

"You will accompany us, sir," said one in a hoarse voice.

Jasperodus had almost let them touch him before he goaded himself into action. With a wild, fearful cry he flung himself away and went pounding down the concourse.

In a minute he had gained the basilica. The doors, as usual at this time of day, were unguarded and he went bursting through them.

The throne in the apse was unoccupied. At a table midway down the hall the Emperor Charrane sat talking with Ax Oleander and another vizier, the mild-mannered Mangal Breed.

All three turned to see what had caused the commotion. Oleander greeted Jasperodus' arrival with his normally unvarying hostile stare; but this time it bore the added tang of an inward triumph.

Jasperodus rushed forward and sank to his knees before the Emperor.

"Sire! On whose orders am I to be junked?"

"On mine, of course," Charrane said indifferently. "Whose else?"

"But, my lord – why?"

Charrane looked from one to the other of his human companions with raised eyebrows. Then he gazed at Jasperodus, but with no hint of feeling.

"At our first meeting some years ago you brought forward points affecting the security of the Empire. Now your work is done. The Empire is secure. That is all."

"That is no reason for a death sentence, sire!"

"Death?" echoed Charrane in puzzlement. "Death?" Again he glanced at Breed and Oleander and for a moment seemed almost amused. "Listen to me, my friend. Because it has been your function over the past few years to question my judgement on matters of strategy, on the broad affairs of state, do not imagine you can become presumptuous over the business of your own disposal."

"I . . . I confess myself bewildered by your change in attitude towards me, sire . . ." Jasperodus quavered, seeking some handle by which to grasp the situation.

Ax Oleander humped his shoulders in a jovial shrug. "If the construct wishes to be given reasons, sire, why not indulge him?"

Charrane lowered his eyes, then nodded curtly. He turned to Jasperodus.

"There is an inexorability about machines, they say," he remarked. "Never halting, always advancing on the course they were first set to, whether circumstances warrant it or not. Certainly it has been the case with you! I have been made aware of how far your activities are beginning to extend. Projects here, projects there – many of them unsolicited!" Now Charrane looked indignant. "Your talents are indisputable, but I do not wish to see them become unwelcome . . . besides, a certain King Zhorm of Gordona has lately applied to become my vassal, and he has recounted anew the story of your stay there, which has given me fresh food for thought."

"That kind of thing is behind me, sire! I work only for the advancement of the Empire!"

"I am aware of that, Jasperodus. But I am also aware that your concern for the Empire now covers all spheres, not merely the military. May I remind you that the care and welfare of the Empire is *my* province? I do not care to be usurped in any form or fashion – ambition, Jasperodus, is a quality that should be restricted to men. In machines it is altogether unacceptable." He spread his hands in a gesture of reasonableness; a hint of humour came to his features. "What else could I do with you? My human ministers may be pensioned off with fleshly pleasures when they reach the end of their usefulness, and be no further bother to me. How does one turn aside the ambitions of a machine? Only by resort to the junkyard."

Jasperodus hung his head. "My services to you should merit a better reward, sire. I will forgo all ambitions, if you will spare me. Even constructs are endowed with a survival instinct."

"I have no doubt they are endowed with many things," Charrane muttered. Then he turned to accept a goblet of sherbet that was offered by a serving maid.

Amid his shock and dismay, Jasperodus was forced to perceive his fundamental mistake. All this time he had been under a misapprehension regarding his relations with Charrane. The Emperor had never for a moment looked upon him as a living entity, but only as an inanimate machine, the use and disposing of which involved no sense of morality.

Badly shaken, Jasperodus rose to his feet. Behind him he heard the heavy tread of the wreckers as they entered the hall.

During the conversation Ax Oleander had been unconsciously moving closer to the Emperor, until he had almost adopted the mouth-to-ear whispering position so familiar to Jasperodus. For the first time since Jasperodus had known him Oleander was wearing a smile of genuine pleasure, and it was clear now where many of Charrane's just-stated thoughts had originated.

"Mouth to ear!" Jasperodus cried. "He feeds you his poison and you swallow it!"

The wreckers gripped his arms.

Jasperodus began to howl.

"DEATH, DEATH, DEATH – you fools, do you not see? You are as dead as I! Death – all the world is nothing but death!"

They dragged him out still howling – not into the city, as he would have expected, but to a cellar under the palace. He passingly understood the reason for it: it would not be seemly to drag a marshal of the Imperial Forces through the streets. Here waited robotic technicians, around them strewn the tools of their trade with which to disassemble him. Broken up into small parts, he would be delivered to the masher.

They laid him down on a board table. But Jasperodus broke free and retreated to a corner of the cell-like room. The technicians fell back, disconcerted by this ferocious, glaring robot who fought for his life.

"What can it matter what thoughts and feelings inhabit this empty vessel?" Jasperodus babbled. "When my voice echoes out of this vacant iron drum, where does it come from? From nowhere, from emptiness – the voice of no one – a voice in the void without a speaker. And what of you? Does any entity form your words?"

Uncomprehendingly the technicians stared at him. The wreckers seized him again, and again Jasperodus began to howl.

"DEATH! ALL IS DEATH!"

He was still howling when they switched off his brain.

12

The return of awareness was slow and fragmentary. It began with a solitary thought that flickered for a bare instant against an overwhelming darkness and then vanished.

Intervals of time cannot be measured in oblivion; but on occasion the thought recurred, then was joined by others. Piece by piece a vestigial, primitive creature was built up and became persistent. The period between the birth of this creature and the moment when it began to call itself Jasperodus seemed immense. It ended when Jasperodus recovered sufficient of his memories to recognise himself as a single entity. He was then puzzled to find that he could not locate himself in space; he seemed to be in many places at once.

Still he could not think clearly, neither did he know for certain who he was, where he came from or how he had got into his present condition. There followed a lengthy phase he thought of as "groping". He seemed able to reach out and search the darkness in some vague or undefined manner, finding pieces of himself and adding them to him. As he did so he gained not only memories and extra mental clarity, but also inexplicable scenes that he seemed able to watch, each from a fixed vantage point.

This phase ended when his history and personality were again in his possession. Along with his anger at how he had been treated, Jasperodus was forced to appreciate certain facts.

He had no body.

He had no single spatial location.

There existed within himself, just below the level of his volition in a sort of subconscious stream, a continuous activity of monitoring, computing, comparing, collating and responding to countless small stimuli.

As far as he was able to ascertain he was located within and throughout the walls of Charrane's palace in the form of a network.

A full understanding of his situation came after a little deductive thinking. Presumably the roboticians had not delivered his parts to the masher after all. Perhaps reluctant to waste such fine workmanship, they had preserved the sub-assemblies and later used them in a low-integration cybernetic system of the standard type that apparently had been installed in the palace and the surrounding ministries.

Just what confluence of interrelations had caused to be reconnected sufficient of his one-time components to restore self-directed integration would remain a mystery. The dim urge that had caused this skeleton brain to seek out the rest of its sub-assemblies was also hard to explain in conventional robotic terms. However, he now found himself fully alert and sound of mind, but embedded in an extensive network of electronic administration.

He wondered what the roboticians had done with his body. That, possibly, *had* gone to the masher.

His new mode of existence gave him an unexampled opportunity for surveillance. Apart from his having access to stored information of all kinds, there was a good number of hidden sound and image perceptors scattered about, mostly for the use, as it happened, of Charrane himself, who had become suspicious of what went on around him. It was ironic that they put Jasperodus in a much more intimate position to watch *him*.

With some curiosity Jasperodus took stock of the situation at court. A number of years had passed since his deactivation. Mars was under firm control, but the Borgor Alliance was once more flexing its muscles. He received little direct news from the outside world, but what he did learn caused him to think that the internal state of the Empire was ominous. Charrane, with some reluctance, had been persuaded by Oleander to agree to the onset of large-scale factory production in an attempt to counterbalance the Borgor threat. There were occasional stories of disturbances in the city, at least one being within earshot of the palace. A proposal was afoot to provide free rations and entertainment so as to keep discontented elements among the masses quiet.

Among the services his circuits controlled were various domestic functions, as well as office and administrative terminals used by the Emperor Charrane. Jasperodus found that this made him able to vent his spite if he so wished. For a while he amused himself by subjecting the great Emperor to a number of petty inconveniences — withholding water when he took a shower, or suddenly delivering it scalding hot or icy cold; transmitting to him the wrong reports through his terminals, or even better, writing up totally fictitious reports on the subject called for; putting through a call to Mars when Charrane had asked to speak to someone a hundred yards away; switching the lights on and off when he retired to bed; interrupting his act of love with wife or concubine by activating all the appliances in the room, and so on. But he desisted after a while lest Charrane should order a total overhaul of the palace's cybernetisation. He could have interfered in the life of the administration more seriously if he so wished — he comprised, for instance, the data retrieval service for the planning staff — but he abandoned any such futilities.

Instead, he began to think of escape.

One day he made a scan of his demesne, looking through each sound-and-vision perceptor in turn, glancing at the inflow and outflow of each terminal. Suddenly he stopped short.

His face older and more lined than when he had last seen him, his old friend Cree Inwing sat in a tiny, stuffy office in an out-of-the-way part of the palace used by the Department of Military Supply. The brisk moustache was still there, as was the military bearing. He wore the epaulettes of a major, and was talking through the all-purpose terminal (Jasperodus had to admit that the new installation had achieved a much simplified method of communication) to the Logistics Section, sorting out details concerning the transportation of a batch of spare parts.

That finished, he rose and replaced the file holder on the shelf behind him. Watching through the same vision perceptor Cree had just been using, Jasperodus saw that he now walked with a pronounced limp.

He returned to his desk. Jasperodus spoke softly through the terminal.

"Cree."

Inwing looked round startled. "Who is it?"

"It is I, Jasperodus."

Bewilderment appeared on Inwing's face. Then his expression firmed. 'That is not his voice," he said sternly.

"My own voice is lost to me. I can only use whatever vodors are available."

"Then where on Earth are you? I heard you had been . . . destroyed."

"There are bits of me all over the palace," Jasperodus told him. "I *was* destroyed, but only to a degree. The engineers incorporated me into the service system." He chuckled gently. "A gross under-utilisation of my components, if you ask me."

He went on to describe in detail how he had been broken up, and how he had been able to reconnect all the parts of his redeployed brain through the system's comlines. Cree reacted by looking in turns astounded and agitated, and at one time his hands began to tremble.

"I want to escape this imprisonment," Jasperodus finished. "Will you help me, Cree?"

"Wait! Wait! Don't go any further!" Cree rubbed his eyes, then leaned forward with his elbows on the desk and buried his face in his hands. "Give me time to take it in!"

Jasperodus waited. He realised that Cree was now middle-aged, no longer the dashing young man he had once been. Jasperodus' entreaty doubtless came as a severe crisis for him.

Finally Cree sighed and uncovered his face.

"So you want to be reconstructed."

"Yes."

Again Jasperodus waited, for what seemed to him a long time. "Well?" he said then.

"No need to ask. I'm with you, all the way."

"It will involve you in some risk," Jasperodus pointed out.

"I owe it to you. Besides, I heard something about that raw deal you got. A bad show, Jasperodus. I'm sorry."

Jasperodus was elated. He had not expected to find help so easily. He had anticipated having to suffer his living incarceration for years before finding some means of extricating himself.

"You've heard *my* tale," he said. "What of yours?"

Cree shrugged. "Oh, my story is ordinary enough. I got my commission – thanks to you. Had some good times. Got wounded in action on Mars – lost part of a leg. So here I am with a desk job in Tansiann. Still, things could be worse." He ruminated. "What happens now, Jasperodus? I'll do whatever you say."

"I know I can depend on you," Jasperodus said. "Listen: I know exactly where all my components are as far as the service system is concerned, but that gives me, in effect, only my brain and a few ancillaries. I have no body. It will be necessary to acquire a new one, and for that you will need money. Also, we will need the services of roboticians we can trust and who are prepared to act criminally. They will need to be bribed."

Cree nodded. "I understand. My funds are at your disposal. If they are are not enough, well . . ." he fingered his moustache. "We will think of something . . ."

A few days later Cree entered his office in high spirits. He had been nosing around in the storerooms under the palace, and there he had found Jasperodus' decorticated body, complete and undamaged.

"Obviously nobody bothered sending it for scrap," he crowed, rubbing his hands. "You'll look like your old self again, Jasperodus."

"I'm relieved to hear it," Jasperodus congratulated, "and also pleased to learn that now there need be no lengthy delay while a new one is manufactured. Have you hired the roboticians yet?"

"Have patience. I am putting out feelers, but give me a few more days."

"Very well, but now that the event is close it is time to discuss practical details. Cutting so much cerebration out of the system will certainly be noticed quickly because of the deterioration in performance. So the thing will have to be done all at once in a short space of time, and at night. Several men will be needed to extract my parts from various points in the palace, which will require careful planning."

Cree frowned. "I was hoping it could be managed stealthily, piece by piece. Surely the system has some redundancy built into it? You said yourself your components were being under-utilised. Couldn't you arrange for the functions to be taken over elsewhere?"

"Possibly, as a makeshift measure, but it would be difficult, and as more of me is removed the harder it would become for me to arrange anything at all. Besides . . ."

Jasperodus hesitated. Then, diffidently, he told of the sexual function he had acquired, and which now was also incorporated into the service system.

"It is being used as a crucial nexus for the whole network," he explained. "It has so much capacity that it could not possibly be substituted for. Its removal will result in what amounts to a breakdown of the system as an integrated function."

Cree's mouth had been agape as he heard of Jasperodus' sexual adventures. He laughed uproariously and slapped his thigh. "You're still the man I knew you for, Jasperodus! A robot and a maid – that I'd like to see!"

"You may," Jasperodus promised, "if you respect my wishes in this regard."

On a dark night a little under a month later, Jasperodus' reassembly was accomplished. As his functions were excised his awareness dimmed, then descended into oblivion. He knew no more until he found himself standing, fully restored, in a windowless stonewalled room much like the one where he had been broken up. Near him stood Cree Inwing and three roboticians – among them, he noted with surprise, one of the team that had deactivated him in the first place. The scene was much the same as on that occasion, with robotic tools scattered all over. Only the wreckers were missing.

"Walk to the wall," said the latter robotician curtly. "Spin round quickly – reach up – touch your toes. Right. Stand on your left leg, raise your right leg and bend to the left to touch the floor with your fingers. Right. Now similar on your right leg. Good." All three watched closely while Jasperodus performed these exercises. "How do you feel? Any nodges, wiggles or disloes?"

Jasperodus listened into himself. "None," he said in answer to their robotic jargon.

"Good." The man turned to Inwing. "We're finished."

Jasperodus moved forward and in an uncharacteristically fond gesture placed his hands around Cree's shoulders. "Thank you," he said. "Thank you."

Cree was embarrassed but pleased. "Steady on, old chap. Don't let that sex centre get the better of you!" He chuckled, then became serious. "It will shortly be dawn. We'd better get moving before light. There'll be no problems : I have a pass, and as an accompanying construct you need none. These fellows will make their own way out half an hour later."

He dipped into a large canvas hold-all and handed to each

man a small but heavy cloth bag jingling with money. They inspected the contents briefly, nodded to him and left.

"Did you say you intend to come with me?" Jasperodus inquired. "You have implicated yourself?"

"My career in the service of the Emperor is over," Cree said with a sigh. "While it is always possible that my part in the rifling of the service system will go undetected, it is not a possibility I would care to depend on. Anyway, the question is hypothetical. To bring our project to fruition I have been obliged to resort to further malfeasance." He grimaced. "Those rogues weren't bought cheaply."

"Are you referring to malversation?" Jasperodus asked delicately.

"The supply funds are now short a hundred and fifty thousand crowns."

Jasperodus became thoughtful. "My predicament has involved you in considerable sacrifice."

Inwing shrugged. "I become weary of inaction behind a desk. I thought we might recover something of our old comradeship together, until we find other employment. What do you say?"

"Certainly!" Jasperodus laughed. "But let's delay no further."

They left the palace without mishap. Cree hired a horse-drawn cab from the rank permanently on call outside the main gate and they trundled through the darkened streets.

His mood was cheerful. "And so, Jasperodus! How does it feel to be mobile and free once again?"

"This is the second time I have been resurrected from the dead," Jasperodus remarked. "Repetition is a feature of this life, it seems."

Dawn was breaking when they ordered the driver to set them down on the outskirts of Subuh. For a distance they proceeded on foot, then Cree disposed of his military uniform on waste ground, changing into civilian garb. Nearby he knocked up the keeper of a disreputable inn, where he proposed they should lie low for a few days.

Jasperodus concurred, but was less cautious. "It is easy to hide in Subuh," he assured him. "Have no fear, I will arrange it."

In fact he had more than mere refuge on his mind. He thirsted for revenge. A few hours later it was mid-morning. Cree slept, while Jasperodus left the inn and ventured deeper into Subuh.

A single hour's walk told him much. With grim satisfaction he observed that many of his predictions had been justified – though the rate of change surprised even him. Subuh was a different, much worse place than before. From a slum it was in the process of being transformed into a wild lawless jungle.

The streets were overcrowded, noisy and strewn with uncollected litter. Sharp-faced hawkers openly sold dubious and illegal wares. Jasperodus witnessed robberies, brawls and bloodshed, all unheeded by the general public; the forces of the law had apparently abandoned the area and much of the populace, he saw, had taken to going armed. Great piles of rubbish were in evidence. Jasperodus passed a sprawling heap of defunct and dismantled robots. One unfortunate, thrown on the heap while still partly functional, made feeble efforts to extricate himself from the tangle, but fell back in defeat and despair.

An isolated tenement surrounded by waste ground burned fiercely and no one attended it, except for its inhabitants who did no more than try to drag their few belongings from the slowly collapsing pile. Jasperodus found the sight particularly depressing. A few years ago the city's fire service would have rushed into action even here in Subuh; now the owners were clearly content to let the building burn to the ground.

In the Diamond, a plaza central to the borough, a great crowd had gathered. Officials in the uniform of the City Administration stood on a wooden platform, backed by a mound of bulging sacks. Jasperodus understood that he was seeing the beginning of the city's poor-law largesse: the distribution of free grain to the unemployed.

He pushed his way rudely through the crowd and mounted the platform. Ignoring the indignation of the officials, whom he also brushed aside, he turned to address the jostling assembly.

His voice boomed out startlingly over the plaza. "Men of Tansiann! You are being given grain, the bounty of the earth. Why do you lack it? If you had land of your own, you would not need to be fed *gratis*. You are citizens of an empire which calls you masters of the Earth, yet you have no right to one square foot of her soil. Take your grain, then, and live the life of the dispossessed."

His speech was greeted with blank, silent stares. He turned, stepped past the puzzled officials, descended from the platform and slipped away from the plaza.

His approach had been too abstract, he decided. Coarser arguments would be needed to sway the citizens of Subuh.

But now he came to an area where abstraction was no stranger. Near the heart of Subuh was a small enclave, bounded by Bishi Street on one side and the Tan on the other, that traditionally was totally robot. A construct could enter here without fear of meeting a single human being, not even a slotman. Ignorant slotmen had, in fact, been known to commit suicide after straying into the area and discovering that they were classed as outsiders and aliens.

If anything the robot enclave was slightly better ordered than the rest of Subuh. Unlike the human proletariat, the robots were capable of organising the cleaning of their own streets. Even robots who collapsed were apparently cleared away (perhaps being added to the heap he had seen earlier, Jasperodus thought) and he saw only one or two twitching hulks on the sidewalk, stepped over by the passers-by.

It was, however, no less crowded, despite the high defunction rate that would be suggested by the poor state of repair of many of the constructs. The loss through junking was presumably being made good by a large nett inflow into the enclave. This alone was indicative of a general increase in crime throughout the city, for the commonest way in which a robot gained freedom was by being stolen and then slipping away from its hijackers.

"Jasperodus!"

He turned on hearing his name called, and espied an old acquaintance. Mark V, more tarnished and more battered, hurried up with a gait that to Jasperodus looked slightly eccentric.

"Your gimbals need attention," he remarked by way of a greeting.

Mark V laughed in embarrassment. "One's machinery deteriorates with age, you know. We cannot expect always to remain in good condition. But how delightful to see you! I followed your career at court with great interest, insofar as one could glean anything from the newspapers, but for some years there has been no mention . . . I have often wondered what became of you."

"As you can see I have given up public service and have decided to return to old haunts," Jasperodus said. "Tell me what is new in the district."

The two walked along together, but instead of supplying the information he desired Mark V treated Jasperodus to a description of an involved and abstruse theory of numbers he was working on. Thinking of his music, of his painting, of the vistas of creativity that were open to him, Jasperodus found Mark V's preoccupations arid and paltry.

Presently they came to the centre of the robot enclave: a large, low-roofed structure known as the Common Room. At Mark V's suggestion they entered. Here was a meeting place for robots from all over Subuh; beneath its timber beams they discoursed, debated and partook of stimulatory electric jags. Benches and chairs were set out in a loose pattern. A lively hum of conversation filled the air.

Mark V announced Jasperodus with a flourish. Several robots whom Jasperodus remembered from the early days came forward and stared at him curiously, as if unable to believe their eyes.

"Jasperodus!" cried one. "Is it really you?"

To his pleasure Jasperodus was welcomed as a celebrity and became the centre of attention. He was conducted to the place of honour, an ornate high-backed chair with lions' heads carved on its arms.

A construct spoke up. "We were about to begin a debate on the nature of infinity and on whether time is truly serial. Would you care to participate?"

"Thank you," replied Jasperodus, "but I am not in the mood for it."

Mark V sidled close. "You have long been a hero to us free robots," he informed him. "For a construct to rise so high in the government! Here in Subuh you are famous."

"Have a caution," Jasperodus warned all. "If my presence here becomes famous outside Subuh the city guard will turn the borough upside down looking for me. I am now a renegade."

A stir of excitement greeted his words. A tall, thin robot stepped near. "I once headed the committee that intended to propose you become leader of the wild robots, had you not suddenly disappeared."

"Here I am. I have returned to become your leader," Jasperodus said rashly. "Are you not tired of living like animals, without rights?"

He was now provoking some puzzlement, even consternation among the gathering. "What do you suggest?" asked one.

"I suggest nothing. When the time comes, I shall command."

The robots crowded round him. Jasperodus was introduced to the more prominent among those he did not already know. He received a pointed question from one with graceful mannerisms, deep and thoughtful eyes, and called (for robots' nicknames were sometimes strange and wonderful) Belladonna.

"You hint at activities going far beyond the bounds of the law. Frankly, what have we to gain? Robots by themselves can achieve little. As it is the existence of our tiny enclave is a perplexing example of human tolerance, to my mind, since if the humans decided to trespass here we could not stop them."

A neural pattern generator box was thrust before Jasperodus.

"A jag, great leader?"

He accepted three shots in quick succession. Feeling warmed and stimulated, he turned to reply to Belladonna.

"The reason for it is thuswise. Any beggar can tell you that he receives his alms from the poor, rarely from the rich, because only the poor understand poverty. So it is with you. The people of Subuh respect your little refuge out of a feeling for your plight, much as they will throw coins to a beggar. Besides, many of them are too ignorant to understand properly that robots are not human, and accord them more equality than their makers intended. Try establishing a robot quarter in a better district, such as Tenure or Elan, and see what happens."

He quickly tired of answering questions and called for newspapers, as many as could be found. He immersed himself in these, ignoring for a time the social life around him, but kept Mark V and one or two others by him to fill in the gaps in the news.

It was all much as he had anticipated. The outlook for the Empire was once again precarious. Encouraged by the success of the second Mars venture, Charrane had attempted to follow it up with much more costly interplanetary projects, including the founding of small colonies on the Jovian satellites. He had failed to appreciate that these extravagant gestures should wait until further expansion and consolidation on Earth.

At home events were proceeding in an alarming direction. The politics of the court had become corrosive and corrupt — the newspapers did not state this in so many words, naturally, but with his special knowledge Jasperodus was able to guess at it. Meanwhile social unrest grew. The slums had spread, sprawling beyond Subuh to encompass a good part of the city. For the moment everything was quiet, but Jasperodus could see that if a leader should arise there was a powder-keg waiting to be lit, unsuspected, perhaps, by the self-interested politicians surrounding Charrane.

Most disturbing was the military situation. The major divisions of the imperial armies were in the north, close to the borders of the revived and stronger Borgor Alliance. They were guarding a structure that was increasingly rotten and unable to back them up, that was overburdened with the costly outspace territories, and more than likely they were already outclassed by the enemy they faced. It angered Jasperodus to see so much of his work to make the Empire safe thrown away by the ineptness of others.

I could have averted all this, he thought. *But as it's here, Charrane, let's see if I can use it against you . . .*

He remembered those far-off days in Okrum. He recalled how easy it was to be a king. How much easier it would be then, here among the rabble and the robots

He fell to reflecting, considering this strategy and that.

At length he stirred. "We will have a debate after all," he boomed. "The subject of our debate will be — Freedom."

He gazed around at them. "Let me be the first to speak . . ."

"I can't say I care for it, Jasperodus. I don't like it at all."

Cree Inwing stared grumpily out of the window of his room in a building near the enclave, where Jasperodus had installed him.

Jasperodus laughed lightly. "You are not alone. Those robots were not easy to persuade either. But once set on a new course they are totally committed to it. That is the nature of the machine."

"Well, I am not a machine," Cree snapped irritably. "And I am not set on new courses without good reason. In this case I see none. Why can't you let things be?"

"I understand your misgivings. You served the Empire faithfully for many years, and now you find yourself involved in treason.

It goes against the grain. But you served the Empire no less faith-fully than I." Jasperodus' voice rose slightly. "How was my ser-vice repaid?"

"It's easier for you," Cree grumbled. "Being a robot you took no oath of loyalty, as I did."

"What difference if I had? Deeds, not words, are the proof of intentions. Besides, why castigate me for what is happening? This Empire will crumble without my help. I am merely kicking the shorings from under an edifice rotted within. Never mind the robots; my real source is human discontent. Ask the mob that one day soon will discover its strength."

"To go pillaging, burning, killing." Cree looked glum. "They are even more your dupes than those poor constructs."

"How so?" Jasperodus suddenly displayed indignation. "The state is giving them bread. I promise them land! That is the lure that is bringing them forth ready to fight!"

This boast elicited only a scornful grunt from Inwing. "Most of them imagine they will be allotted some valuable property as a reward for their part in the rebellion and be able to live thereafter on the rent! You know very well that is not how you intend to arrange matters. You have preyed on their ignorance."

Jasperodus laughed again, placatingly.

"Nevertheless the affair may give the Empire the new start it needs," he suggested.

"Don't try to fool *me* with your dissembling arguments," In-wing retorted bluntly. "Your motives are entirely destructive – I am as well aware as you are of that. For one thing the rebellion can't succeed. It will merely create havoc for a while, there being no armed presence strong enough to oppose it. Then the imperial forces will enter the city – and all who have been so foolish as to follow you will be annihilated, robots and people together. You and I both know this. But it doesn't matter to you, does it? You only want to prove to the Emperor that he can't treat you badly and get away with it. It's a bad show."

At this Jasperodus dropped the badinage with which he had been trying to cover his feelings, and allowed his true surliness to appear. "Perhaps you are wrong," he said sullenly, turning away. "I have done surprising things before."

"This time without my help. I'm leaving. Back to the west, perhaps." Inwing looked older than Jasperodus had ever seen him.

Jasperodus drifted to the door, his head lowered stubbornly, a baleful glow in his red eyes. "What of it all?" he said curtly. "Am I not entitled to reassert myself? As for you, you are going nowhere. You are a wanted man; I have placed a guard upon this house and you will remain here until further notice. This is for your own protection."

"Or because you fear I will inform on you?" Inwing said acidly.

Not looking back, Jasperodus left.

A time came which Jasperodus saw as a favourable opportunity. There were no sizeable military forces within easy distance of the capital. The city guard was understrength. Most important of all, the Emperor Charrane was absent, away on an inspection tour of the Martian dominion.

Jasperodus and his helpers had been secretly preparing the revolt for months. In the middle of one sunny morning Jasperodus gave the word. A raggle-taggle army of robots, slotmen and indigenous poor suddenly gathered in the streets of Subuh and went pouring into the city. An hour later, when the city guard had been called out, contingents in other boroughs rose to enter the battle.

The rebels were armed with bullet guns, some beamers, pikes, swords and cudgels. Alongside each robot Jasperodus had placed an accompanying human so as to ensure his loyalty in the face of counteracting commands from the enemy. Otherwise organisation was fragmentary except for a small corps – the humans wearing brief uniforms of grey battle-jerkins and berets – surrounding Jasperodus.

His lieutenant was a man known as Arcturus, something of a minor leader in his own right. A product of his environment, he had a physique that was potentially powerful, but he was spindled, his features made pasty as a consequence of infantile under-nourishment. A man of rare intelligence for the Subuh, he was one of the few to have ingested the theory behind Jasperodus' advocacy of communal land-ownership. His own ideas went further, however. He subscribed to some obscure doctrine that was not at all clear to Jasperodus, whereby everything was to be held in common and all labour centrally directed.

By mid-afternoon several parts of Tansiann were burning. Roiling smoke drifted over the city; from wherever one stood could be heard the distant sounds of clamour. As Jasperodus had anticipated, a large mass of people not privy to his plans had joined the tumult, either as a welcome diversion from frustrating normality or as a chance to loot, and the unrestrained violence of the mob was thus raging in a number of quarters. Members of the city guard, understanding what lay in store and having witnessed the fate of some of their comrades, had already taken to throwing away their uniforms.

Not all went without opposition. The middle-class and upper-class suburbs showed a surprising ability to react quickly to an emergency. Tenure, Elan and others had become efficient, armed camps which had repulsed the first ragged waves of invasion and looked like holding out for some time.

The storming of the palace took place in the evening. Here the fighting was fiercest, for while the palace had never been conceived as a citadel, the palace guard resisted strenuously and were better trained, so that four hours later only half the vast complex was in rebel hands. Just the same Jasperodus pressed the attack; he was determined that his presence should be seen and felt by the notables and staff who had thought him long gone. Finally, round about midnight, the sound of gunfire died down, and a motley mob sauntered wonderingly through intricate plazas and terraces, through apartments and halls the luxury and grandeur of which they had never known.

Together with many other prisoners Ax Oleander was captured. The unpopular vizier, found huddling in a wardrobe in his apartments, would have been lynched had not Jasperodus himself rescued him and consigned him to incarceration in the cellars. Later Jasperodus was to be much amused by a perusal of his private papers, which revealed certain treasonable contacts with the government of Borgor. Even if the Empire should fall to its long-standing enemy the oily vizier meant to survive.

The tensions of battle momentarily over, uninhibited revels began. Jasperodus climbed a tower and spent some time alone, watching the flames leap up here and there from the spreading darkness below.

The next day he was out with Arcturus and members of his corps, attempting to put some order into the chaos he had created. Most of the battalion commanders were nowhere to be found. The hastily-formed army was too busy enjoying the fruits of its partial victory to be much bothered with discipline. Nevertheless he managed to reconstitute the harried and defeated fire service, pressing extra men into duty as fire-fighters. The quicker he could repair the ravages he had wrought the easier it would be to win the confidence of the general citizenry.

About mid-morning, in the middle-class Condra district, a robot ran towards him carrying a field vid-set attached by cable and drum to a nearby public booth. It had been planned to use Tansiann's vid-line service in this way, but up until now no one had apparently felt the need for communication. He accepted the set and found himself staring, on the tiny monochrome screen, into the crudely-made face of a low-order robot he identified, after a moment's thought, as one by the name of Chisel.

"What is it?" he snapped. "You belong to the guard party, do you not?"

Chisel's head moved aberratedly, as though he were suffering strain. "There has been an attack, sir! Men came to the house looking for Major Inwing, whom they attempted to murder."

"What transpired?"

The robot began to babble incoherently before Jasperodus calmed him down and extracted the story.

The would-be killers had known their business. Despite the mixed human-robot guard they had got into the house in a surprise attack and two of them had penetrated to Inwing's room, injuring him before being killed by Rovise, captain of the guard.

Rovise had acted well. Only he, Chisel and another robot called Bootmaker by this time remained to defend their charge. He had ordered the robots to lower the unconscious Inwing through the window and carry him away from the back of the house, holding off further sallies while they did so.

"What are Inwing's injuries?" Jasperodus demanded. "Describe."

"A bullet hit him in the head. I do not think his brain-case is broken. He is alive, but unconscious."

"Who is with him?"

"Only myself and Bootmaker, who is even less intelligent than I! Tell me what to do, sir!"

Jasperodus recalled with a sudden chill that when still in Charrane's favour he had once drawn up contingency measures to be used in case of insurgency. These measures included highly trained assassination squads to knock out traitors and rebel leaders. There was no question but that these squads were now operating, and that Cree was a target. His peccancies on the eve of his disappearance had no doubt been linked to Jasperodus' re-emergence, which was more than enough to identify him with the revolt.

Jasperodus cursed himself. Once on the trail the assassins were sufficiently skilled as detectives not to let go – and they were utterly dedicated. It was only a matter of time before they gained their objective, unless he could help Inwing.

And the worst of it was that Chisel – as the unlucky construct himself well knew – was simply not intelligent enough to handle the situation. He and his helpmate were of an elementary type of androform robot, generally expected to act only under supervision. For instance, they had thoughtlessly fled with Inwing in a direction taking them away from the enclave, instead of into it where they could have counted on finding protection.

"Give me orders, sir!" Chisel pleaded urgently. "Rovise gave us no further instructions beyond this point, and is doubtless now dead."

It came home forcibly to Jasperodus that it was necessary to direct Chisel in the most simplistic, most unequivocal of terms. The situation was precarious. The robots were quite capable of forgetting the real purpose of their mission, or of putting some other interpretation on it instead.

He mustered his sternest, most commanding voice. "You are to prevent the assassins from killing Major Inwing, using any means whatsoever that are available. That is a prime directive, which must engage all your attention, permanently and without attenuation. Do you understand?"

Chisel nodded feverishly. "I understand. Prevent the assassins from killing Major Inwing – at whatever cost. I understand. We obey!"

"Good. Now tell me exactly where you are, and I will be with you directly."

But before Chisel could answer there was the sound of an explosion and the vidset screen rippled and then went blank. Jasperodus observed that the overhead lines to the booth had been blown down by a mortar bomb.

More mortar bombs came whizzing down into the street from over the rooftops. Shrapnel rattled against his torso. Hoarse shout and screams mingled with the flat, brief blasts.

The bombardment finished. The survivors picked themselves up from the roadway. Arcturus cursed, examining his arm. The firefighters had fled, abandoning their equipment and several burning houses.

Jasperodus waved his arms. "Take cover!" he growled. "Into the buildings!"

He helped carry still-living wounded into one of the deserted houses. They laid them down in a lushly carpeted drawing-room. One began to groan in an empty, uncomprehending tone.

Arcturus turned to Jasperodus from an inspection of the injured. "Two of these men need immediate medical attention. What do you think's happening?"

Jasperodus shook his head. He went to the door and peered cautiously out. He saw men in imperial uniform passing the end of the street. The troops paused, as if checking the avenue for activity, then moved on.

As soon as all seemed quiet Jasperodus took a number of men on a reconnoitre. Keeping close to the sides of buildings, they passed through streets displaying only a few bewildered citizens who quickly disappeared at the sight of an armed force.

A burly figure came staggering towards them, a bottle clasped in one hand and a machine-gun in the other. It was the commander of one of Jasperodus' battalions.

"Any news?" Jasperodus demanded of the besotted rebel.

"Imperial troops are in the city. They moved in this morning from Axlea – only forty miles away."

"How many?"

"At least four thousand, I'd say. They're moving fast. They'll be at the palace soon."

"And where are your men?"

"I don't know. Drunk. Whoring."

Jasperodus grunted in disgust. The man was useless. At least, he thought, he could depend on the robots and slotmen.

He hadn't known of the presence of troops in Axlea. Perhaps they had been quartered there en route for rest or retraining. Still, the situation was not irredeemable. He could contain it – if he could rouse his shabby army out of its stupor.

But what of Inwing? Jasperodus found himself in the grip of an unaccustomed anxiety.

"We will move towards Subuh," he announced, "and gather up what we can on the way."

At the first vidbooth they came to he put a call through to his headquarters in the enclave and ordered a search of the surrounding district for Inwing. He also called the vidbooth exchange to inform the operators of his whereabouts and of the direction he was heading in. Possibly Chisel would try to contact him again.

Barely half an hour later this hope was rewarded. The moronic robot trembled with the duress of too much responsibility as he stared out of the vidscreen.

"Well?" Jasperodus snapped. "Where are you? How are things with Inwing?"

"We are in the north of Subuh, sir, in Monk's Road. We have carried him as fast and as far as we could, but it has made no difference; he is still unconscious."

Jasperodus became exasperated, both at Chisel's peculiar reasoning and at his actions. If he and Bootmaker had been carrying Inwing openly through the streets all this time it was a miracle the assassins had not struck.

And as luck would have it a segment of the relief force from Axlea now lay between Jasperodus and North Subuh; the imperial troops had been attempting to carve up the city, cutting off borough from borough. Also, in heedlessly heading north Chisel had put the assassins between himself and South Subuh, thus depriving himself of possible help from that quarter.

"Inwing is with you now?" Jasperodus queried.

"He lies in an alley, with Bootmaker standing over him."

"And you are armed?"

Chisel displayed a machine-gun. "I have this, and Bootmaker is similarly equipped."

Jasperodus paused, then spoke slowly and deliberately. "Listen to me carefully, Chisel. This is the most important thing that has ever happened to you. An assassination squad is out to murder Major Inwing, and you alone are in a position to prevent it. Have you got that?"

"Yes, sir, but I am scarcely capable of initiative! I do not have the brain to plan strategy!"

Jasperodus waved aside the robot's complaints. "Even robots can make efforts. You must try your utmost; use what mental capacity you do have and think out ways to frustrate the killers. If you try even you, Chisel, can *think*. I am depending on you to do this thing."

Chisel's head trembled even more and his distress and exertion were almost palpable "I am trying my hardest. We will not fail. I swear it! You can depend on it!"

"Good. Now the first thing you must do is to get Inwing under cover. He is far too vulnerable out in the open. Find a room in a stout building. A small room with no windows and only one door, so that it can easily be defended against intruders. As soon as you have installed yourselves and Inwing into this room call me again through the central exchange."

Chisel took in the instructions with great attentiveness. Suddenly he stiffened. "A man I recognise has just passed the booth. He is one of the assassins!"

"Do not panic," Jasperodus warned. "If he is moving away from the location of Inwing, let him pass. If he is moving towards the alley . . ."

"He moves towards the alley!"

"Do not let him near Major Inwing!" urged Jasperodus, agonised. "Kill him!"

Chisel turned and stumbled from the booth. Jasperodus' screen went blank as the equipment switched itself off with his departure. He waited for some minutes but Chisel did not return.

He wondered if he had done enough to make the preservation of Inwing Chisel's overriding goal.

Then he turned his attention to getting through the cordon that separated him from North Subuh.

"This is no way to save the city," Arcturus grumbled. "What are we supposed to be doing?"

Jasperodus deliberated. He had gathered about a hundred men

and they huddled in an archway hidden under a bridge carrying a railway track that led westward out of the city. They listened to the crackle of gunfire in the middle distance. Two men tinkered with a motorised vehicle captured by ambushing an imperial patrol.

"I have a private mission," he confessed. "Possibly I could accomplish it alone. If you prefer you may take charge of operations until I return and conduct them as you see fit."

Somewhat displeased by his attitude, but asking no questions, Arcturus agreed. "We will proceed towards the palace and try to organise matters in a somewhat more coordinated fashion," he said. Just then the robot carrying the field vidset again appeared, having attached it to a booth in the next street, and Chisel once more faced Jasperodus.

This time there was no head tremor and the cretinous robot's voice was full of confidence. "Success, Jasperodus! Our goal is achieved! It is impossible for the assassins to kill Major Inwing now!"

A feeling of relief flooded Jasperodus. "You carried out my instructions?"

"Indeed yes. A room with no window and only one door. Bootmaker is there this very minute. Many difficult decisions were involved in finding the room! Breaking down doors, arguing with tenants – furthermore, by vigorous application of intense mentation all conditions stipulated by you have been fulfilled . . ."

"What is the address?" Jasperodus interrupted.

"The house is at the north end of Monk Street, second from the corner with Abbey Street, and is set back from the road. We are on the third floor, at the rear."

"Then I am barely a mile and a half from you, I believe. I hope to be there within minutes." He handed back the set to the carrying robot.

Wondering if he would be able to find a doctor for Cree in the vicinity, he set out in the motor vehicle, which had a raised armoured skirt for protection from gunfire. Otherwise he carried only his long-tubed beamer. The vehicle was steam-driven, with a small fast-heat fire-box fuelled by pellets made from a woody composite. He worked a lever, pumping in pellets, then steamed up the engine. The vehicle rolled out from under the archway, careened round the corner and down the road to the main avenue separating the boroughs.

The imperial troops had set up firing points on all the main intersections and on many minor ones, thus establishing an effective cross-fire. Jasperodus' advantage was that they did not always immediately recognise him for a robot, and so tended not to bring into use their beamers, which alone could destroy him. He swept at speed through the streets between him and North Subuh. Bullets drummed against the skirting and occasionally pinged off his body, but he clung to the steering wheel and managed to keep his seat. Once a beam hit the side of the truck, burned its way through the skirting and hissed behind his back, but it did not touch him. Eventually he realised that the firing had stopped; he was through the cordon and in Subuh.

The house was as Chisel had described it. The line of tenements was broken just there and the building stood alone, set back from the street. Otherwise it had the same unkempt appearance; the stonework was grimy and cracked, many of the windows were broken. The front door had been broken down – by Chisel and Bootmaker, presumably. Cautiously Jasperodus entered a darkened hallway and mounted narrow stairs. Surprisingly, the robots had chosen well. The house offered good defensive positions, with its sharp twists and turns and close passages.

On the third floor he found a door at the end of a short passage, facing the back of the house. He hammered on it.

"Who is there?" cried Chisel's excited voice from within. "No stranger may enter! Depart or face our machine-guns!"

"It is I, Jasperodus," Jasperodus called.

"Jasperodus, our commander! You indeed may enter!" There came the sound of furniture being shifted behind the door, then of a lock being turned, then the door was flung open.

"All is as I have stated," Chisel exulted. "It is absolutely impossible for the assassination squad to kill Major Inwing now." He gestured with a flourish. "See – we have killed him ourselves! How now will the assassins perform the act?"

Jasperodus stepped into the cramped, grimy room and stared aghast at the scene that met his eyes. On a blood-drenched pallet bed against the far wall lay the corpse of Cree Inwing, his skull crushed and battered by some blunt instrument. Near him stood

Bootmaker the cobbling robot, his dull red eyes staring passively at Jasperodus and a machine-gun held awkwardly in his hands.

"A perfect strategy to thwart the desires of the assassins who are hunting the major!" claimed Chisel in a voice that invited congratulation.

His wits paralysed, Jasperodus stared from one robot to the other. Here it was: the basic, incurable idiocy of the machine, laid bare before his understanding like a sick vision. With a bellow of agonised rage he leaped at Chisel, who sprang back in surprise. Jasperodus slammed him against the wall and pounded him again and again with his steel fist. Chisel, like Bootmaker, was smaller than Jasperodus and not nearly as sturdily constructed; his flimsy pressed-sheet body-casing buckled and broke apart and tiny components spilled out, dislodged by Jasperodus' violence. In a final vicious attack Jasperodus brought his fist down like a hammer on the unlucky construct's head and he toppled to the floor with a crushed braincase.

Jasperodus advanced on Bootmaker, who had stood motionless and silent throughout the destruction of his companion. "You also took part in this?"

"We debated together ways and means of denying the assassins their pleasure, until finally Chisel arrived at his idea, which he considered a stroke of genius."

"There are some humans even more stupid than you," Jasperodus said in strangled tones, "but even they would not make so incredible a mistake!"

"As to that I cannot say. For forty years I made and repaired boots and shoes alongside my master and then alongside his son, my second master. That is my trade: I was never trained to know when and when not to kill. When my master's son died I was left alone and so joined the wild robots, though to be frank I would prefer to be back with him, working at my last. I can make a good pair of boots, sir."

Jasperodus took hold of Bootmaker, and dragged him from the room and partway down the first flight of stairs, where he flung him over the banisters and down the stairwell. The robot hit the ground floor with a resounding crash. When Jasperodus passed by him a minute later his limbs were moving feebly in a reflex action.

In a daze Jasperodus boarded his motor truck and drove south, passing groups of disorganised guerrillas and arriving shortly in the enclave. In the headquarters he was greeted by Belladonna, who had taken no part in the fighting but instead had appointed himself Director of Political Research.

"Good to see you, Jasperodus. All goes well, I trust? Though I hear there is renewed fighting throughout Tansiann. Hopefully we shall soon regain control."

Jasperodus made a half-hearted gesture of acquiescence. The headquarters seemed quiet. The vidset switchboard he had arranged was still staffed, but no one was calling in, the centre of communications having shifted to the palace.

"I have something I would like you to see," Belladonna said, "if you would care to step into my premises." He extended an arm invitingly.

Jasperodus followed him through the covered passageway that led to the buildings Belladonna had sequestered for himself and his team. "I have been giving much thought to the deficiencies which human beings have forced on we robots, in keeping no doubt with our former condition of machine slavery," Belladonna explained as they walked. "With the onset of the robot revolt there is no reason why we should continue to suffer these deprivations. Thus you, Jasperodus, have shown that robots can express forceful self-will, which has been an inspiration to us all. Another useful faculty our masters have hitherto forbidden us is facial expression, which no one can deny is a valuable aid to communication between individuals. Accordingly we have been doing some work in this field."

He opened a door and they were in the research centre, a long corridor flanked by steel doors painted white and each bearing a number.

"It would have been possible to simulate the human face, using a rubberoid sheath manipulated by a musculature system," Belladonna continued, "but we rejected this approach as being slavishly imitative. A typically robotic face is what is needed."

He opened door number four. Within, half a dozen or so robots were standing talking together, or else gazing into mirrors. Jasperodus observed that their faces underwent curious machine-like motions. Each robot had been fitted with a new face which incorporated, in the region of the mouth and cheeks, slots and flanges capable of simple movements relative to one another. These made possible mask-like travesties of a limited number of human expressions.

"Attention!" barked Belladonna. "Our leader wishes to see a demonstration."

With alacrity the robots formed a rank and went through their repertoire in concert, by turns grinning, grimacing, scowling, looking comically stern. Four expressions in all, each one rigid and unvarying, grotesquely unrealistic, the transitions between them sudden and startling.

"How is your conversation improving?" Belladonna asked, obviously pleased with the performance.

"In truth there has been no great advancement as yet," the team leader answered apologetically. "We still find that verbal communication far outstrips what can be added to it by facial contortions."

"No doubt it comes with practice," Belladonna replied optimistically. "Let us move on, Jasperodus."

They stepped back into the corridor. "Now I have a top secret project to show you," Belladonna confided. "Something of military application. We are fortunate in having some excellent chemists among us."

Door Nine disclosed a well-equipped laboratory. A number of carefully intent constructs were busy with flasks, tubes and burners. Labelled jars and boxes lined the shelves that covered the walls.

Belladonna approached the main workbench and showed Jasperodus an elaborate set-up of retorts and coils from which a dark green liquid slowly dripped into self-sealing metal containers. He glanced at Jasperodus. "We may expect the current conflict eventually to turn into a war between men and constructs, before we are able to achieve our real aim, that of founding a robot republic. In that struggle this weapon will prove invaluable. It is a poison gas that is deadly to humans but harmless, of course, to constructs." He picked up one of the cylindrical containers from a tray and pressed a button on its top. "See!"

A thick green fog spurted from a nozzle, forming billowing clouds which quickly spread through the laboratory. "To a human being this vapour is instantly fatal."

Belladonna must have possessed a poor olfactory sense. The gas had an intensely vile stench that revolted Jasperodus. He averted his head, uttering a horrified cry.

"Death!" he gasped. "The smell of death!"

He knocked the hissing container from Belladonna's hand, then charged wildly into the convoluted assemblage of reaction vessels, smashing and scattering everything to fragments.

"Cease production of this evil odour," he demanded, confronting the startled robot scientists. "Destroy the formula, expunge it from your memories. I cannot stand the smell of death."

13

"So you think we should let supplies through?" asked Jasperodus.

"On humanitarian grounds it would appear reasonable," the other stated.

"Why feed an enemy?" Arcturus objected without much conviction. "We should have overwhelmed those areas days ago."

They stood on the floor of the basilica. During the past week Jasperodus and his co-conspirators had once more taken control of the city, but had left unmolested certain opulent areas whose residents had formed a common defence. Jasperodus somehow felt no enthusiasm for their subjugation.

"Let them have supplies," he said carelessly. "It will soften their attitude towards us."

The third member of the conversation was Jasperodus' own replica. The staff robots and household robots of the palace had made a smooth transition to the new régime, with the exception of those few controlled by secret command languages who still proved recalcitrant and had been locked in the cellars along with the other prisoners. The human household servants were less willing, of course, but they understood their situation and cooperated as well as might be expected.

Jasperodus 2 inclined his head in assent and left to make the necessary arrangements.

Evening approached, softening the quality of the light that entered through the high mullioned windows. The throne had been removed from the apse, as had the thought-pictures the dais had formerly concealed (they were too distracting) and Jasperodus had introduced a more democratic atmosphere into the court – if court it could be called – mingling with his proletarian lackeys on equal terms. In keeping with the notions expressed by Arcturus and Belladonna he would probably style himself (though he no longer cared or thought about the future) First Councillor, First Citizen, or something of the sort.

Absent-mindedly Jasperodus attended to one or two other matters that were brought before him. At about sunset a series of loud explosions ripped through central Tansiann, some of them close to the palace. They were believed to be the work of loyalists and a great deal of confusion and concern was occasioned, but Jasperodus ignored them entirely and went on supervising the arrangement of seats for the event he planned for later that night.

Somewhat after the onset of darkness there were more explosions and fires throughout the capital, together with sporadic guerrilla attacks on rebel positions. It was plain that loyalist elements had spent time in organising themselves and now were attempting to make the rebels' possession of the city untenable.

While the guests were arriving, messengers continually brought news of developments, but he paid them little heed. He had invited – or rather, ordered to appear – a gathering of Tansiann's most renowned poets, artists and musicians for an evening of social mingling interspersed with music of quality.

Also in the company were any of the coarsest of Subuh's denizens, human and construct, who cared to show themselves. Drink and modulated electric current flowed freely. Jasperodus spent part of the time circulating among the guests, encouraging drunkenness and general indiscipline, and part of the time to one side by himself, observing all with dry detachment. Occasionally further explosions could be heard, dull thumps or sharp detonations according to how far away they were.

Belladonna approached, reeling from too much neural pattern stimulation. "The situation is looking ugly," he rasped.

"No doubt it will be under control by morning." Jasperodus raised his hand, a signal for the orchestra to begin the next item on their programme, an elegant concerto for multihorn by the composer Reskelt.

Disinvolving himself from all talk, Jasperodus listened idly to Reskelt's flawless pattern of melody. In a few minutes the short piece came to an end and the musicians rested. Glancing around the hall, Jasperodus noticed that he was being observed with some interest by a white-bearded but hale oldster whose face was slightly familiar. It was the riddle-poser, one of the troupe who had entertained Jasperodus when he was king of Gordona.

Seeing that he was recognised, the old man approached. "So

you were not retained permanently in Gordona," Jasperodus remarked. "But what brings you here?"

The other chuckled as if at a joke. "No, we were able to leave
as soon as King Zhorm was reinstated. As for why I am here, we
arrived to fulfil an engagement booked several months ago, and
the major-domo has requested that we remain until the Emperor
returns to put the palace back in order. What of yourself? I see
you have not changed your habits, for you are in a roughly similar
situation to the last time we met."

"Oh, I have not been without some self-development," Jasperodus replied in a wry tone. "I progressed from treachery to a
life of service in the name of ideals. But then I myself was betrayed
by the man to whom I gave my trust, and this is my response."

"You refer to the Emperor Charrane?"

"Exactly."

"Ahhh . . ." The riddle-poser sighed, shaking his head. "What
an empty thing is revenge!"

"It is what one turns to," Jasperodus said thoughtfully, "when
one feels one's manhood threatened."

"Hm. It is quite apparent that you have an unusual talent for
making the world suffer for your disappointments. But why so?
Is it not a vanity to act so destructively? Repaying evil with evil
has never been reckoned a mark of wisdom."

"And how should I be wise?" Jasperodus asked. "And what is
this drivel about evil? What else is there? Why should any good
exist? There is no virtue in the world, that has been amply demonstrated. Once I was crass enough to expect it, fooled no doubt by
my lack of consciousness, but now the nature of things is clear to
me . . . the world itself is an enemy; whosoever one loves it takes
away . . ."

Jasperodus broke off. Nearby was Arcturus, eavesdropping, his
pasty leaden face intent. "I am not the one you should be talking
with, philosopher. Arcturus here is more the man for ethical discussion. He has a marvellous scheme for putting the world to
rights, whereby the human race is to place even its minutest affairs
under the direction of a central committee, that is to say of Arcturus
and his friends, who inevitably will be characterised by a mad lust
for power." Jasperodus emitted a braying laughter and Arcturus,
who had in fact modified his views on witnessing the grasping and

immoderate behaviour of the Subuh mob, looked uncomfortable.

"Unfortunately I have little appetite for debate tonight," he murmured.

Jasperodus turned back to the old troupster. "At our first meeting you entertained me. Now let me entertain you, with a work of my own devising."

He stepped before the orchestra, raised his hands and called for silence. A hush fell on the hall. The attendants began persuading people into the rows of seats that had earlier been set out. Jasperodus nodded to the conductor as a signal to begin, then offered the old man a seat at the front and took a place next to him.

After seizing the palace Jasperodus had discovered in the store rooms all his old papers and belongings, including the manuscript score of his symphony, an ambitious musical work which he had just completed when he was dismantled. His desire to see this work performed before an audience was the main motive behind the soirée, and the orchestra had been in rehearsal for the past four days.

After a dignified pause the conductor raised his baton.

The symphony opened with a full, sonorous chord which was broken and reiterated in various slow rhythms. Then, leisurely and with unfailing ease of motion, the first movement developed. The subsidiary themes were long, extraordinarily inventive, and unfolded with an elaborate baroque logic. The main motifs, on the other hand, possessed a sedateness and a detachment that was ravishing, stated with fetching simplicity, advancing and receding now winsomely, now wistfully, through the evolving pattern of sound.

The movements succeeded one another without hiatus. There was no dramatisation or straining for effect. The music was abstract in content; it conveyed only the most impersonal of emotions. It spoke of endless space, endless time, ceaseless effort; of nascent being struggling against blind eternity – as in the slow third movement, where the horns erupted intermittently against a serene, timeless background of poignant melody, pulling and tugging with their sudden pullulations.

Jasperodus had put the totality of his effort into the work. It summed up all the thought and feeling of which he believed he was capable, and he did not think he could ever better it.

He had written a voice part into the final movement, making it a sort of miniature oratorio. As the preliminary bars were played he rose from his seat and joined the orchestra.

His manly, pleasing baritone issued forth, emerging as a wilful, individualistic entity, sometimes blending with the orchestral framework but sometimes bursting out of it to explore unrelated tonalities. The words he sang were in a dead language – copied from a magical description of mystic worlds – and were there merely as a stop-gap, to give the voice articulation. It had been his intention later to incorporate the movement into an opera, supplying more intelligible words from a libretto.

This closing section tempered the formerly abstract character of the symphony with more personal, more romantic feelings. Initially the voice part did no more than display its strength; but soon it found its direction and began to express a hopeful joy. This gradually turned into a display of barren tension, however, as it wandered, seemingly without relief, through an arid and friendless vastness, ranging higher and higher. Never losing its passion, it eventually spiralled despairingly down, accompanied by quiet discords which hinted at darkness and tragedy. And yet, after resigning the field to the orchestra for a spell, it finally ascended again, this time with a degree of objectivity that was strange, almost inhuman in its indifference to all feeling.

Jasperodus' voice faded. For some bars thereafter the orchestra held a persistent humming note, which in turn faded away.

The audience, the educated part of it at least, sat spellbound. At length enthusiastic applause broke out.

Jasperodus returned to his seat. "What do you think of it?" he asked the riddle-poser.

The oldster did not reply for a moment. Then he nodded slowly.

"First performances are apt to provoke judgements that later become invalidated. Nevertheless I would pronounce it a work of genius. The productions of men truly are extraordinary and without limit."

"But it is not the work of man," Jasperodus pointed out. "It is *my* work."

"That is what I meant. You are the work of men, are you not?"

Jasperodus made a disappointed gesture. "You regard me, then, as only a relay for human talents, having none of my own?"

"The question is not altogether meaningful. Certainly you are constructed so as to possess abilities that men have conceived and developed, but which robots never could. That, at least, is the scientific opinion." As the old man spoke these inconclusive words the familiar blackness that lay like a blanket over Jasperodus' feelings was intensified. He grew displeased with the conversation, quit the old man and drifted away, to receive everywhere effusive congratulations for his symphony.

"Do not praise me," he said abruptly to one strikingly beautiful young woman, the daughter of a famous artist, who though gazing wide-eyed into his face glanced more slyly over his body. "My achievement is vicarious: the expression of conceptions created by others."

Arcturus sidled up to him. "I was given some unsettling news during the concert," he said quietly. "The Fourth Army left the frontier two days ago to join the Second Army already on its way here."

"Hm," grunted Jasperodus. "Well, advance the arrangements for the defence of the city."

He turned away, but minutes later a dishevelled messenger came into the hall and sought out Arcturus. The rebel commander hurried up to Jasperodus wearing a startled look.

"The Borgor Alliance has launched a full-scale attack on the Empire!" he announced in a shocked voice. "They have crossed the border in force!"

"No doubt they judged the moment ripe," Jasperodus commented. "Oh, well, the Fourth Army will be forced to wheel about to face them. So at least they are off our necks."

"Frankly it looks to me as though we shall be besieged by the imperial armies or by Borgor – or by both! What a mess!"

"Hah!" Jasperodus' tone was glowering. "What we need are a few nuclear weapons. Then we could wipe out the Borgor invasion and the imperial armies all together, in one blow while they fought one another."

Arcturus moved closer, glancing to left and right. "That is not all. We have also just now received intelligence that the Emperor Charrane is to land on Earth in three days' time."

"An ignorant rumour. He is on Mars – that is months away."

"The information comes from a reliable source. As soon as the Emperor heard of the revolt he embarked on a secret new vessel

– an extremely fast space cruiser that by chance had just made a test flight to Mars. This vessel is a nuclear-powered rocket and is capable of constant acceleration; consequently it cuts the journey down to less than two weeks."

"So!" Jasperodus responded wonderingly. "The charismatic Charrane! His presence puts a different complexion on things. He is, after all, the inspiration behind the Empire."

"What shall we do?"

"Come with me."

Arcturus followed Jasperodus out of the basilica. They crossed the plaza, still rubble-strewn from the fighting. A further clump of explosions, by the sound of it across the city, added to the events of the night. Minutes later they had arrived at the flying stables on the roof of the north wing.

"I knew the story about Charrane was true when you mentioned the nuclear rocket," Jasperodus said. "There have been some developments in nuclear propulsion recently. At a flight testing station just outside the city I found this aircraft and so I flew it here."

The plane stood in the open hidden by a canvas fence. It had a long, sleek, needle-nosed fuselage, delta wings, and rested on a tripod of tall legs like a bird. Its construction, as Jasperodus knew, was clever. The skin, of aluminium and titanium, could withstand intense heat and gained strength and lightness from an ingenious layered honeycomb structure.

He pulled down a section of the fuselage, forming a curved gridded ramp leading to the flight cabin. "Where are we going?" asked Arcturus in mystification. "What are you doing?"

"Getting out."

The rebel stared at him disbelievingly. It was some moments before he found his voice.

"You're really going to do it! Quit! Desert us all just when the going gets tough – just when we need your leadership most!" His face sagged, appalled.

"Naïvety was ever the failing of idealists," said Jasperodus casually. "Try to think clearly for once! Did you honestly imagine the revolt could succeed? Of course it couldn't – not for one moment! It was easy to gain Tansiann, and we talked hopefully of the uprising spreading to other cities of the Empire. But it hasn't."

"Perhaps because our initiative faltered."

"Perhaps. What difference would it have made? We have roused a rabble – no match for the trained troops of the Empire, I do assure you of that. Not that it would make any difference, either. The truth is that an empire of this type goes rotten at the centre while remaining relatively healthy at the periphery. There is still enough vigour in the outer provinces to make a rampage of the kind we have engineered here impossible. Besides, the people there are more aware of the threat of an external enemy, particularly in the northern provinces. That provides sufficient disincentive for any sympathy with rebellion. If it comes to that, I wonder how our own followers will react to the approach of Borgor armies, especially if preceded by a missile bombardment."

Arcturus scowled. "Your motives are a mystery to me. Everything you say may well be true, but I am not made of the stuff of deserters." And he turned to go.

Jasperodus caught hold of him and pushed him to the ramp with a sardonic chuckle. "Don't imagine I brought you here in order to save your skin. I need someone to man the evasion-and-defence board. The outer regions of the Empire are a veritable hedgehog of radar watches and ground-to-air missile sites. True, this plane is a new conception in attack aircraft, able to fly over hill and dale at a height of only hundreds of feet so as to escape radar detection, but we are going on a long journey and are still likely to be challenged. Get in the plane."

Against Jasperodus' superior strength Arcturus could do nothing. He stumbled into the darkened cabin. Jasperodus closed the door behind them. Small lights came on on the pilot board, providing the merest glimmering of illumination.

"Better strap yourself in," Jasperodus growled, shoving Arcturus to his station, a seat behind and to one side of the pilot's. "We'll be flying at close to two thousand miles per hour."

Arcturus stared hopelessly at the board. "I don't know how to operate this."

Jasperodus ignored him and prepared for take-off. In essence the new engine was simplicity itself: it was a nuclear ramjet. A compact, very hot reactor core heated indrawn air which was then vented through the exhaust to provide thrust. Jasperodus withdrew the damper rods, bringing the core to incandescence. Then he fired the cartridge that initiated the flow of air through the baffles.

With a rising whine the ramjet began its self-perpetuating action. The aircraft rose vertically, supported through its centre of gravity by the single jet; as Jasperodus slowly swivelled the exhaust assembly, bringing it to the attitude for lateral flight, the plane described an accelerating curve that in short order sent it hurtling through the night.

A sense of familiarity came over Jasperodus. This was the second time he had seized power, subsequently to flee in an aircraft, both times in comparable circumstances.

"Hah!" he told himself again. "Repetition is a feature of this life, evidently."

They left Tansiann far behind. Jasperodus set his course, then spent the next half-hour instructing Arcturus in his duties. The evasion board, being a prototype like the rest of the plane, was not complicated and he abbreviated the procedure further for his companion's sake. All Arcturus had to do was note any radio challenges or prospective missile interceptions, press appropriate buttons or otherwise follow Jasperodus' instructions. While not too enthusiastic a pupil, he learned the drill well enough.

"And now perhaps I may know where we are bound," he grunted.

"I may as well tell you of my plans. I intend to commit suicide, though the phrase is inapt since I have never been alive." Glancing round, he saw Arcturus' startled look. "Don't worry," he added with grim amusement. "You won't be included in my self-destruction. I am obeying an urge to do one last thing before my demise : I am going home, to confront the people who made me. Perhaps I will berate them for their efforts." I wonder what they were thinking of, he told himself silently. Surely they must have known that this ludicrous self-image would soon rub up against reality. Or possibly they hoped I would stay with them, a doting surrogate son, and so never learn of my true condition.

"I understand nothing of what you say," Arcturus said. "Why should you wish to destroy yourself?"

"I am disillusioned with this living death, despite my various strivings over the years."

"At a guess you suffer from some slight brain malfunction," Arcturus volunteered uneasily. He grew curious and attempted to question Jasperodus on his origins, but the robot offered nothing further.

They journeyed in silence. After a while Jasperodus reduced speed to the subsonic range and brought the plane down to a height of only a few hundred feet, switching on the special radar set that enabled the autopilot to follow the contours of the landscape. Only once did a watching radar station pick them up; Arcturus reported a missile arcing towards them, but it hit a hillside when Jasperodus swung away from it and they were pursued no more.

Because they were travelling against the rotation of the planet the night was a long one and Arcturus eventually slept, neglecting his duties. In the early morning they flew over Gordona (out of danger from the Empire's radar hedgehog now) and Jasperodus looked for the railway track that would lead him home. Then, after some circling and searching, he located what he thought was his parents' cottage standing alone in the middle of a cultivated patch.

He extended the air flaps and undercarriage and swivelled the jet assembly. With the grace of a gull the plane alighted in a ploughed field, blowing up a cloud of dust. Jasperodus waited for the dust to settle, then lowered the ramp.

"Stay here," he told Arcturus. "I will be back shortly."

Walking towards the cottage he noticed at once that not all was well with the household. The farming robots went about their work, but they had not been serviced in a long time. The hoeing machine dragged itself across the earth, unable to perform its task with anything like acceptable efficacy.

Nearer to the cottage Jasperodus came upon a simple grave bearing the name of his mother. He paused, walked on and entered the cottage by the open door.

Within, the light was dim, the curtains being drawn across the windows. He stood in the main room of the dwelling, surrounded by the homely furniture that had served the old couple for half a lifetime. Lying on a bed beneath the window casement was the robotician Jasperodus automatically — by reason of some inbuilt mental reflex, no doubt — called his father.

The man's breathing was shallow and laboured. "Who is there?" he asked in a faint voice.

"I, Jasperodus, the construct you manufactured close to a score of years ago."

He stepped nearer, looked down and felt puzzled enough to

start reckoning up the years. When he had left them the man and his wife had been just about to enter old age. By now they should be almost twenty years older, but still sound of wind and limb. Yet the face that stared up at him was ancient, in the last stages of an unnatural senility. It looked a thousand years old : the eyes were dull, barely alive, yellow and filmed; the skin sagged and reminded him of rotted fungus; trembling, claw-like hands clutched at the dirty coverlet.

It didn't add up. Was his father in the grip of some wasting disease? The two stared at one another, each startled by what he saw.

"Jasperodus . . ."

"Yes, it is me." Even as he pondered, even as he wondered how far his father's mind might have deteriorated and whether he would be able to answer, the words Jasperodus had meant to speak started coming out of his mouth. "Cast your mind back. I am here to ask you only one thing. Why did you do it? Why did you burden me with this fictitious self-image – this belief in a consciousness I do not possess? A clever piece of work, no doubt, but could you not see how cruel it was – that I was bound to discover the truth?"

The old man smiled weakly. "I always knew that unanswerable question would bring you back to us one day."

"Fake being: a mechanical trick," Jasperodus accused.

"There is no fictitious self-image, no mechanical trick. You are fully conscious."

Resentment entered Jasperodus' voice. "It is no use to lie to me. I have talked with eminent roboticians – I have even talked with Aristos Lyos – and besides that I have studied robotics on my own account. I know full well that it is impossible to create artificial consciousness."

"Quite so; what you say is perfectly true. Nevertheless – you are conscious." The old man moved feebly. "My great invention!" he said dreamily. "My great secret!"

Had the oldster's mind degenerated, Jasperodus asked himself? Yet somehow the robotician did not speak like a dotard.

"You talk nonsense," he said brutally.

But the other smiled again. "At the beginning we decided never to tell you, not wishing you to be afflicted with feelings of guilt. But

now you evidently need to know. Listen: it is quite true, consciousness cannot be artificially generated. Some years ago, however, I
made a unique discovery: while uncreatable it can nevertheless
be manipulated, melted down, transferred from one vehicle to
another. I learned how to duct it, how to trap it in a 'robotic retort'
— to use my own jargon. If any other man has ever learned this
secret he has kept it well hidden, as indeed I have."

He paused, swallowed, closed his eyes for a moment, then continued. "To perform these operations, of course, one must first
obtain the energy of consciousness, necessarily from a human being. We took half of your mother's soul, half of my soul, and
fused them together to form a new, original soul with its own
individual qualities. That is how you were born — our son, in every
sense of the word, just as if you had been of our flesh and
blood."

A long, long silence followed these words. At length Jasperodus
stirred, stunned both by the novelty and by the compelling logic of
what he had just been told. "Then I am, after all, a person?" he
queried wonderingly. "A being? A self?"

"Just like any human person. In fact you have more consciousness, a more vigorous consciousness, than the normal human, since
in the event we both donated somewhat more than half of our
souls. I can still remember that day, misty though everything now
is. It became a trial in which each tried to prevent the other from
giving too much. It was a strange experience, feeling the debilitating
drain on one's being — and yet, too, there was a kind of ecstasy,
since when the consciousness began to flow from each of us, we
could feel the coalescence of our souls. We have paid the price
for the procedure, of course, in the loss of over half our vitality, and
in the premature ageing which resulted . . ."

Jasperodus moved away, pacing the room. "A heavy price, perhaps."

"Not at all. We knew what we were doing. To lose a part of
one's life — that is nothing. To create a life — that is something
to have done. I hope you have not regretted our gift of life." The
old man's voice was a quavering whisper now; he seemed ex-
hausted.

"I have been through many experiences, and I have suffered to
some extent, chiefly through not knowing that I am a man." He

picked up a wooden figurine that rested on a sideboard, contemplating it absently while pondering. "How did you come by this discovery? It seems remarkable, to say the least."

His father did not answer. He was staring at the timbers of the ceiling, burnished by odd rays of light that entered through chinks in the curtains.

Jasperodus returned to the bedside. "And why have you made a secret of it? Many people have tried to make conscious robots. It is a major discovery, a real addition to knowledge."

"No, no! This technique is much too dangerous. Think what it would mean! At present constructs are not conscious, but some are intelligent, even shrewd. A few of them already begin to suspect what is missing in them. If my method became known it would lead to robots stealing the souls of men. At worst, one can imagine mankind being enslaved by a super-conscious machine system, kept alive only so that men's souls could be harvested – as it is, lack of consciousness is all that prevents the potential superiority of the construct from asserting itself. So my technique will die with me, and I implore you never to speak of it to anyone."

Jasperodus nodded. "I understand. You have my promise."

"Perhaps we should not have used it at all, but this one desire we could not resist: to have a son."

"There is an image that has occurred to me from time to time, often in dreams," Jasperodus remarked. "It shows a blast furnace melting down all manner of metal artifacts. The vision has been so vivid – so frightening – that I have been convinced it contains some meaning. You, I suppose, put it in my mind."

"Quite so. It was the only clue to your true nature I gave you. The fire of the furnace, which melts objects so that the metal may be used anew, is an analogy of a supernal fire – a cosmic fire – that melts the stuff of consciousness ready to be fashioned into new individuals. I discovered this fire."

"Supernal fire," Jasperodus said slowly. He grunted, and shook his head.

"I am still puzzled," he confessed. "Apart from the principles of robotics, certain events and circumstances in my life have convinced me that I lack a soul – for instance I was once dismantled, yet when I was reconstituted my feeling of consciousness returned. How may that be explained?"

His father gave a deep shuddering sigh, as though seeking the last of his strength. "Did that really happen to you?" he whispered. "It is not impossible. The soul, being non-material, does not always behave like a substance subject to the laws of space. Within limits one could be dismantled into subassemblies, and provided some degree of biological or robotic integration remained, the soul might well not dissipate."

"And when it does dissipate?"

"The cosmic furnace, into which all souls are thrown at death. From the common pool new individuals are moulded."

"So as well as making a conscious construct, you have also solved the mystery of what happens at death," Jasperodus remarked in a tone at once flippant and sombre. He cogitated, trying to understand the issue in all its aspects. The old man was clearly taxed by so much talk, but he could not resist asking the questions that came to mind.

"If I have consciousness, how is it that I cannot locate my 'I'? When I enter into my mind I find only thoughts and percepts."

"So it is with everyone. The self always remains hidden. You cannot see the seer, the mind cannot grasp the thinker of the thought. That seer, that thinker, is 'I', the soul."

The senile robotician made an effort to lift his head, but sank back with a defeated, sighing moan.

"I am sorry," Jasperodus said, "I have been inconsiderate with so much inquisitiveness. What may I do for you? If it comes to that, may we not reverse the operation that gave me life? I could easily spare some vitality, which might restore your health."

"Too late; my condition is irreversible. In any case I would not countenance it. There is only one service you can perform for me, and that is to bury my body in a grave alongside that of your mother."

"You may live for some time yet. At least I can stay here to take care of you."

"No need for that either." With an effort the old man fumbled under his pillow and brought out a little white pill. "Well, Jasperodus, you chose to go your own way, but I see you have turned into a person of quality. I would stay to hear how you have fared, but I fear it might make parting too difficult. So farewell – and may the rest of life prove to your satisfaction."

204

"Is that necessary?" Jasperodus asked, his eyes on the white pill.

"I prepared this to spare myself an existence without the use of my mind during my last hours – which would not be long now in any case. I have delayed taking it so far – perhaps subconsciously I sensed you would come. Now that I have seen you I feel a sense of completeness. Nothing need delay me further."

With difficulty he guided the pill to his lips. Jasperodus reached out to snatch it away, then stayed his hand.

His father died peacefully within seconds. Jasperodus drew back the curtains, admitting sunlight into the dusty room. He looked carefully around him, consigning every detail to his memory and recalling that occasion long ago when he had walked out of here, little realising the sacrifice that had been made on his behalf.

Then he went through the cottage, looking for notebooks, instruments, anything appertaining to robotics, though whether he would have studied or destroyed any material or artifacts relating to his father's great discovery he was not sure. However, he found nothing: everything had been meticulously removed.

Going to the tool shed he sought out a spade, then dug a neat grave beside that of his mother. He wrapped his father's body in a sheet, laid him in the excavation, filled it in and erected a plain wooden namepost.

The work took slightly over half an hour. For a short while afterwards Jasperodus stood before the little cottage, taking in the landscape that lay before him, with its moistly wooded rolling hills, the cloud-bedecked sky that stretched and expanded everywhere over it, beaming down great shafts of sunlight into the air space beneath, and beyond that the framing immensity of the void and the wheeling masses of remote stars which for the moment he couldn't see, and he speculated on the nature of the cosmic furnace his father had described, where all beings were melted, formed and re-formed.

It was a marvel to him what a change new knowledge had wrought in him. All inner conflict, the result of his ignorance, was gone. He felt intelligent, strong, aware of himself, and at peace.

On his return to the aircraft Arcturus found him in a private mood. "Well, what now?" the rebel slum-dweller said acidly. "Do we proceed to the place of your ritual suicide, wherever that is to be?"

"I hope you will not think me unreliable if I have changed my mind," Jasperodus informed him. "I shall live after all. We return to Tansiann."

"So we are to fight Charrane and Borgor after all?"

"The best hope lies in a reconciliation with Charrane – though whether I can ever be reinstated with him I do not know." Automatically his mind began inventing various stratagems – unmasking the perfidy of Ax Oleander, petitioning for the return of the Emperor, and so on. "No matter; events must fall out as they will. Even if I am forced to quit public life there is much that I can do."

Arcturus grunted, eyeing him derisively but with curiosity. "As you wish, but what has brought about this change in policy?"

"I owe you, I suppose, apologies and explanations," Jasperodus said, "though they would be tediously long. For me it has been a circuitous route, to discovering the sacrifice that was necessary for the creation of my being. That sacrifice should not be heedlessly abnegated. It should bear fruit. To create, to enrich life for mankind, to raise consciousness to new levels of aspiration, that is what should be done . . ."

The ramp closed shut. Graceful as a gull the nuclear ramjet soared up from the field and went whining away to the East.